I0819423

In the SPIRIT *of* FRENCH MURDER

The Phyllida Bright Mysteries

Murder at Mallowan Hall

A Trace of Poison

Murder by Invitation Only

Murder Takes the Stage

Two Truths and a Murder

The American in Paris Mysteries

Mastering the Art of French Murder

A Murder Most French

A Fashionably French Murder

In the Spirit of French Murder

The Quinn & Gates Mysteries

Murder at Lincon's Gala

Murder in Lincoln's Library

Murder at the Capitol

In the SPIRIT *of* FRENCH MURDER

Colleen Cambridge

kensingtonbooks.com

KENSINGTON BOOKS are published by

Kensington Publishing Corp.
900 Third Avenue
New York, NY 10022

All Kensington titles, imprints and distributed lines are available at special quantity discounts for bulk purchases for sales promotion, premiums, fund-raising, educational or institutional use. Special book excerpts or customized printings can also be created to fit specific needs. For details, write or phone the office of the Kensington Special Sales Manager: Kensington Publishing Corp., 900 Third Avenue, New York, NY, 10022. Attn. Special Sales Department. Phone: 1-800-221-2647.

KENSINGTON and the K with book logo Reg. US Pat & TM Off.

Library of Congress Control Number: On file

ISBN: 978-1-4967-5122-5

First Kensington Hardcover Edition: May 2026

ISBN: 978-1-4967-5124-9 (ebook)

10 9 8 7 6 5 4 3 2 1

Printed in the United States of America

The authorized representative in the EU for product safety and compliance
is eucomply OU, Parnu mnt 139b-14, Apt 123
Tallinn, Berlin 11317, hello@eucompliancepartner.com

AUTHOR'S NOTE

Although Julia Child and her husband, Paul, lived on rue de l'Université in Paris in March 1950, as far as the author is aware, she never visited a medium, had her fortune told, or encountered a dead body. She was, however, a wonderful, enthusiastic, and engaging cook who loved sharing her skills and the fruits of her labor in the kitchen with friends.

—Colleen Cambridge, May 2026

In the SPIRIT *of* FRENCH MURDER

CHAPTER 1

Paris
1950

"It was an *absolute disaster*!" Julia cried, gripping my arm in desperation. "I was completely *mortified*! I simply can't *believe* what a muck I made of it!" Her bright blue eyes were wild with emotion, and her curly brown hair seemed to vibrate with emphasis.

I blinked. I had merely asked how the luncheon she had cooked yesterday for her friend had gone, and apparently, it had not gone well at all. "Well, what happened?" I asked cautiously, and also with a healthy bit of skepticism.

After all, what Julia Child might consider to be an "absolute disaster" in the kitchen was probably little more than a bit of eggshell in an omelette or the top of a cake that was not as level as she might want. Maybe she'd put too much, I don't know, thyme or chervil or salt in something?

My friend, who was studying at Le Cordon Bleu, was a wiz *dans la cuisine*, and some—very little, but some—of her skills and education had been rubbing off on me. I still had my own absolute disasters, like a cheese soufflé that had collapsed like a hot air balloon; what on earth had I been thinking to even try making such a delicate dish?—but I was certain her troubles would pale in comparison to anything I had done.

"Oh, good *heavens,* I don't even know if I want to tell you!" Julia finally released my arm and plopped into a chair, coffee cups, plates, and flatware rattling as her arms and elbows settled onto the table.

We were in her kitchen on the second level of the apartment she shared with her husband, Paul. It was a very small space, hardly more than a galley, and it didn't have hot running water (something I'd taken for granted back home in Michigan but learned was a luxury in Paris). But it did have a massive stove, soapstone counters, and an entire bank of windows on one wall. Today, on this cold, crisp day in the first week of March, the sun shined through those windows and bathed the room in warm light, and I was beginning to think that spring might actually come once again to my adopted city. It had been a long, tough, *cold* winter—and, astonishingly and sadly, for Julia and me, it had also been filled with murder.

I was more than ready for the warmth and light of spring.

"Oh," Julia moaned. The table rocked, and its burden clinked again under the shift of her arms.

I had taken a seat as soon as I came into the kitchen. It was a requirement in La Cuisine de Scheeld (as Paul Child called it, using the French pronunciation of their surname), for there was simply no room for more than one person to stand in the space, especially when Julia was cooking—which she was always doing, and always doing in such an energetic, choreographed fashion that you just needed to stay out of her way. Not to mention it was a good idea to be sitting so you could be lucky enough to sample whatever delicacy she was cooking.

The fact that Julia was actually *sitting* in her kitchen with nothing in front of her to cut, chop, or knead was shocking all on its own. Whatever happened must have really been bad.

"All right, I'll tell you. I'll confess it all—I'll give you the *bald truth*—and then we'll never *speak* of it again, all right, Tabitha? Promise me! And this," she went on, shaking her head, her eyes wide and fixed on me, "is precisely why I am so *relieved* I didn't accept the offer from your messieurs to cook for their little soirée tomorrow night! My God, if Chef Bugnard ever *heard* about this . . . !" She moaned once more, thinking of her teacher at the cooking school.

"What happened?" I said again, lifting my cup of coffee to drink. French *café* was one of my favorite things about the City of Light—and I had many favorite things. I tended to add a healthy amount of sugar to it to make it even better. It was rich and nutty and robust—a far cry from the Folgers I used to drink back home.

"Well, I was making eggs Florentine. Do you know *how* many times I've *made* eggs Florentine, Tabitha? Do you have any idea how many times I've *cooked* that dish? Probably a hundred! Maybe two hundred! It was one of the first things I learned from my *dear* and *wise* Ali-Bab," she said, gesturing impatiently toward the massive tome sitting on a shelf. *Gastronomie pratique,* by Henri Babinski, written under the pseudonym Ali-Bab, was a dark, aged book the size of a cinder block. It was this "bible" for French housewives that had launched Julia's interest in cooking.

"You've made it for me," I said. "And it was wonderful!"

"Yes. It usually is. But yesterday . . . Good heavens, Tabs, I simply don't know what I was *thinking*! I just *chucked* everything I know about cooking right out those windows." She flapped a hand at them. "What does Chef Bugnard say? What has he *drilled* into my head every single day at class? *Measure, measure, measure . . . taste, taste, taste*! And did I do any of that?" She gave me a look, demanding me to answer her question.

"Um . . . no?"

"That's right. I didn't measure a damned thing. I just—oh, God, Tabitha—I just *slopped* and tossed and *flung* everything about like a mad *scientist*! It was like I was trying to make Frankenstein's *monster* or something! I thought I didn't need to measure or to taste or to look at the recipe, I'd done it so many times. I mean, who *doesn't* know how to make eggs Florentine . . . ?"

"I don't," I said with a grin.

"I'll teach you," she said. "It'll be my penance for mucking up lunch for Winnie yesterday. Oh, I don't mean it's a penance to teach *you*, Tabs, I just mean it's *my* penance because I'm going to make myself go over it and over it and over it again because I was such a fool to think I could just *whip* things up and ignore everything I know!"

"So . . . what happened after you made the eggs and they didn't turn out?"

Julia made a strangled sound. "We ate them. I *served* them. I actually served that mess—that floppy, gloppy, disgusting mess! The *sauce Mornay* was . . . Ugh, it was like *glue*! We just sat there and choked it down, and I didn't say a *word* about it. And neither did Winnie."

"Oh," I replied, then clamped my mouth closed with a heartfelt grimace. What else could I say?

"It was *miserable*, Tabs! Absolutely *miserable*! But do you know what? I decided then and there, I wasn't going to apologize. I'm *not* going to be one of those—those *fluttery* cooks who go around apologizing for every little thing that's wrong or didn't turn out *perfectly* or anything. I'm *never* going to apologize for anything I make in the kitchen!" She slammed her palm onto the table. *Clink-rattle.*

"We ate it, and neither of us is dead—well, at least I'm not dead. And I certainly hope Winnie isn't dead! Oh, heavens, that's all I would need! God knows you and I have run into enough dead people, haven't we?" She huffed out a laugh that turned into a half-sob.

And then, all at once, we were laughing together.

We weren't laughing at the murders she and I had gotten caught up in over the past few months, but at the entire situation of gloppy, floppy eggs Florentine and miserably choking them down one's throat without saying a word.

Once the hilarity had eased, I said, "Well, I, for one, am disappointed that you aren't going to be there tomorrow night for the soirée."

"Oh, I'm going to be there. And, Tabitha, remember what I said! We aren't to speak of the Debacle of the Eggs Florentine ever again, and definitely *not* to your messieurs! I simply can't have that delicious light of adoration for my cooking fade from their eyes." She chuckled. "Anyway, even though I'm not going to be *cooking* exactly, I am going to be working with Chef Debord *dans la cuisine* at Maison de Verre tomorrow night. I'll be assisting him. I think I'm making one dish on my own."

"You are?" I exclaimed. "That's wonderful, Julia! I'm so happy to hear that."

"Chef Bugnard arranged it. He and Debord go way back, from before the war. I am going to learn *so much*! It's going to be *fabulous*! And the *food*! It's going to be *spectacular*!"

I was nearly as excited as Julia was about the event. My *grand-père* and Oncle Rafe—both of whom had warmly and lovingly welcomed me to live with them in the gorgeous mansion across rue de l'Université from Julia and Paul Child's apartment—had recently purchased and remodeled a restaurant. Maison de Verre had been one of Paris's premiere *restaurants gastronomiques* before the war and the German Occupation—apparently on the same par as La Tour d'Argent and Le Grand Véfour. It had also been one of my messieurs' favorite places to eat, for it was within a three-block walking distance and the food was incredible. The restaurant had closed down during the war, when the chef-owner decided he couldn't welcome or even tolerate the Germans, and it had been abandoned—well, mostly abandoned—ever since.

I had had my own harrowing experiences inside Maison de Verre recently, but the fact that it would soon reopen and that surely we would frequent the place didn't bother me at all. The so-called ghosts had been exorcised from the place, for it had been lovingly cleaned and remodeled into a stupendously and consummately French establishment.

Tomorrow night my messieurs were having a small gathering with some close friends as a sort of pre-opening for the restaurant. It was also their opportunity to debut Chef Debord to those whom they hoped would be their patrons.

I'd been delighted when Grand-père had originally suggested Julia might want to cook a dish or two for the little gathering, but she had declined, and in the end, it had been the best decision. Not because of the Debacle of the Eggs Florentine, but because it really was more appropriate for Chef Debord to present the menu since he was going to be running things. I suspected Grand-père had made the offer simply because he was sweet and kind and very grateful for all the meals Julia had cooked for them (particularly when I was off poking around into murder investigations).

"Do you know everyone who is coming tomorrow night?" asked Julia from over her shoulder. Having confessed the details of her debacle and feeling absolved—or resolved—she'd risen and returned to the stove, where she belonged. I didn't know what she was cooking, but it smelled divine, and it was comforting to see her back to work.

"I don't think so. Some of them I've met before, I'm sure. Most of them are old friends of Grand-père and Oncle Rafe from before the war," I replied. I had been living with my messieurs for nearly a month before I realized that Oncle Rafe was no blood relation to me but instead was a very close longtime friend of my grandfather's. His partner in every way.

"Do you think some of them were in the Resistance?" Julia said, turning from the stove even as she continued to stir the contents of a pot.

"Maybe. I'm not sure. You know it can be a difficult subject for them to talk about," I replied. Both Julia and I had been witness to more than one tense exchange between my grandfather, who was a partner at a large, respected bank and had had to carefully balance his interactions with the Germans while remaining loyal to and protective of his countrymen, and Oncle Rafe, who'd been a staunch member of the Resistance and who tended to see things as far more definitively black or white.

"Yes," Julia said thoughtfully. "I can't help but think about what it must have been like . . . the sorts of decisions people had to make about what to do and when. Keep your head down and avoid the Germans and try and go about your daily life without getting killed or sent away to prison, or get involved trying to fight back." She gave a little shudder.

I knew how she felt. We had recently been involved in a murder investigation that brought home to both of us how terrible it had been living here during the Occupation—and navigating and understanding the emotions and memories Parisians still struggled with five years later. Neither of us could imagine what it would have been like to live in a nation suddenly put under the rule of another country.

"We were lucky neither of us lived here during that time," I replied. I had worked at the Willow Run Bomber Plant outside of Detroit, riveting large parts of airplanes. Julia had met Paul when they both worked for the OSS—the Office of Strategic Services—in Asia. Although we'd both been involved in the war effort, neither Julia nor I had had it thrust in our faces like it had been here in Europe. Especially France.

"We really were," Julia said with great feeling.

I looked at the clock and shot up from my chair. "Yikes! I'm going to be late for my appointment if I don't get going," I said, already shoving my arms into my coat sleeves. I had a number of American students to whom I was teaching French in private lessons. My French was native and flawless, for I'd grown up learning the language with my mama and my *grand-mère* back in Michigan.

I glanced at the stove, but whatever Julia was cooking was obviously not ready to be eaten, and it probably wasn't something I could take with me, anyway. I'd have to get a sandwich at one of the cafés after my tutoring appointment.

Or . . . I could pop into the kitchen at home and see whether Bet or Blythe—our daily maids—had left something I could eat. I had to get my car, anyway, which was parked under the portico attached to the house.

"Ta-ta!" I said, standing on tiptoes to smoosh a kiss on Julia's cheek. "If I don't see you before tomorrow night, I'll see you then! Cook well!"

"Bye, Tabs! And don't you worry—if I have any of this gorgeous boeuf bourguignon left over, which I'm certain I will—do you *see* how much is in this dish?—I'll call, and you can take it over to your gentlemen."

I called a thanks as the elevator doors closed between Julia's apartment and me. As often happened when I was in this particular elevator, I couldn't help but remember back in December, when I'd ridden down in it with a young woman who was later murdered in the cellar of this very building. Besides the killer, I had been the last person to see her alive.

That incident had been the catalyst for my involvement in several murder cases over the past few months. Despite what some people might think, I hadn't gone looking for crimes and homicides to get involved in—they just kept showing up in my and Julia's lives. And in every case so far, I'd been compelled to poke around because of that connection.

The cold, crisp air bit at my nose and cheeks as I hustled across rue de l'Université. The home I shared with Grand-père and Oncle Rafe was a majestic three-story building made from creamy Parisian limestone. Like much of the city's architecture, it boasted high ceilings and many windows and dormers decorated with ornate iron railings.

The front door opened into an elegant two-story foyer with a rose, black, and white marble floor and an ornate fin de siècle chandelier with electric lights. A kitchen three times the size of Julia's took up the back of that level (and included an actual refrigerator, over which she often expressed her envy) and opened onto the gated courtyard behind. There was a small sitting room and a study on that floor as well, but we never used those spaces.

Grand-père and Oncle Rafe were somewhere near eighty and they preferred to spend most of their time on the first floor—the one above the ground floor. That was something I'd had to get used to here in Europe: that the first floor was one floor *above* the ground floor, unlike back home.

Except lately, when they'd been over at Maison de Verre, overseeing (and arguing) about the decor and decisions, my messieurs tended to sit in the well-appointed salon that took up a large part of the first floor. It had a large fireplace as well as a furnace that did a pretty good job of keeping them toasty warm, even during the coldest days. There was also the added benefit of the door opening into Grand-père's little greenhouse, which had been built on top of the portico roof. He loved to putter about with his *bébés délicieux,* as he called them: herbs and small fruit trees, as well as a pleasant little pond with large goldfish.

I had been given the entire top floor for my living space, and it was mostly made up of a large, airy room that had originally housed the staff. I had a bathroom of my own up there, too, with running water—hot water, all the time, just like at home—and a large tub that I liked to soak in. I had no idea how my messieurs arranged for the luxury of hot water at the turn of the tap, but I enjoyed every moment of it. Along with that, I also noticed that for some reason, our house was never included in the scheduled electricity blackouts that plagued a city still recovering from war and occupation.

Just as I was crossing the street, the front door of our house swung open. A woman bundled up in coat, scarf, and mittens rushed out, and I could hear someone calling after her from inside. She ignored them and continued on her way, nearly running into me on the walkway leading to the house.

"Ah, pardon, *mademoiselle,*" she said. She glanced at me, then suddenly stopped and gripped my arm with fingers in thick knitted mittens. "*You.* Are you the granddaughter?"

The woman had to be at least fifty or sixty, much older than me but still younger than my grand-père and Oncle Rafe. Her coat was a bulky old wool thing that smelled strongly of cigarettes and some other pungent, musky scent. Her head and neck and part of her angular, olive-skinned face were wrapped in a thick woven scarf of dark blue. Even so, I could see that she had been beautiful once, many years ago.

Startled by the intense look in her eyes and her agitation, I pulled my arm away. "I am Maurice Saint-Léger's granddaughter, yes." I felt in my coat pocket for my Swiss Army knife and curled my fingers around it, just in case.

"Ah, but you must tell them! You must tell them to *heed what I say,*" she said. Her eyes were dark and wild, gleaming with something that made a shiver go down my spine. "He—ah, he does not listen! But I tell you, I have heard from them!"

"Heard from who?" I echoed, wondering if I ought to back away and rush into the house to see whether everything was all right.

"From the spirits! They've told me I must warn them. And I've done so, and—"

The front door flew open.

Oncle Rafe stood there, his eyes dark with fury. "Go on with you, Vierca! Go! Tabitha, come inside."

I had never been spoken to in that tone of voice by Oncle Rafe—or Grand-père, for that matter—and my stomach lurched in my middle. I didn't even hesitate; I obeyed.

I glanced at the woman as I brushed past, and saw not madness, not fury . . . but fear in her eyes.

CHAPTER 2

I was barely inside when Oncle Rafe closed the door with a sharp click.

"What is it? Has she gone? Tabitha! What did she say to you?"

It was Grand-père, standing at the top of the sweeping staircase on the first floor. His gnarled hand gripped the newel post, and the hem of his house robe trembled against his trousers. Monsieur Oscar Wilde, the tiny dog my honorary oncle called a pet, was standing on one of the steps, barking his head off.

"She has gone, Maurice," Oncle Rafe said. He sounded a bit out of breath, and I noticed he was wearing his slippers and the knitted cap he often donned in the winter to protect his bald head—both very informal items that were never present during social visits.

Based on their relaxed attire of dressing robes over loose trousers and house slippers, I concluded my gentlemen hadn't intended to leave the house, nor had they expected visitors. Was this why they were so upset? Because someone had interrupted their day or seen them in such deshabille?

"Oscar, *silence*!" Oncle Rafe shouted, still in that same terrible voice he'd used to order me inside.

The dog immediately, and shockingly, stopped barking. But he didn't sit, and he continued to watch with eyes that seemed filled with worry.

Before I could say anything—I was still trying to figure out *what* to say, for I was so confused and shocked by this display—one of the housemaids emerged from the kitchen.

I say "one" because Bet and Blythe are identical twins, and none of us could tell them apart.

"Monsieur, what is it? What has happened?" Her eyes were wide, and she was carrying a feather duster and a broom. She was in her forties and had brown hair pulled back in a tight chignon. Her face was long, with creases alongside each corner of her mouth. The apron tied over a dark blue skirt and light blue blouse was impeccably white. She wore very sensible black shoes and heavy wool stockings.

Oncle Rafe collected himself and waved her off. "It is nothing," he said. "Only a misunderstanding." He glanced at me, then up the stairs toward Grand-père, but offered nothing more.

Bet or Blythe appeared skeptical, but she gave a little curtsy and disappeared back into the kitchen.

"Grand-père?" I said, looking up at him. The flush of agitation had faded from his face, but even from where I was standing, I could see that his hand gripped the velvet collar of his robe.

"It's all right," he said, but I didn't miss the look exchanged between the two men. "Did that woman speak to you, Tabitha?"

"Yes. Who was she? What did she want? Why are you two so upset?"

I started up the stairs, scooping up Oscar Wilde along the way. He didn't weigh more than seven or eight pounds, but what he didn't have in bulk, he made up for with huge ears that looked like butterfly wings. They were brown tipped with black around the top edges, like a painter's outline. His fur—mostly white, but with splotches of brown and black—was silky and soft and grew in long hairlike strands from his ears, tail, and trunk. He usually wore a bow tie of some jaunty color, and even a little tuxedo jacket or vest on occasion. Today his tie was a somber black. As one might guess, he was terribly spoiled.

"What did she say to you?" Grand-père demanded.

"Not much," I said carefully, feeling my way. I wasn't going to lie, but I didn't want to upset them any further. "She just said that you needed to listen to her. What is she talking about? Listen to her about what?" I said as Grand-père muttered an irritated "*Peh*!"

"It was nothing," Oncle Rafe said from behind me. "Don't you have a tutoring appointment, Tabitha? You mustn't be late."

Stung by the abrupt dismissal of both myself and the event I'd witnessed, I released Oscar Wilde onto the floor of the salon without even giving him a treat. I barely noticed that he didn't bark or whine over this omission. That was yet another testament to his sense that this was an unusual situation.

I have to admit, I felt a little shaky. I'd seen my messieurs become agitated over things as minor as the color of the drapes at the restaurant and as serious as who had done what to resist and who had collaborated during the Occupation, but in the eleven months I'd lived with them, I'd never seen them so upset, angry, and dismissive—especially with me.

"Yes, of course," I said. "I was already running late when I saw . . . when . . . Well, I'll be off. I'll see you both later. And Julia has promised some leftovers of her boeuf bourguignon!" I added brightly, but this statement didn't evoke the usual raptures of delight from my messieurs over the prospect of a meal cooked by Madame Child. My heart sank further.

I managed to press a kiss to Grand-père's soft, hairless cheek and one above Oncle Rafe's beard, but it felt awkward, and neither of them gave me the quick one-armed embrace I normally received. Even though I knew I hadn't done anything to upset them, I realized my knees were shaking and my palms were damp. As I went down the stairs, I heard the two moving to take their seats in the salon and the low, intense rapid-fire of their voices.

I glanced at the clock and saw that I should have left for my appointment—which was on the Right Bank, across the river—five minutes ago. Fortunately, this lesson was with Mrs. Woodward, an American expatriate whose husband worked with Paul Child at the US embassy. She had been late every time I arrived at their flat for the French lessons I was giving her, so for once, I didn't feel the need to rush. She could wait for me—if she was even ready at the appointed time, which had never happened yet.

I went into the kitchen and found Bet or Blythe in there, cleaning up dishes from what had probably been a small luncheon for my messieurs.

"Who was that woman? Do you know?" I asked.

She stopped what she was doing and dried her hands on the towel stuck behind the ties of her apron. Her eyes were worried. "That I do not know, mademoiselle. She rang the bell, and I answered, of course, and she wished to see the gentlemen, and so I went up the stairs to ask if they would speak to this woman. They were not expecting visitors, you see. But she said she was from *le restaurant*, and so of course they would see her, *non*? But then she went up there, and I heard the voices. They were surprised, I think, that it was her. Whoever she was.

"It seemed, I thought, they did know her somehow but had not expected her. And I don't think . . . I don't think she *was* from the restaurant. At first, it was quiet, the voices, besides the surprise. They did not ring for me or Bet to bring coffee, mademoiselle, and so I went about my business, and Bet, as well. She was up on the second floor, of course, tending to your bathroom. And then at once there were the loud voices and stomping of footsteps, and the barking and yowling!"

Her eyes went wide, and her hands fluttered at the sides of her face as she demonstrated the chaos. The yowling, I suspected, had come not only from Oscar Wilde but also from Madame X, Grand-père's sleek black cat, who wore a diamond-encrusted collar. "And then someone came down the stairs so quickly and loudly I even thought they were falling—but it was just the woman leaving very quickly. There was much shouting."

And Oncle Rafe had, for some reason, come after the visitor—to make certain she left, I supposed. Or to give one more verbal parting shot, whatever it might have been, for whatever she'd done to upset them. I didn't like the idea of either of my messieurs being so upset, but I was even more concerned about the fact that it seemed Oncle Rafe had stomped down the stairs after her. He was far too old to be so agitated and angry and hurrying down steps. Thank God it hadn't been Grand-père, who was even more rickety and arthritic than Oncle Rafe. My stomach squeezed at the thought of how easy it would have been for either of them to trip or slip and take a tumble, especially with Oncle Rafe wearing slippers!

"Did the woman tell you her name?" I asked.

Blythe (at least I knew which one she was now) shook her head. "No, mademoiselle. She said only that she was from the restaurant and needed to speak with them."

"Thank you. I appreciate everything you've told me." I looked up at the ceiling. "If Bet heard anything about what happened when she was upstairs, I would want to know."

"Of course, mademoiselle," she replied, giving me a little curtsy. "Now, I will give you a little bite to eat, *oui*? And you must be on your way. You will be late."

Ignoring the fact that everyone seemed far too knowledgeable about my schedule, I gratefully accepted the piece of baguette, slices of Gruyère, and the wrinkled red apple she pressed upon me, then headed out the door. She even gave me a thermos of coffee. I hadn't even taken off my coat and hat during the entire debacle, so I was a little hot and sweaty as I climbed into my cherry-red Renault, managing my burden.

As I navigated the traffic from the seventh arrondissement, where we lived, over the Pont au Change to the fourth arrondissement, I went over the encounter I'd had with the woman. Somehow, she had known I was "the granddaughter"—a fact which I'd chosen not to mention to Grand-père. Had that just been a guess on her part? I was, after all, approaching the house as she came bursting out the front door. Or had she somehow known who I was? But, no, no, she'd *asked* if I was the granddaughter. So she hadn't known for sure, but she'd known I existed.

And what had she said? It had sounded mad and crazy. *They must heed what I say! I have told them.*

And something about spirits . . .

The hair on the back of my neck lifted, and a little squiggle went down my spine. *From the spirits,* she'd said when I asked where she'd gotten her information. At least, that was what I *thought* she'd said. I wasn't going to mention *that* to Grand-père and Oncle Rafe—at least not yet.

You'd think a crazy experience like that would have had all the details imprinted on my mind, emblazoned in my memory, but it had happened so fast, and it had been so weird and intense, that I wasn't completely certain I remembered everything right.

I did know for certain she'd asked if I was the granddaughter. And I also knew for sure she'd said something about "the spirits," because it had been so startling.

I heaved a breath and decided I needed to put the incident away for now. I was shortly going to arrive at a professional appointment, and I needed to focus on my job—at least for the moment.

It's not easy eating while driving and having to shift the car's gears, one hand on the steering, one hand to shift—especially when one is distracted by the memories of being accosted by a lunatic—but I managed to scarf down my little lunch before I got to Mrs. Woodward's place. I was even lucky enough to find a parking place on the street, which was a miracle in itself.

Since the war had ended, Americans, in particular, but Europeans, as well, had flooded into the city. That meant more people in a place that was still strapped for resources (like coffee, hot water, and electricity) and more cars filling the streets. I'd heard plenty of complaints from Parisians about how thick the traffic was, and how it was nearly impossible to cross the street at times or to find a parking place. Until I had my Renault, which was a gift from Grand-père and Oncle Rafe, I had walked, bicycled, or taken the *métro* everywhere.

Fortunately, Paris is a pleasure in which to be on foot, or at least out in the open air. I loved my adopted city and even on the coldest, most miserable days in December when I was on foot in the ice and sleet, I was filled with gratitude for being here, *living* here . . . and also relieved that the City of Light had truly begun to awaken after the horrors of the Occupation.

As I'd hoped, Mrs. Woodward was late for our appointment. And as I arrived only eight minutes after the scheduled time, I don't think she even realized I'd been tardy.

Even so, our meeting went well—she was really improving with her verb conjugations—and at the end, she gave me the name and address of a British expat who wanted French lessons for her teenaged twins. I took the information and tucked it away with a smile. I doubted I would be hired for that job, for I'd discovered that English people didn't want to learn French with an American accent. Still, I was grateful for her referral and thanked her profusely.

Despite my work with Mrs. Woodward, all during our lesson, the strange incident at home had perked in the back of my mind like a pot of coffee on the stove. Who was that woman? I couldn't think of any way to find out without further upsetting my messieurs. I knew without a doubt *they* weren't going to tell me.

As I drove back home, I had a moment to be even more grateful for Julia's offer to provide dinner tonight. I had a sort of date this evening, which I had purposely not mentioned to my friend due to the inordinate amount of interest she—and most of the vendors at the food market—took in my love life. And because of my tutoring schedule today, I hadn't gone to the market with Julia, as I usually did, which meant I hadn't planned what to cook for dinner—or, more accurately, had *her* tell me what I should make for dinner based on what we found at the market and my limited skills *dans la cuisine.* Shopping for fresh food in early March was a challenge.

Grand-père and Oncle Rafe had had a live-in housekeeper, along with the day maids, but shortly after I arrived in April of 1949—on Easter weekend, when the lights of Paris were finally turned back on for the first time since the Occupation—the housekeeper had had to leave to care for an ailing sister in the South. Although I am not anywhere near as practiced as Julia, I could fumble my way through the kitchen (or so I'd thought). At least, I had done pretty well back home, where we relied on Campbell's soup, Spam, and white bread that was so flimsy you could crush the entire loaf and fit it into a coffee mug. Despite being French, neither my mother nor my grandmother had been motivated to be excellent cooks, and we'd eaten in the American way. With the loss of the housekeeper and with my gratitude to Grand-père for letting me live there for free, I'd happily and enthusiastically taken on the role of cooking dinner for us every night. Bet and Blythe came in each morning, but they left by midafternoon, and as I'd learned in Paris, we didn't eat dinner until seven or eight . . . and it was an *event.*

I learned very quickly that my fumbling in the kitchen with jars of Ragú, cans of soup, and rubbery eggs was not going to cut it with my beloved French messieurs. (Fortunately, I never even broached the subject of finding a local source to buy Spam.) Meeting Julia Child was a miracle in more than one way. We became close friends, partly due to the proximity of our homes and the fact that we shopped most often at the same street market. I helped her with her French and fixed a few things in her flat (thanks to my Swiss Army knife), and she not only began to teach me how to cook, but she often—*very* often—shared the meals she cooked for her and Paul, as well.

Especially when I was involved in a murder investigation.

Which had not happened for, oh, more than three weeks now and surely wouldn't happen again. Three murder investigations was three more than any normal person needed.

Back home, with my car tucked under the portico, next to the sleek black Bentley my messieurs drove—albeit very rarely—I discovered with delight that Bet and Blythe had not yet left.

I found them both in the kitchen, just packing up their things and drawing on their coats, hats, and gloves.

"Thank you very much," I told them, gesturing to the kitchen, which was sparkling clean, as usual. All the dishes I had used for my quick breakfast had been put away, and there was a pot of fresh coffee on the stove. A small apple pastry sat on the counter, its crust bumpy and golden and glittering with coarse sugar. It smelled delicious, and I knew one of them had cooked it instead of picking it up at the patisserie. "Did anything else happen while I was gone?" I glanced up toward the ceiling to indicate my messieurs.

"*Non, mademoiselle,*" said one of them. "It has been quiet since you left."

"Perhaps too quiet, eh?" added the other, and they both nodded sagely.

I wanted to ask Bet if she had heard anything when she was up on the top floor, but I didn't know which of them she was. I gritted my teeth and plunged on, trying not to give away that I had no clue whom I'd talked to in the kitchen before I left. "Do either of you remember anything that was said? Anything else?"

One of them looked at the other and made a face that seemed to encourage her to speak. Blythe looking at Bet, I concluded.

"I heard them," said Bet. She hunched her shoulders a little, as if uncertain whether she should continue.

"It's not eavesdropping if they're shouting," I told her. "Their voices can be loud."

She nodded. "*Oui.* They were loud. And angry. I couldn't really hear what they said except *absurdité! Ridicule!*"

"Did you hear anything that might give a clue to who the woman was? Did they know her, do you think?"

"Oh, *mais oui*, it was certain they knew her. They were surprised to see her, you see, but they were not angry—not at first. But then." She spread her hands and wiggled her fingers near her face, exactly as her sister had done to describe the bombastic conversation. "*La madame* was . . . she was not so loud, you see, as *les messieurs*, but she was insistent, and she sat on the chair near the stairs." Bet gave me a wary look.

"And you were near the top of the stairs, of course, sweeping or dusting," I said with an encouraging smile. "And so you could not help but hear some of what she said."

"*Bien entendu.* She was . . . she was speaking of the spirits. The ghosts, I think. The, eh, the voices?" She rotated her hands, as if to extract the word from midair. "And *les messieurs*, they were not . . . They did not like to hear that. M. Fautrier, he was not so loud about it, but M. Saint-Léger, why, he laughed. It was not a funny laugh, you see, but he scoffed at her as if he were angry or did not like what she was saying."

I nodded, remaining silent, hoping she'd say more.

"I think . . . I think they called her Vierca. Madame Vierca. But I cannot be certain, you see, for they were not so loud at first." Bet gave an abrupt nod, looked at her sister, and I realized that was all the information she had to impart.

"One more question. Have you ever seen that woman before? Either here or anywhere else?" I sounded like Hercule Poirot or Sam Spade. Apparently, my experience involving murders had turned me into a skilled interrogator.

They both shook their heads, and I smiled and thanked them once again before bidding them bonsoir as they finished pulling soft knitted hats down over their ears.

After they left, my attention fell on the apple pastry. I decided it looked too delicious to just leave sitting there, so I made up a little tray including the tart and a pot of fresh coffee. It was far too early for dinner, but surely my messieurs would like what the English would call a "tea" and what I would call my afternoon snack. I put the tray in the dumbwaiter; then, with some trepidation, I climbed the stairs to the salon.

"Bonsoir!" I called gaily as I came across the landing into the sitting room, whose two doors were wide open, as usual.

It was a comfortable and well-appointed room and very French, with its heavy tasseled draperies cloaking the tall windows, paisleys strewn over side tables and the back of the sofa, and Louis XV curved furnishings. A thick rug covered the worn wooden floor, and a huge fin de siècle cabinet of ornate mahogany and glass housed a variety of spirits and wine, as well as cocktail pitchers, shakers, strainers, glassware, and small serving dishes. Each gentleman sat in a comfortable chair whose upholstery and cushion had long conformed to the shapes of their respective bodies, with small tables within easy reach for cat and dog treats, ashtrays, and books or newspapers. A large, low table completed the sitting area, sitting between the sofa and their seats. The room was toasty warm and smelled of cigarettes and the grooming products my messieurs used.

Next to the fireplace, which contained a crackling fire, was a set of narrow double doors that led into the small greenhouse. The glass was fogged with steam from the warmth inside, helped, I knew, by the very same fireplace that heated the salon, as well as by some other warming element Grand-père had conceived. Every morning a young man came to bring upstairs the day's supply of wood, the remains of which sat in a large metal tub next to the hearth.

The draperies on the windows lining one long wall were open, allowing the light from the cold gray day to filter into the room, assisted by several floor lamps with shades of dangling fringe and by table lights with colorful Tiffany glass.

Oscar Wilde, who had not heard me come into the house, for I'd entered through the back kitchen door, was delighted by my appearance. He sprang off Oncle Rafe's lap and launched himself toward me with barks and wild, springing leaps. Since I'd neglected him earlier, I succumbed to his adorableness this time and offered him one of the tiny biscuits Oncle Rafe kept on the table next to his chair.

Acting as if the events earlier today had never happened, I leaned over to kiss Oncle Rafe on the cheek where he sat smoking one of the dark cigarettes he favored. It smelled spicy and musky.

"*Bonsoir, ma chérie,*" he said, patting me on the hand with a quiet smile. Monsieur Wilde jumped back into his master's lap with the ease of a cat, hopeful for another chance at a biscuit.

"Blythe made an apple tart, and it looks delicious," I said, navigating past the small furnace, which offered a wave of heat, in order to greet my grandfather, as well. "I made a tray."

He smiled up at me and offered a cheek for my greeting, waving his cigarette, a different brand, away from me. "I thought I smelled something delicious. That is very kind of you, *ma mie.*"

I was breathing easier now that they were both calmer and things seemed to have gone back to normal. It took no time to pull the dumbwaiter and its burden up to the salon level, and soon we each had a small plate with some of the delicate tart, coffee, and a lace-trimmed napkin. Madame X eyed me with her cool green eyes from her post on the back of the sofa, and I realized I'd neglected to give her one of the catnip treats as was her due. I quickly rectified this error and sat down next to her.

"And how was your appointment, then, Tabi?" asked Grand-père. "Was Madame Woodward on time for once?"

I found it mildly surprising that he would remember this detail and know whom I had been meeting with today, especially considering the state of his mind when I'd left. But then again, for a man over eighty, he was still very sharp mentally, if not quite as spry physically. Both of them were.

My heart squeezed as I thought yet again how much I'd come to love them over the past eleven months, and how close I'd come to losing them back in January. I hoped whatever had upset them was no longer a worry.

I told them about my appointment and about the referral for a British student. They chuckled when I explained that it would probably go nowhere due to my gauche American accent, and they assured me that I had hardly any accent at all. Then I casually mentioned that I was meeting up with Jean-Luc Héroux tonight.

"That is the veterinarian, *non*?" Grand-père asked, eyeing me keenly. "We have not met him yet."

"But we have met *le bon inspecteur* Merveille," said Oncle Rafe, giving me a pointed look. "Why do you not go on a date with him, *chérie*? He is very charming and very handsome."

My cheeks heated, but I kept my expression and voice casual. "*Bien entendu, oncle.* He is a very nice man, but he is also engaged to be married," I reminded him—for the umpteenth time.

Yes, Étienne Merveille was a very nice, very intelligent, very polite, and sometimes wryly amusing man whom I'd come to know during those three murder investigations. He was too formal and reserved to be considered charming, whatever my *oncle* might suggest. Nor was he classically handsome, although he certainly wasn't unattractive. Merveille and I had even shared two meals tête-à-tête—and several others, crowded around the table in Julia's kitchen. Recently, to my intense embarrassment, and despite the number of uncomfortable interactions we'd had (mostly with him lecturing me about not getting involved in murder investigations), I'd realized that I was terribly attracted to him. Of course, I had admitted this to no one, especially Julia.

"Eh." Grand-père flapped an indolent hand at the concept of Marguerite, Merveille's fiancée, whose photograph had until recently sat on his desk at *la police judiciaire.* The fact that the picture had been missing from the desk the last time I was in his office was a point I had *not* mentioned to Julia—or anyone. "What are engagements but to be broken?"

I rolled my eyes, and Grand-père muttered something to Oncle Rafe. They chuckled, and the look they exchanged was one of long, comfortable intimacy and shared secrets.

"As I was saying, I am meeting Jean-Luc—yes, he is the veterinarian—a little bit later tonight."

"He is not bringing you the cat," said Grand-père, pausing in the process of lighting a cigarette and fixing me with a sharp look.

Madame X hissed at me, then sprang off the sofa onto a table, then up to the fireplace mantel. Her diamond collar glittered like the fallen straps of the evening gown worn by her namesake, the woman in a famous John Singer Sargent painting. An artist's copy of the original hung on the wall here in the salon. Heaven knew how much Grand-père and Oncle Rafe had paid for the piece, which portrayed the woman as Singer Sargent had originally painted her—with a strap falling down on one shoulder. That version of the painting had been deemed too provocative for the American public, so the artist had "fixed" the strap, setting it back on the woman's shoulder, before the image was displayed in a museum in Chicago.

Just as haughty and elegant as her namesake, Madame glared

at me from her perch. She gave another hiss, this time silent but wide enough that I saw needle-sharp teeth.

I didn't know why she was so upset. I'd never even brought the bedraggled alley cat who'd saved my life anywhere near the house. But somehow *madame le chat* knew the possibility had been discussed.

"No, Madame X, you don't need to worry that Lupin will be invading your household," I said. I had named the cat after Arséne Lupin, the mysterious and cunning cat burglar of French fiction. It was a fitting name for a scrappy but heroic feline who'd lived on the streets and in the alleys.

He—the cat, not the fictional character—had taken great exception to being abducted and brought to Jean-Luc's veterinary practice in my misguided attempt to have him treated for a nasty infection. Presumably, he shared Patrick Henry's opinion of "Give me liberty or give me death" when it came to his streetwise life.

Lupin had taken the first opportunity for a jailbreak—after he'd been treated—and, so far as I knew, was still living a dissolute life on the streets near the vet's office. I had caught sight of him last week, but he'd refused to come down from a nearby balcony to thank me for all I'd done—or for the number of francs I'd spent getting him healthy, just so he could go back out and cruise the *rues* and alleys.

Grand-père grunted and took a drag on his newly lit cigarette. "Very well, then. If you do not intend to come home tonight, then you will telephone us, *non*?" He gave me a keen look.

I blushed again. Damn it, these Frenchmen were just too much. If it wasn't food or wine on their minds, it was sex. Despite their openness about lovemaking, *I* didn't feel comfortable discussing my love life with my grandfather. Not that I had a love life. Jean-Luc Héroux was the first man . . . well, other than a killer . . . that I had even considered going out with since arriving in the City of Light.

"I'll be home, and probably early," I replied firmly. "Tomorrow is a very important day, and I've kept my schedule clear so that I can help you."

"What? Help us? With what?" Oncle Rafe seemed genuinely confused.

"Why, with the gathering at Maison de Verre," I said, just as confused. "There must be plenty of things to do."

"Oh, no, no, no, Tabi, there is nothing for you to do but to arrive," Grand-père told me. "It is all managed. The flowers, the settings, the menu. Chef Debord and Madame Child will be there *dans la cuisine*, preparing, and we have the maître d', Monsieur Barbier, and *le vin* . . . No, there is nothing for you but to be there. And you will wear the Dior, *non*?" His eyes gleamed with appreciation at the thought.

I hadn't thought to wear the haute couture frock my messieurs had insisted on buying for me from Maison Dior—and which had somehow been handsewn, created especially for me in far less time than usual due to some miracle they'd wrought. I hadn't expected to get it for months, but after two fittings in less than three weeks, the frock had been boxed up and sent home with me—much to my messieurs' delight.

"Isn't it a bit formal for the gathering tomorrow night?" I ventured. I had to admit, I *was* looking forward to wearing the gorgeous confection of hand-pleated creamy fabric that looked like a collection of clamshells beautifully arranged to create skirt and bodice. But to a small gathering in the restaurant? What if I got food or wine on it?

"But of *course* you will wear it!" Oncle Rafe exclaimed.

At the same time Grand-père said, "But that is why we pressed Christian to have it made so quickly, *chérie*! For you to wear tomorrow night."

"Then of course I will wear it," I said with a smile and a dart of excitement. It was the most gorgeous item of clothing—and the most expensive—I'd ever owned. I'd simply not eat or drink a thing.

"And you will have the Mademoiselle Feydeau to help with your hair?" Grand-père asked.

I reached up automatically to touch my hair, which I'd recently had cut into a short, very chic, very French style. It was short in the back and longer around the front, framing my face with sexy tendrils and skimming the nape of my neck, leaving it bare.

"I can do it myself," I replied, albeit a little uncertainly. Was there something I didn't know about my new style? My friend Lisette Feydeau had cut it for me about a month ago, and although it had taken some getting used to, I loved it. My head no longer looked like an explosion of curls, wild with static electricity, when I took off my hat. I felt as if I truly looked Parisian, at least as far as my hair. I still wore my American boots, which did cause comment sometimes, as they were equipped with chunky dark heels and very clearly *not* fashionable.

"Only it is getting a bit long, you see," Oncle Rafe told me. "Perhaps it needs a bit of a trimming?"

I stifled a smile. Not only were my messieurs obsessed with my sex life, but they were also deeply involved in my fashion and style. I supposed that wasn't very surprising for a pair of Frenchmen who had their own consummate styles.

"I'm sure I can get her to give me a trim before tomorrow night," I replied. "I'll call her hotel and leave a message. Now, I think I'll take a soak in the tub before I leave to meet Jean-Luc. I'll take the tray down when I go."

They waved me off, and I gave Monsieur Wilde one more little pat on his silky head before I jogged up the steps. I did not even consider offering one to Madame X, who had continued to eyeball me with a furious green stare.

A couple of hours later, it was after six, and Jean-Luc and I were sitting in a cozy but crowded bistro around the corner from his veterinary office, which was just three blocks from rue de l'Université.

It was dark outside, and the *rue* was filled with cars rumbling past. The sidewalk was clogged with pedestrians walking their dogs or heading to dinner and drinks—sometimes both. More than one dog lay tucked beneath the tables here at the bistro as his or her master ate, drank, and visited with companions. A policeman rode by on his bicycle, its lantern bobbing and swaying from where it hung on the handlebars.

Our table, pushed up next to a steamy window, was so small our knees touched. Neither of us seemed to feel the urge to shift away. In fact, Jean-Luc was smiling warmly at me as he drew on a cigarette, and I was smiling right back.

I liked him quite a lot. He was charming, as most Frenchmen were, and funny, and his love for animals shined through in his words and actions. He was good-looking without being suavely handsome, with a straight, neatly trimmed mustache and dark hair that always seemed unable to stay combed back. A stray lock often fell over his left temple, and I imagined that was because he spent so much time looking down at his patients—or struggling with them.

"And the poor pussycat—well, she was *not* having it. She did not want to be held, and she certainly did not want to be jabbed with a needle," he was telling me with a smile. "I could not hold her still, and I did not want to poke her more than once, which might happen if she was squirming. And there was no one to help me," he added, giving me a sort of woeful look. "And so, me? I had to become a genius."

I grinned, sipping from a tiny glass of vermouth. "And what sort of genius thing did you do?"

"Why, I put *le petite chat* into a cage, you see, but then I found a piece of wood that fit inside, as well. I crowded her, *le chat,* into the cage and used the wood to hold her very tight to the one side, you see? And so her fur and her skin, they bulged out through the openings of the cage like a woman's breasts spilling over her brassiere!" His eyes danced, and I managed not to blush over his comment. "*Et voilà*! I could push the needle right into her skin. She could not move away, and she could not claw or bite me, eh, you see? And it was over in a minute."

"I'll bet she had plenty to say about that afterward, though," I replied, thinking of Madame X's hissing earlier today and Lupin's yowling when I captured him and put him in a cage, as well.

"Oh, *oui,* she was very loud. She was *dying*, she told me. *Dying*! And she was quite mortified, too, you know. *Les chats,* they have much dignity. Far more than *les chiens.*" He nodded sagely and settled back into his chair, eyeing me. "This is nice, here, with you. Very nice, Tabitha." His mustache curved with his smile.

"It is."

Our knees bumped together, and he moved one of his so that it was rubbing gently against mine, sending little ripples of warmth up my thigh. I took another sip of my vermouth. It was sweet without being cloying. Until I came to Paris, I'd only ever had the aperitif as a mixer in a vodka martini, but here it was a common sipping liquor—and Julia used it in a lot of dishes she cooked, as well.

A couple walked by close to our window, talking and laughing so loudly that I could hear them through the glass, and despite the attractive and charming man across from me, my attention was drawn to the window. As the couple passed by, my gaze fell on a figure standing just across the sidewalk from my window.

She stood under a streetlight, smoking a cigarette, bundled in the same coat and scarf she'd been wearing when she accosted me earlier today.

CHAPTER 3

I gasped, surging up from my chair, and Jean-Luc hastened to follow suit, bumping the little table.

"What is it? Tabitha?"

"That woman," I said, yanking up my coat from where it was hanging over the back of my seat. "Out there. She—I need to speak to her. Excuse me."

I was still pulling on my coat as I rushed out the front of the little eatery, the bell atop the door jangling wildly.

She didn't seem surprised to see me rushing toward her. She took one last drag on her cigarette, then tossed it to the ground in a glowing arc.

"Who are you?" I asked before she could speak. My breath made rapid white puffs in the cold air. "Are you following me? Spying on me? What do you want?"

"I am Madame Vierca, and I want only to help you—and Monsieur Saint-Léger and Monsieur Fautrier." Her gaze was as intense as it had been this afternoon. She fixed it on me with deep, dark eyes set in sunken cavities. They were hypnotic and alluring when they captured my gaze in the pool of light from above. I felt a little shiver of something jitter through me.

"What do you mean, help them? Help me?" I demanded, blinking to break the connection between us.

By now, Jean-Luc had clomped up behind me. "Who is this?" he asked, handing me the woolen beret and scarf I'd left by the table.

I held up a hand, silently asking him to wait, never pulling my attention away from the woman. I was getting a better look at her now.

She was old, but not as old as Grand-père and Oncle Rafe. Maybe sixty? Her skin was a dusky olive shade, shiny in the low light. It was a face that that still held beauty in its sharp cheekbones and elegant nose. Her skin was lined with age but not covered by grid marks of wrinkles. A lock of thick, very dark hair had escaped from the scarf around her face and curled at her dusky cheek. Her eye makeup was smudged, but she still wore red lipstick. She smelled of cigarette and some other scent I couldn't identify, but it was smoky and musky, exotic. It emanated from the heavy woolen coat in which she was bundled.

"Your grand-père is in danger. I have tried to warn him, but he does not listen. He is not open, you see. But I think you . . . you are, mademoiselle. You are open, yes?"

Madame Vierca continued to hold my gaze with hers and reached out to close her hand, in a fingerless glove, around my wrist. I didn't feel threatened; Jean-Luc was right there, and we were under a streetlamp on the sidewalk, with many people walking nearby. Instead, I felt another shock of energy rush through me from her touch.

"I—I don't know," I replied, pulling my hand away. I wasn't certain exactly what she meant by *open*. "And what makes you think—How do you know he's in danger? What sort of danger?"

"I see such things," she said.

"You have ESP? You're a psychic?" I wasn't certain whether to laugh or to be impressed. "A fortune teller?"

"I am a medium, mademoiselle. When they choose, those who have gone before us speak through me . . . from beyond the veil. When they have a message, I must deliver it. It is my duty because it is my gift."

My head was spinning. I had so many questions and thoughts. I settled on one. "Do you know my grand-père?"

"Ah, *oui*, I have known Maurice Saint-Léger for many years.

And Monsieur Fautrier, too. And the others." She reached for me again, this time more gently, and this time held my hand palm up so that my fingers curled, creating a sort of cup out of my hand. "Monsieur Saint-Léger, he is not open to hearing these messages I have received. He is not a believer. But you . . ." She fixed me with her eyes once more and nodded. "You . . . I should like to do a reading for you, too, mademoiselle. Will you allow it?"

"A reading?" The hair on the back of my neck—bare in the chill evening due to my short hair—lifted. But it wasn't from the cold. It was because of what she said. "What do you mean?"

"I have said it—I am a medium. I speak to those who have gone before us . . . those who are on the other side of the veil. They . . ." She paused and fixed her eyes on a point over my shoulder, as if listening to someone. Her brows lifted. "Ah, *oui*, there are those who wish to speak to you."

Aware of Jean-Luc standing there vibrating with interest and surprise, I pulled my wrist from her grip. "I—I don't think so," I said, not very firmly. I was intrigued in spite of myself, and that jittering feeling continued to sweep through me even when she was no longer touching me.

Those dark eyes gleamed, holding my gaze for a long moment. Then she looked again over my shoulder. "It is . . . *oui*, it is your grand-mère, I believe. She is here. She wishes you to listen."

Now I took a full step back. Jean-Luc's solid, warm presence behind me was welcome. "I don't believe you."

"But she says . . ." Madame tilted her head slightly, looking once again over my shoulder into nothing. "Ah, *oui*," she murmured, then returned her attention to my face. "She says that the car on the lake, it was . . ." She frowned, tilting her head the other way, straining, as if to listen. "Ah, that it was amusing and bold. Like you, mademoiselle. She is proud of you, you see."

My body went cold, then hot, and a rush of prickles swarmed me. I gaped at her. "How . . . ?"

The faraway look in her eyes, the straining to see *something* that I could not see or understand, eased. And they focused on me once more. "As I say, mademoiselle, I receive messages." Those *eyes.* They were so dark, so knowing, as they delved into my gaze, I found it difficult to breathe.

"I . . . I don't know," I managed to say, still stunned. There was no way, absolutely *no way*, this random woman knew that I'd driven a car on a frozen lake *back home in Michigan.*

"Come to me, mademoiselle. Come tomorrow. I will not charge you for the reading. You are Maurice Saint-Léger's *petite-fille.* I wish only to help some old friends." She took my hand once more, but this time, she pressed a small card into it. "Please do not wait. There isn't much time, mademoiselle. *Les neuf bleuets* . . . they lose their blooms."

She gave me one last look, a silently impassioned one. Then looking at Jean-Luc hovering behind me, she said, "Bonsoir, monsieur. Tell her she must heed me." And then she walked away.

Jean-Luc took my ungloved hand as I stared after her for a long moment. His fingers, though covered, were warm and comforting.

Finally, I shook myself out of the stupor, out of that very strange time of murky thoughts and tingling energy skittering through me.

Without speaking, Jean-Luc and I went back inside the bistro, only to find that our table had been given away. The waiter eyed us with irritation and presented Jean-Luc with the bill. He waited, tapping his foot, nose in the air, while my date paid for our drinks and the small bowl of peanuts on which we'd munched.

"I think I'd better go home," I told him as we came back out onto the street. "I . . . I feel like I ought to be near my grand-père."

"Of course I understand," he replied, lighting a cigarette. He took my hand—now gloved—with his free one, and I let him.

My head was filled with thoughts, questions, worries. Part of me wondered what Jean-Luc thought about the whole "speaking to dead people" thing, but part of me didn't want to talk about it. Not yet . . . because I wasn't sure what *I* thought.

We had walked only a few steps when Jean-Luc said, "Now, what is this about a car on a lake?" His voice held laughter and confusion.

I chuckled, relieved to have a distraction from all of the thoughts weaving through my head. I nudged my shoulder companionably against his arm while we walked. We had not yet kissed, but I suspected that was soon to change.

"I drove my fiancé's sedan onto the frozen lake in the small town where I lived back in America," I explained.

Jean-Luc halted to look down at me in shock. "You have a fiancé?"

"Not anymore," I replied. "Mostly due to me driving his car onto the lake." I chuckled.

"Ah, I am *quite* relieved to hear that." He moved in a little closer, and I felt the brick wall of a building behind me as I eased back against it.

I looked up at him, saw the intent in his eyes, and lifted my face to meet his lips. He leaned in, his cigarette hand propped against the wall above my head, his other hand still holding mine. Those fingers tightened on mine as our lips met. His mustache was soft and silky and hardly prickled against my skin. His lips were chilly from the air, but the rest of him was not. He smelled of cigarette and something fresh and spicy and tasted of vermouth and tobacco.

It was a very nice, rather thorough kiss, and when we separated, we were both smiling. Several people walked past, giving us not the least bit of notice. The French were not at all shy about public displays of affection; they happened all the time, everywhere, and sometimes were nearly pornographic in their explicitness.

"Now you will tell to me how this happened. This car on the lake," he said, waving his cigarette in a circle, as we started to walk once more.

"It was a Ford, and it belonged to Henry McKinnon, the man

I was engaged to. Another friend bet me fifty dollars that I wouldn't do it, and of course, that spurred me on. You see, Jean-Luc, I should warn you. I have this little imp inside of me that nudges me into doing careless and impetuous things." I grinned up at him as we meandered along.

"Ah, yes, like the snooping around of the murder investigations," he replied, chuckling, as he spewed out a stream of smoke. "I like the idea of this little imp, this little fairy, or *le lutin*, bounding about inside of you like a little pussycat, poking at you to do these bold and daring things. This little imp, does she have a name?"

I shook my head, still smiling. "No, she hasn't got a name."

"Ah. That is a shame. She, like every other pet, ought to have a name." He clicked his tongue. "And so tell me, then . . . you drove onto the ice and you won the bet and your fiancé was very angry."

"That's pretty much what happened. But you have to understand, I did all the mathematical calculations and measured the depth of the ice, and so I knew it was safe. And I was going to give Henry the fifty dollars because the Ford needed new tires."

He grunted with understanding as we turned the corner onto rue de l'Université. "But of course. And he did not accept the money, then?"

"No. But he did accept my engagement ring back, and it was worth more than fifty dollars. So I think he got the tires, after all."

"And then you came to Paris to nurse your broken heart?" He looked down hopefully at me. "And to find the perfect French lover to help you forget this Henri?"

I laughed, my breath making white puffs in the air. "My heart was not the least bit broken, Jean-Luc. Henry and I were both different people after the war, and I think that . . . well, that disagreement, that fight, whatever you want to call it, was just the impetus for us both to do something we knew was right."

"Ah, *oui*. To end a relationship when its time has come is a difficult but necessary thing. But it is always exciting to begin a new one, *non*?"

We had reached the walkway leading to my house and stopped there. He tossed aside his cigarette and took advantage of having both hands free to ease me into his arms, fully against his warm body.

Just as we were getting into a good, delicious kiss, the door to the house opened. I jolted back, pulling away more from surprise and concern than embarrassment at being caught making out on the street. Like I said, the French encourage lovemaking on any level, in any way or anytime.

A man was coming out of the house. It was neither Oncle Rafe nor Grand-père. He had a cane, and he was dressed very elegantly in a long, swinging coat, a muffler, and a homburg.

"Inspecteur Devré!" I said when I recognized him. For some reason, my face exploded with heat.

It probably had to do with the fact that this elderly man—about the same age as my messieurs and their close friend—was the great-uncle of Inspecteur Étienne Merveille, and he had just caught me making out with a man on the street. Not that anyone knew about my attraction to Merveille, and there was no reason for me to be embarrassed . . . but we aren't always logical in our reactions, are we?

Guillaume Devré was long retired from working at the *police judiciaire*, but I suspected he often advised his nephew on cases. He was, as I understood it, a legend at what was called la Sûreté when he was on the force as a homicide detective. I had met him a few weeks ago, when he'd come to visit my messieurs during the murder investigation with the poisoned wine. I'd been impressed by his thoughtful intelligence.

"Mademoiselle Knight," he said, pausing to greet us. His hand went to the brim of his hat in polite salute. "And monsieur. Bonsoir."

"Is everything all right?" I asked. "With Grand-père and Oncle Rafe?"

His eyes, just as intense and knowing as his nephew's, caught mine. "Yes, of course, mademoiselle. Why do you ask?"

I felt the bottom of my stomach drop a little under that penetrating stare. I honestly didn't know whether to believe him, and he was obviously intent on learning what I knew. "They had a visitor today, and she upset them quite a bit. I just wondered if that's why you were here."

"Ah, mademoiselle, do not worry yourself about the visitor. That woman—she is harmless. But tomorrow night it will be quite pleasant, *non*?"

His swift change of subject felt suspicious to me. Perhaps he simply didn't want to discuss the matter in front of Jean-Luc, a stranger to him.

"Yes. I am very much looking forward to it," I replied.

"Ah, my taxi has arrived. I must bid you au revoir until tomorrow, then, mademoiselle. Monsieur." He tipped his hat again and continued on his way to the street, where a cab had just pulled up.

"He is from the police?" Jean-Luc said, watching the taxi drive away.

"He's retired. But he's a longtime friend of my messieurs."

"Ah, I see. And I see also that my intention to ask you to dinner tomorrow night will be in vain, *hein*?" He gave me a crooked grin.

"Yes, sorry." I quickly explained about the little soirée at Maison de Verre and made it clear that I didn't have the freedom to invite anyone as a guest, as it was very small and very much my messieurs' gathering and I would be playing hostess. I didn't want Jean-Luc to think I wouldn't have invited him if I could have, for I would've. Probably.

We said good night with another prolonged, delicious kiss, which almost made me want to invite him inside to the ground floor sitting room. It had been a long while since I'd had a boyfriend—or, as my Grand-père would say, a lover.

My hand was on the door latch when Jean-Luc said, "Are you going to see her? The woman, the medium?"

I turned back to him. I had been wondering the same thing. "I don't know," I said, and that was the truth.

"And you waited until *now* to tell me all of this?" Julia cried, taking my arm so I'd stop and look at her.

It was early the next morning, and we were clomping down the sidewalk in our boots, on our way to the food market on rue de Bourgogne. She'd just returned from her morning class at Le Cordon Bleu, and as was her habit—and had become mine—we were going to see what the merchants in the market had to offer.

Normally, Julia would be buying all the ingredients for whatever dish she'd learned in her morning class with Chef Bugnard, in order to make it for Paul when he came home for lunch. But because of the soirée at Maison de Verre this evening, she would be prepping some of the dishes for that event instead. Paul, she said, would have to bite the bullet and eat lunch with his coworkers today. "There will be no special nap for us after lunch, either," she'd added with a saucy grin.

Now she continued to laughingly berate me. "A strange woman shows up and starts talking about danger for Monsieur Saint-Léger, and she gets chased out of the house by Monsieur Fautrier, and then she *follows* you on your date! Which you didn't *bother* to tell me about, either, yesterday, Tabitha." Her blue eyes danced with humor and mild reprimand. "And then the woman *accosts* you while you were on a *date*?"

"I didn't want to call you and interrupt your evening," I said lamely.

"Ridiculous! These are the sorts of things *friends* tell each other. Immediately! That's why we have *telephones*. I'm simply *astonished* that you kept all of this to yourself until now."

We'd started walking again, Julia in her six-foot-three glory looming over my five-foot-five as our arms bumped against each other. Each of us carried a large market bag of heavy canvas, and thankfully, the day wasn't terribly cold and there was no wind. It was actually almost pleasant and quite pretty—a bright blue sky with warm, bright sunshine. The snow had melted, leaving gray slush mixing with mud along the edges of the sidewalk and street. Gray-brown grass and spindly bushes suggested that spring might be just around the corner.

"It was just all so strange, with the way the messieurs were upset and then pretended nothing happened—and then Madame Vierca showing up outside the bistro where I was with Jean-Luc. It's creepy."

"I'll say! But it's also really very *interesting*, isn't it? She *must* be legitimate if she knew about you *driving* the car over the lake!"

"That's what really got to me. But . . . it *is* possible she knew about it. Grand-père knows because I told him, and maybe he mentioned it to her, or to someone else, who mentioned it to her. They've known each other for a long time, she said." I had turned those thoughts over and over in my head all night, trying to figure out a way Madame Vierca might have discovered the information. I wasn't quite ready to believe my deceased grand-mère had actually *told* her about it . . . although, honestly, there was a part of me that wanted it to be true. After all, I was no stranger to playing around with a Ouija board or having a palm reader look at my hands or getting a tarot reading during a carnival.

"That's a big stretch, Tabs," Julia said. "A *really* big stretch."

"But that's the sort of thing so-called clairvoyants *do*," I replied. "They do their research so they can, I don't know, ingratiate themselves with their targets. Make it seem like they're legitimate."

Julia stopped and looked down at me. "But why? For what purpose? What will she gain by all this? She told you she wouldn't charge you for the reading, and she's been very persistent, especially after that *scene* at your house yesterday. She seems really worried about your grandfather."

"Yes, she is persistent. But remember, Grand-père is very, very rich . . . so what better way to wiggle her way into his confidences—and his bank account—than by hooking his granddaughter first?"

Julia boomed a laugh, shaking her head. "I never knew what a cynical person you are, Tabitha!"

"My dad's a detective—I learned at a young age not to trust just anyone. And he taught me a lot about con artists so I wouldn't ever be taken in." I shrugged. "I guess it's in my blood."

"And so, it seems, is investigating murders. Anyhow, you *are* going to go, aren't you, Tabs? Are you going today? I want to go with you when you do! I've got until one or so before I have to get *cracking*."

"Oh, I don't know," I moaned, throwing my arms wide. My market bag swung out, then clunked back against my side.

"What do you have to lose?" Julia asked—quite reasonably. "Maybe she *does* know something. And if you don't go and something happens to your grand-père, how are you going to feel about that?"

"I know," I said miserably. "I thought about that, too."

"Bonjour, Madame Marie!" Julia cried suddenly, her voice carrying across the way.

She was waving to Madame Marie, known throughout the market as Marie des Quatre Saisons because she always had the best produce throughout the year—even now, in the winter, when pickings were slim.

Julia and I approached the large wagon where Madame Marie sat, as she always did, on a stool, with her cigarette and a small fire in a metal pail to keep her hands warm. She was a tiny, round, but wizened old lady of uncertain age—surely well into her sixties or seventies—bundled up in a heavy wool coat, fingerless gloves, and a thick muffler. Today she wore a stretchy wool hat pulled down over her gray hair, which stuck out like little tufted wings over her ears.

"*Bonjour, madame et mademoiselle!*" Madame Marie cried, beckoning us to come closer, the smoke from her cigarette making snakelike streaks in the air. "I have something you will really love, Madame Child. You will want to kiss me on the cheeks, *hein!*" She tapped both of her round, wrinkled cheeks with gusto, somehow managing not to singe her hair with the cigarette. "And how are you today, eh? Did you have a nice evening, eh?"

This last was, as always, directed at me—and what she was really asking was, Were there any men in my life?

Somehow—mostly due to Julia's gregariousness with everyone she met and her determination to get me married off as happily as she was—my love life had become *le grand sujet* for the entire market. Also surely contributing to the collective interest was that I was the granddaughter of Maurice Saint-Léger and was half French, so I really was one of *them.*

I should explain that shopping for food in Paris is nothing like going to the grocery store back home. In Paris you walked to a street market that was usually a combination of wagons and carts, storefronts, and vendor stalls. Everyone knew everyone, and the merchants and their customers—all local, most living within a few blocks—were a little community of their own. Madame Marie had the best produce; Mademoiselle Fidelia offered fresh eggs of all sizes and colors, from chicken to duck to quail and so on; Mademoiselle Yvette owned a small cart with a variety of flowers (obviously far more limited in March than in June or July); Monsieur Gérard offered his mead; and Monsieur Michel displayed all the gorgeous mushrooms he grew in the catacombs. There was a fishmonger, a *fromagerie*, a *cellier de vin,* a *tabac*, a *pâtisserie,* and a boulangerie—and more. It was a lively and colorful experience, shopping at the market.

I smiled at Madame Marie as I began to poke through a basket of potatoes. At least I knew how to pick out a good spud. "I had a very nice evening. Thank you, madame."

"Ah, *oui,* it seemed that way, indeed," she replied, her rheumy eyes glinting with delight. "That was Monsieur Héroux escorting you along the street, was it not?"

My gaze shot to hers. "You saw us?"

"Ah, *oui,* indeed, mademoiselle." She was grinning, revealing crooked, tobacco-stained teeth. "It is very good to have a nice young man, eh? So tall and strong makes for a good lover, *non?*" She tossed her cigarette stub into the little fire.

I started to demur and explain that we'd been on only a few dates, but decided, Why bother? She would think what she liked, anyway, and maybe she wouldn't have so many questions if she thought I was deep in a relationship. "He is very nice," I replied, ignoring the comment about a "good lover."

"What is it you *have* for me, madame?" asked Julia. "I am ready to kiss your cheeks!" She had already started a collection of items she meant to purchase, piling up tiny blue and red potatoes, fat purple and white turnips with little strings of root still clinging to them, a rather sad-looking cabbage if you asked me, and several beets with wilting greens.

Wilting.

I remembered suddenly, in a flash, what Madame Vierca had said last night, during her rantings and ravings.

Les neuf bleuets . . . they lose their blooms.

It sounded like nonsense to me, but for some reason, it came back to my mind now, as I looked at the sad, straggly beet greens. A little prickle ran down my spine—not so very different from what I'd felt when Madame Vierca took me by the hand last night.

I knew a *bleuet* was a small flower, a cornflower or a bachelor's button, I think is what we called them back home. I didn't know why she would have been talking about flowers wilting.

"Madame Marie, when you saw me and Monsieur Héroux last night, did you see a woman?" I realized that was a vague question—surely there had been many other women out and about—and so I added, "Someone who was following me? She was older than me and bundled up in a scarf and coat." I struggled to think of any other detail, for those could describe any number of people on the street in the winter. "Um . . . her scarf was dark blue, and she wore bright red lipstick." Which also described any woman one might see in Paris.

"Someone was following you, eh?" said Madame, glancing up at me sidewise as she withdrew a small wooden basket from beneath her counter. "Not a jealous lover of the good Monsieur Héroux?"

Julia exploded with excited shrieks when she saw that the basket was filled with strawberries. Luscious, ripe red strawberries. I joined her in her delight. *Strawberries! In March!*

"Oh my God! Where did you get these? You are a *goddess*, Madame Marie! A *genius*! An *angel*! *Merci, merci, merci*! Ye gods, they're going to cost the world, aren't they? But I'll *pay* it!" She lunged for Madame, planting two loud, smacking kisses on her cheeks, nearly bowling the little woman off her stool.

A little breathless, Madame righted herself and gave me a little nod. But she spoke to Julia first. "*Oui*, they are not cheap, madame." She named a figure that had Julia's eyes goggling.

Julia clapped a hand to her chest, gasping, as if she were having a heart attack, even as her eyes continued to dance with delight. She began to dig in her purse to withdraw the funds. "Where did you get them?" she asked again.

"Ah, well, I have many friends, you see," Madame replied. "And there was a shipment into Les Halles from Algeria, and someone owed me a favor. It is always good to have the favors owed, *non*?" She grinned and shrugged. Then she turned to me in a sudden movement. Like those of the woman last night, Madame Marie's eyes held none of the cloudiness of age. "Do you speak of the woman Madame Vierca?"

I jolted. "Yes. You know her?"

"*Mais oui*. Eh, I know *of* her," Madame clarified. "Who does not?" She waved a hand to encompass the market, the neighborhood, the city. . . .

"She followed me last night. What do you know about her?" I asked.

Madame took the francs Julia had counted out, and shoved them into a deep pocket. "What is it you want to know, mademoiselle? If she is who she says she is? What she says she is?"

"Yes." I ignored Julia, who was hugging the small basket to her chest, still in vocal raptures over the unexpected bounty. "She wants to give me a reading."

"Ah, *je comprends*." Madame eased back slightly, eyeing me closely. "Well, mademoiselle, all I can tell you is that I know of many who have spoken to Madame Vierca and none of them call her a fraud." She shrugged and extracted a rumpled pack of Gauloises to light a new one. "*Mais bien sûr*, I have not paid the exorbitant fees she charges to listen to her," she said, ignoring the irony that she'd just charged a fortune for a basket of strawberries.

"I'm not sure I believe in that sort of thing," I said, even though . . . well, I kind of did. And I thought I maybe *wanted* to.

Madame leaned forward. "I have lived many years, mademoiselle, and I have seen many things, and there is one thing that I know. Many, many parts of the life are not meant to be understood or explained. So many strange things in this world . . . The watchmaker in rue Zacharie for one, eh?" Her eyes gleamed. "With the special watch? But if Madame Vierca, if she has something to tell you, I think you must find out what it is."

CHAPTER 4

"Well, that was very exciting," Julia said as we clomped along, heading back after a few more stops at the market.

I wasn't certain whether she was referring to the strawberries or to what Madame Marie had said about Madame Vierca, but I suspected she was talking about the strawberries. After all, she *was* Julia Child.

"I can't *wait* to get these fat, juicy little *jewels* into my kitchen," Julia went on, confirming my suspicion. "I sneaked one, Tab, and it was like—like *ambrosia* on my tongue! Like *summer* exploding in my mouth! I'll give you one of these juicy little nuggets *if* you promise you won't go to see this Madame Vierca without me."

I laughed. "For the price of a strawberry, I'll make sure you can come with me. We'll go right away—as soon as we drop everything off at home. But wait a minute." I stopped.

We had just passed Madame Marie's stall, which was at the beginning of the market and thus on our way toward home. Near her was the small cart belonging to Mademoiselle Yvette, the flower seller. That was what had caused me to halt.

I went over to Mademoiselle Yvette, and as always, she greeted me with a sweet smile. Since it was March, her offerings were limited, but I noticed she did have some white and pink carnations. There were buckets (without water in them, for it would freeze) containing boxwood, holly, and evergreens, as well as some eucalyptus and dried flowers that I couldn't identify.

"Bonjour, mademoiselle," she said, responding to my greeting. She was younger than me, but not by much. She wore a dark blue coat and a scarlet knit cap over her springy dark hair. Her fingerless gloves were knitted in a red and white chevron pattern. She had a round, button-tipped nose and a number of freckles scattered over her pink cheeks. She, too, had a small fire going in a little metal pail and a cigarette in one hand. "And what is it I can help you with today?"

"I'd like some of the pink carnations," I replied. "Six please. I think Grand-père would appreciate something brightening up the salon. And some of that boxwood, too, I think."

"Of course, mademoiselle. And you had the nice date last night, eh?" she said, casting me a grin as she carefully began to pluck the flowers from their bucket while holding her cigarette. The chill in the air kept the blooms fresh without the need for water.

I didn't bother to be exasperated by her question. Instead, I gave her a saucy smile and a wink. "It was *very* nice," I purred, deciding that if I couldn't beat the gossip, I might as well feed it. "Do you know who Madame Vierca is? The woman who speaks to the dead?"

"Mm. Perhaps," replied Mademoiselle Yvette as she deftly wrapped my flowers in crinkling brown paper. She wasn't looking at me, which I found interesting. "Perhaps I have heard of her." She shrugged.

"She was following me on my date last night so she could speak to me, and she said something about wilting *bleuets*—no, that the nine *bleuets* were losing their blooms. I thought I would ask you about it, since you are an expert on flowers. I wondered if it meant something in particular."

Now she looked up, frowning. "The wilting *bleuets*? Nine bluets? No, no, I do not think I have ever heard of something like that."

"What kind of flower is a *bleuet*? I think it's a cornflower, or I think we call them bachelor's buttons. Is that correct?"

Mademoiselle Yvette nodded. "*Oui.* It is a small flower with many frilly petals. It looks much like the carnations, but not so big." She showed me a circle with her fingers about the size of an American quarter. "It has a long stem, you see. It is very nice for the vases, because it will last a long time. And there are not so many blue flowers, *hein*?"

I nodded. "And a *bleuet*—that's what people wear on the Eleventh of November, right? Little *bleuet* flowers made from felt or paper."

"*Oui, oui.* These *bleuets de France*, they are in remembrance, you see, for the young men who fought in the Great War. The first terrible war," she said, amending her statement with a grimace. "It is sad that we have had two such terrible wars, and both with Germany taking parts of our country, *non*?"

"It is," I replied with great feeling—and a familiar wave of gratitude that America had mostly been spared bombing or other attacks on its soil.

"But *le bleuet*, he even grew in the destroyed fields, the wasteland of the Western Front, after the fighting. He was strong and resilient—the first sign of life after so much destructions! And he represented us, the French, for *we* are strong and resilient, and we are still here, even after all the . . . *egh*!" She made a disgusted noise and spat on the ground.

I was sure she was thinking of the Germans and their occupation of the city, as well as of the terrors of the First World War.

"*Le bleuet* was a bright spot of color and hope springing forth in the muddy, ruined trenches, and so that is why he became the symbol of hope. And, too, for the young men who came in late to fight—they wore the blue trousers instead of the red *pantalons*. Many of them were not even twenty years old."

I nodded thoughtfully. I hadn't known most of that, only that on November eleventh, the posies were sold and worn all over the country in honor of the veterans and anyone who'd been affected by the war. Widows. Children. Anyone.

"You've never heard of *les neuf bleuets*?"

"*Non.* It means nothing to me, mademoiselle." She smiled apologetically, then gestured to the paper-wrapped carnations in a subtle indication that she had nothing more to add to our conversation. I dug out my money.

Thanking her, I gathered up the flowers and rejoined Julia, who'd been standing by, waiting.

"I had another one," she confessed, her eyes dancing. "They're *impossible* to resist! They're just so *sweet* and juicy and *fresh*!"

"I don't blame you," I said, and we started walking back.

She asked me what I had been talking about to Mademoiselle Yvette, and I explained.

"The nine blue flowers," she said. "They're dying? You didn't tell me Madame Vierca said *that*."

"I almost forgot about it. She was saying so many things, and I was so taken aback by them. It was the sad looking beet greens that made me think of it. Does the phrase mean anything to you?"

"Sadly, no. I suppose I'd better have another strawberry to *drown* my sorrows," she said with a chuckle.

"At the rate you're going, they'll all be gone before we get back," I teased, but I gratefully accepted a plump berry when she offered one.

"There aren't very many left," she said, looking morosely into the basket. "Not enough to actually *do* anything with them."

"I suppose we'd best eat them, then," I replied hopefully. "If you can't make a tart or pastry with what's left, you know."

"My *poor* Paulski! He won't get any of these *happy* little gems," she gushed and popped another one into her mouth. To be honest, she didn't sound too sad about it. "I could save him one or two, but only one or two wouldn't really be worth it, and so we might just as well eat them all. That way he won't even know what he's missing!"

We both laughed, and yes, by the time we got back, the small basket of sweet berries was empty of everything but strawberry juice stains and one little green star-like stem.

The card Madame Vierca had pressed upon me gave her address as being near Place Maubert, on rue des Grands-Degrés. This was on the same side of the river but a mile or so east from where we lived. I had looked it up on Julia's map and figured it would take about thirty minutes to walk there. Since it was cold and Julia had a schedule to keep, we decided to drive to Place Maubert.

Driving was one thing, but finding a place to tuck my little Renault was another. The streets in that part of the Left Bank, not far from boulevard Saint-Germain and in what was known as the Quartier Latin, were narrow, crooked, and often dark. They were some of the oldest of the *rues* in Paris, where the medieval scholars had studied and where students still gathered today, at La Sorbonne and other educational establishments. Grand-père had once told me that one of the roads here in the Latin Quarter still led directly to Rome.

I ended up parking several blocks away from our destination and just west of the market at Place Maubert. "At least it isn't too cold," I said to Julia as we met up on the sidewalk next to my car.

"I don't mind a brisk walk—My God, what is that *incredible smell?*" she said, stopping to spin around slowly as she sniffed at the air.

Such a question never had a simple answer when you were in Paris, because there was always something delightful to smell. If it wasn't baking bread or crisping buttery pastries, it was cigarettes or *café* or some other libation . . . or sizzling sausages or stewing chicken or poaching fish. Somewhere, everywhere, someone was cooking or basting or frying or smoking or drinking, and the scents mingled with the chill of the wintry air and the coal and woodsmoke and car exhaust . . . and, of course, the river.

Whatever Julia had scented must have come from the market that filled the street at Place Maubert, which was an elongated, triangular sort of square. I counted eight different streets, some narrow enough that you'd barely fit a car through, that came together in a haphazard way to create this large space. I could even see the spire of Notre-Dame and her north rose window right down the street from us.

The *marché*, which was the oldest produce market in the city, was bustling with people going about their business, just as at our smaller one on rue de Bourgogne. Even though Julia moaned low in her throat, her eyes bouncing from a market stall filled with wheels of cheese to the *poissonnière*'s counter, to a small spice shop, she stuck by my side. That was true friendship.

Once we got past Place Maubert and its market, heading toward the river on rue Maître Albert, the streets became narrower, just wide enough for a car to pass through and not hit the heavy black iron posts set into the ground. Here the buildings—dark with soot and age, plastered with torn posters, painted with advertisements—were nearly on top of each other. They cut off the bright winter's sun even now, in the late morning, and made it seem as if we were approaching twilight. The uneven, rolling cobbled streets jutted off crookedly, adding to the dim lighting. There were fewer cars in this area, but many pedestrians and some cyclists.

I could imagine the monks of days past hunched in their flowing vestments, cloaks rippling at their ankles, as they made their way down these passages. The clip-clop of horse's hooves on the cobblestones, the smells of cooking stews and baking breads, woodsmoke, and horse dung would have filled these narrow streets. Yet to those monks, surely these passages wouldn't have felt as narrow and crowded as they did to me, who lived in a world of grand-sized automobiles and bomber planes.

I wasn't nervous about being in this dark, narrow, and close place. Not really. I was with Julia, and it wasn't even noon; in my mind, anyone who had nefarious thoughts or plans would still be sleeping off the previous night's nefarious activities. Still, I did find myself looking around more diligently than when I was walking to the market or to one of my tutoring appointments. I also had to make certain to keep an eye on the sidewalk in order to avoid stepping in dog leavings, which were notoriously plentiful in Paris.

"Where is this place?" Julia asked as we came to rue des Grands-Degrés. Maître Albert ended here in a narrow cobblestone walk crowded with trees that led to the quai de la Tournelle, and it turned west into Grands-Degrés. "If you ask me, wherever we're going doesn't seem like the place where a semi-famous medium has her office. It's kind of off the beaten path, don't you think? How many of her customers are going to come to this part of the city?"

"What makes you think she's semi-famous?" I asked.

"Madame Vierca knows your messieurs, and Madame Marie knew who she was right away, without you even telling her." Julia shrugged. "That's a pretty broad range of types of people."

I nodded thoughtfully. "Interesting. When I asked Mademoiselle Yvette whether she knew Madame Vierca, she said she might have heard of her, although she wouldn't tell me any more than that."

"See what I mean? This woman seems to have a reputation. I'm just thinking that this seems like a very unusual place to have an office, or whatever she uses to meet with clients." Julia's normally ebullient, lilting voice was more hushed and even than usual.

I checked the card Madame Vierca had given me and then my street map. Yes, we were going in the right direction. Along the river, parallel to the quai.

The little *rue* was narrow and crowded with buildings, so there was little space to walk between them and the equally narrow street. The structures were built up against each other, sharing side walls all down the way. This created a long, uneven, unbroken stretch of windows, entrances, and facades, with nowhere to turn but around. There was less foot traffic—or any vehicular traffic—here. I felt extremely aware of my surroundings and wondered how many eyes were watching us from some of these windows.

"This is such an old part of the city . . . I don't know, it sort of makes sense to me. Old places, old traditions—"

"Witchcraft and the occult?" Julia said. "Monks and alchemists? Mad scientists in their labs, studying here at the university?"

"Maybe. Old cities teem with ancient secrets, don't they? They must, as they've been here for centuries, collecting history and bits of people and memories. Knowledge. Who knows what happened here over the centuries? There must be so many stories . . ." I didn't realize I'd come to a stop, my voice trailing off into thought, until Julia nudged me.

"You all right?"

I shook off the little skitter of a shiver over the backs of my shoulders. This quiet little street, with its tall, close wall of buildings, was definitely having an effect on me. "Yes. I just feel like there are lots of things we don't know or understand in this world."

"That's what Madame Marie said."

I nodded. "This is it." I'd stopped, whether consciously or unconsciously, in front of the address on Madame Vierca's card.

I approached the green door, set into a building of striated creamy stone. Not Haussmann style—no, not here in this area—but still made from the quintessential Parisian limestone. Julia crowded up behind me, casting a shadow over me and onto the green-painted wooden door.

I rang the bell and waited, aware that my heart seemed to be thundering all the way up in my throat.

Why did I feel as if I was going to find another dead body?

CHAPTER 5

The green door swung open.

"Ah, mademoiselle. You came."

Madame Vierca was mostly hidden by the door as she gestured us to come inside.

Julia and I found ourselves stepping into a dim hallway lit only by a single naked light bulb that dangled alarmingly from the ceiling. A warm yellow glow emitted from beneath a door at the far end of the passage. A line of mismatched woven rugs covered the floor, and the warped paneled walls needed a paint job. They might have been pale blue at one time, but now they were dingy gray, with stains and water spots. The hallway was cold; I could see the short, nervous puffs of air I was emitting. I smelled cigarette smoke, burning wood, and the same unfamiliar musky scent that had clung to Madame Vierca last night. Someone in the vicinity was boiling cabbage.

Julia and I exchanged looks, but my spirited little internal imp wasn't going to allow me to back out now. I recognized the same determined, curious light in my friend's eyes and grinned at her.

"Come. This way, if you please."

Madame led us down the hall, moving quickly and soundlessly. She wore a burgundy paisley shawl over a long dark skirt that flowed over her shoes and dragged behind on the floor. I might have seen something skitter off in the shadows as we passed by, but I decided to pretend I hadn't.

We trailed her past several tightly closed doors all the way to the end, where light seeped from around the edges of a final door. After such a spartan and worn passageway, the room beyond the door was a surprise. It was well lit with a number of electric lamps on tables and standing on the floor, each of them shaded with creams and pinks and golds. A thick woven rug that looked like the Aubusson in my messieurs' salon covered the floor. The furnishings consisted of a divan facing a low table with two chairs on the other side, like in any other well-appointed parlor. There was a vase of flowers on the table, as well as an ashtray and a small wooden figurine. An oversized, worn deck of cards sat next to them. In the corner was another small table, next to a comfortable high-backed chair that looked like the perfect place to read.

Except for the doors—there were two of them, including the one through which we'd entered—the walls were draped, completely covered, with more rugs and tapestries, all in rich colors and with organic patterns. There was a single window on what I was sure was the only exterior wall of the room. It was swathed with floor-length drapes, but I could see a hint of sunlight—such as it was amongst the tall, close buildings—outside.

A coal-burning stove sat in one corner and emitted enough heat to make the room feel close and stifling as soon as we stepped inside. Creamy white candles sat in groupings on the low table between the divan and chairs and on other side tables. A haze of scented smoke filtered through the air—the same scent that, along with tobacco, clung to Madame Vierca. I couldn't see where it was coming from; it seemed to have permeated the room like oxygen.

"Sit." She gestured to the divan, and Julia and I did so.

I felt smothered by the closeness and the heavy, scented air and pulled off my hat and gloves and shrugged out of my coat, letting it crumple behind me on the sofa. Julia did the same with a grateful sigh.

Madame had taken one of the chairs across from us and, picking up the cigarette that sat smoldering in a nearby ashtray, eyed me and then Julia in turn.

"And who are you, madame?" she asked, fastening her dark eyes on my friend.

Here, for the first time, I saw Madame Vierca without the swathing of her muffler and the murkiness of evening light. She had pasty olive skin and large eyes topped with thick dark brows. Her hair was long and thick and dark, but there were strands of silver coursing through it. She wore it down and caught back in a scarf tied at the nape. Large gold and silver bangles clinked on her forearms; I thought with an internal grin that those might be too obvious an accessory for a fortune teller or psychic.

"I'm Julia Child, a friend of Tabitha's."

"Ah." Madame drew on her cigarette, still scrutinizing Julia with those fathomless dark eyes. She nodded, then reached out, her palm upright. "You have a grand energy around you, Madame. It—it *sings.* Please. May I?" She gestured again with her open hand, and Julia glanced at me.

I shrugged, and she shrugged back and offered her own hand.

Madame didn't turn Julia's hand over to look at her palm, as I'd expected her to do. Instead, she put her cigarette back in the ashtray, then gently clasped both her hands around Julia's. She closed her eyes.

"Please say your full unmarried name three times, madame. And your date of birth."

Julia spoke quietly and steadily.

When she finished, the room went very still and very silent. A prickle danced down my spine as I tried to breathe in the heavy, warm space.

Madame opened her eyes after a moment, but she didn't look at either Julia or me. Instead, in the same way she had done with me last night, she fixed her attention on a spot over Julia's shoulder. Nothing happened for a moment; then Madame murmured something I couldn't discern. She tilted her head and waited, then nodded, then murmured again, closing her eyes. She was silent for another long moment, maybe a minute or two. Then she smiled faintly and, opening her eyes, released Julia's hand.

She focused her gaze on the present. "Madame Child, you have the great energy around you, as I have said. It is a big bright light that spills onto many, many people in many places. Somehow, you will go to many people. You will . . . Eh, I am not certain how it will be . . . It makes no sense . . . but this is how I see it . . . You will go into many, many homes and bring much pleasure into them. It is strange . . . I see you standing in so very many parlors and sitting rooms." Her thick dark brows drew together, then rose into perfect arches. She shrugged, spreading her hands. "I do not know what it means, madame, or how it is possible, but it is what I see. It is what the ancient records are showing me."

Julia and I exchanged glances, but we didn't speak. I couldn't fathom what it all meant, and from the look on her face, I could tell my friend hadn't the foggiest idea, either.

"You will be happy," she said, and Julia looked at me again, her eyes popping wide, as she smiled and shrugged.

"Now, mademoiselle." Madame Vierca's grave tone drew my attention back to her gaze. "You love your grand-père very much, I know . . . or you would not have come here to see the strange old woman, eh? You are not as stubborn as he is."

"I don't know about the stubborn part, but yes, I do love him very much. What is it you want to tell me? Why is he in danger? From who? Or what?"

"Ah. The impatient one, are you? Please." As she'd done to Julia, she held out her hand toward me.

I knew what to expect, so I didn't hesitate and offered my hand.

Her dark fingers were warm and surprisingly soft around mine; for some reason, I'd expected them to be rough and knobby and skeletally cold.

"Now say your full name three times, mademoiselle, and recite your birth date."

I complied, and as I finished with my birth date, I felt a huge rush of tingling energy course through me—into my fingers and up along my arm, then through my entire body. I didn't pull my hand away from hers.

After what seemed like forever—and felt longer than when Madame had held Julia's hand—she released mine and opened her eyes.

She nodded as if someone was telling her something she already knew. Her eyes were fixed over my left shoulder as she listened to something only she could hear.

At last she turned her attention to me. "You, too, have the energy around you. But it is different." She glanced at Julia, then back at me. "It is quieter but no weaker. You have . . . It is death, I see. *Non, non, non,* not yours, mademoiselle. But you . . . how is it . . . it comes to you, death."

I scoffed, giving Julia a wry look. "I'll say."

But Madame didn't seem to hear me. She was once again focused on something I couldn't see. "But you see, death—it does not come *for* you, eh? It comes *to* you." Now she looked at me. "It *seeks* you . . . For some reason, it looks for you."

I nodded slowly, a strange calm settling over me. "Yes, that seems to be the case. But . . . I already know about that."

"Your grand-mère is here, mademoiselle. She is with you always. She watches over you, eh? And she is smiling."

I shook my head and waved a hand—this sort of weirdness was not what I'd come for. Whether my grandmother was with me or not—and I guess I believed she was—it wasn't relevant. "Tell me about my grandfather."

"He is in danger, I've said, mademoiselle. He must take care, for it will come. Like the snake in the grass, it will come, do you see? He trusts, he does. And Monsieur Fautrier . . . they sometimes do not see the threat. They believe it is over, now that *les Boches* have gone."

"What does this have to do with the Germans?" I said, surprised. Since the end of the war five years ago, there had been no threat from the former occupiers.

"No, no, it is not *les Boches.* You misunderstand. It is another threat. From within. It will come quickly, suddenly." She made a slashing movement, as if she held a sword and was beheading someone in front of her. Her expression was intense as she caught my gaze. "I have known *les messieurs* for many years. They are kind and generous men, and very smart. At one time, he—*le* Fautrier—he was more open to the 'other,' you see. The . . . other side. He was not so stubborn as the other.

"Ah, but that is over. Your messieurs—they trust, mademoiselle. They trust too easily . . . even when they should not. They believe . . . I think they believe that their age, their wisdom, and their connections, they protect them. But their lives . . . they are in danger."

Frustration rose inside me. She was making no sense and rambling on. She was telling me nothing solid, nothing credible. I wondered again whether Julia had been right—that Madame was somehow spouting information and then manufacturing vague hints in order to make me believe in her or crave more information, more details, so I would return again and again . . . and eventually begin to pay her.

Those dark eyes speared me. "You do not trust me, I see, mademoiselle."

I flushed, going even hotter than I already was in this stuffy room. "I'm sorry, but you aren't telling me anything to help, Madame."

She spread her hands and leaned forward. "Mademoiselle, I can only tell you what the spirits show me. I see a great darkness, a hot, dark red, in front of your grand-père, and there is no light. And there is a silver snake weaving between his ankles. It is a warning. That is all I can tell you."

I shook my head, still frustrated. "You said something about *les neuf bleuets*. About them, um, losing their blooms."

"What is this?" She squinted at me.

I frowned. "Last night outside the café, you said the nine bluets were dying, losing their blooms. *Les bleuets.*"

She shook her head slowly. "I do not . . . I do not remember that, mademoiselle. I am sorry."

I stared at her. "But that's what you said. I heard you say that the bluets were wilting and that my grand-père was in danger."

Madame sat back abruptly, hooking up a new cigarette with her finger from some pocket hidden beneath her shawl. "I tell you, I do not remember what you are saying, mademoiselle. Sometimes I do not remember all that I hear from the spirits, eh? But I do not *lie*," she added fiercely, brandishing the unlit smoke. "I do not cheat or make the con, mademoiselle. I see that you wonder now . . . but it is my name. Vierca. In my language, it means 'truth.' And that is what I give to you—the truth of what I see. Whether you like it or not. Whether you *believe* it or not."

I looked at her for a moment, then shrugged. "All right. I'll see what I can do about my grandfather. I'll try to keep him safe—but from what, I'm not certain."

Suddenly desperate to escape the stifling room, I rose and began to gather up my things. Julia, who'd remained silent during this exchange, did the same.

"I believe you want to help my grandfather, Madame," I said as I pulled on my coat. "I only wish I understood more what you were trying to say. What the threat is. How to protect him."

"If there is more that comes to me, mademoiselle, I will tell you. I give you my word."

Julia and I didn't speak until we were back out through the green door and into the fresh, crisp air.

"Oh my God, I can *breathe* again!" Julia exclaimed. "Wasn't that the creepiest, *strangest*, most interesting thing ever? And the whole time, I felt like I was being *smothered* like a pork chop in a sweet vermouth-mushroom sauce."

I nodded, unable to find words. I was still thinking about everything that had transpired—especially Madame not remembering what she'd said about the bluets.

"Was I the only one who thought we were going to go in there and find another dead body?" Julia asked on a half laugh, half heartfelt groan. "I think you're beginning to rub off on me,

Tabs! I'm *so* glad we didn't this time. Maybe you've broken the curse. But, ye gods, she sure had you nailed—finding death all over." She gave a little shiver I thought had nothing to do with the wintry breeze that had kicked up and was running, trapped, down the narrow *rue.*

"I hope so, too," I replied. As much as my little internal sprite was insistent that I poke around whenever a dead body showed up in my life, it still didn't make up for the fact that it was terrible and horrible and so sad that violent death seemed to find me. Maybe I should have asked Madame Vierca why that was so.

"And just *how* am I going to be in everyone's *living* room?" Julia continued, marching along. I had to hustle to keep up with her long legs—legs that clearly seemed determined to put space between us and the home of the medium. "That's *preposterous*! She was *kooky*, and a little scary. But it was all so interesting—what an experience!—and I'm going to wait and see if her predictions come true. At least she said I'm going to be *happy*."

"I can't imagine what she meant by all that . . . except . . . Well, wait a minute. You know how FDR was on the radio every night for his fireside chats? It was like him being in our living rooms during the war. Maybe you're going to be on the radio," I said.

"On the *radio*? Doing *what*? Singing?" Julia burst into raucous laughter, which caused a passerby to look over at us. "I suppose I could be cast in a radio play. 'Julia Child, *formidable* actress'!" She was still laughing. "Good grief, I just want to *cook*. Forget about being famous. If I get to work in a restaurant someday, I'll be *happy* as a sassy little clam in a herby white wine sauce." She realized she was charging ahead of me and slowed down. "And that stuff about the flowers and her not remembering saying it? She must go into a trance when she does these things—whatever you want to call them, readings?—and she doesn't remember what she says when she's in the trance."

"I guess so," I said as we reached the market at Place Maubert. "She said she doesn't remember everything the spirits tell her. Her eyes were sort of glazed over, and she was looking . . . I don't know . . . *somewhere,* somewhere else, when she was talking to us."

"She said your grandmother was with you," Julia said after a moment. "Did she mean . . . well, Monsieur Saint-Léger's wife?"

I understood the unasked question. "Yes, I'm sure she meant my grandmother Léonie. My other grandmother is still alive. Grand-mère is—was, I mean—Grand-père's wife. She died a little more than a year ago."

Julia and I hadn't talked much about the fact that I had been born and raised in Michigan, and that my grandmother had come to live with my parents when they got married just after the Great War. It was my grandmother who'd urged me to come to Paris after the war and to stay with Grand-père. She knew I felt very out of sorts and lost about what to do with my life, especially once I broke off my engagement to Henry. Grand-mère died in January 1949, and by April I had arrived in Paris.

It was the best decision I had ever made—even with all the dead bodies that kept crossing my path—or that my path crossed. I wasn't sure which was true.

"There were no hard feelings about Grand-mère coming to America with my mother and leaving Grand-père here. I think she understood the, uh, situation. I have all the letters they wrote to each other over the years. I think—I mean, I *know*—they loved each other. Just not in a romantic way. They were happy living apart. Living their separate lives. But they were very close friends."

Even though I had become completely comfortable, even delighted, by the fact that my grandfather loved Rafe Fautrier, and vice versa, in the same deep, devoted way my parents loved each other, I knew not everyone was as accepting of that situation. Julia had never given me any indication that she thought otherwise, either, but I supposed she must have been wondering about whether my grandmother was hurt or bitter about their separation. I was glad to have assuaged her fears.

"Well, now what are you going to do?" she asked.

"If I could stick Grand-père and Oncle Rafe in a bomb shelter or an army tank or—I don't know—a bank vault to keep them safe, I would. But I don't see that happening. They'd laugh me out of the room if I suggested they should take care or stay home, especially with Maison de Verre opening so soon."

"Yes, that's true. *Try* and put it out of your mind for tonight, anyway," Julia said. "You'll be able to keep a close eye on them while you're eating all ofthe *magnificent* food Chef Debord and I are making. Tabs, I swear, you're going to *love* it. It's going to be like—what is it?—nirvana for *un gastronome*!"

Despite my worries, I couldn't help but smile at Julia's enthusiasm. I gave her a great, lusty one-armed hug as we walked, and replied, "I'm looking forward to it—except that I'm going to be wearing Dior, and I don't *dare* eat or drink anything. You'll have to save me a plate."

My messieurs' renovated version of Maison de Verre was a completely different place than it was the first time I had set foot inside.

Everything was beautiful, elegant, simple, and yet breathtaking. Although it might seem strange to say it, I was so proud of my messieurs for remaking this place, one that held terrible memories within its brick walls and scarred wooden floor, including removing the swastika that had been stamped in the concrete of the front stoop during the Occupation.

The only thing that remained the same was the space's footprint, its three built-in booths, and the tall bow window that gave the restaurant its name. Made of six vertical bars of glass panels, every other section was made of textured and patterned glass. Some of the sections had glass that looked like the bottoms of wine bottles, some were mottled; others were wavy, and so on. The alternating sections were clear. These six vertical panels created a shallow bow that took up most of the front wall. This mixture of textured and smooth glass gave anyone who might look through the grand window from the sidewalk only a peek of what might be inside.

The interior had been redone, and the decor was understated

elegance: rich blues and lush greens mingled with silver and white, along with the palest of yellows, bringing the theme of crystal and glass from the window into the softer parts of the seating area. The walls had been painted a vibrant midnight blue. Simple glass sconces hung at intervals so as not to compete with the focal point of the tall, faceted window. A single chandelier of emerald-green glass had been strung low in the back, at the center of the restaurant, with small hurricane candle holders in a similar style on each table.

The upholstery of the chairs and the booths, as well as that of a long bench seat that had been constructed along the front wall, was a paisley fabric with every shade of dark blue. The tables, made from blond wood with heavy walnut bases, gleamed—ready to be laden with food and drink.

To my surprise, I noticed that the last of the three booths at the back of the room had a small silver cross embedded in the floor just beneath it—right where I'd discovered a woman who'd been poisoned and left to die. My messieurs had honored her memory, permanently marking the place of her death. Tears welled in my eyes, and I blinked them back, suddenly angry at anyone who meant these good, softhearted men harm. If Madame Vierca was right, I had to vigilantly watch over my elderly gentlemen—but even so, I couldn't believe anyone here tonight would be a threat to them.

I'd hardly come in through the door to the place when I was swept up by my grandfather. He insisted that every one of his friends—most in their late sixties, seventies, or eighties, which meant that I was the youngest person present by thirty years—must meet me, which really meant that every one of them must gush and fawn over me. But they were all so charming and witty, it was difficult not to enjoy it, especially when Monsieur Dior went into raptures over the fact that I had "honored him" by wearing his creation. That helped me feel less self-conscious of the fact that I was wearing a frock that had cost thousands of francs.

I hadn't moved more than a foot from the front door since arriving. Between the zillions of kisses on my cheeks, everyone clasping my gloved hands, and the delight with which the guests were greeting my gentlemen, it was an uproar. There were only about twenty people who'd been invited to this little soirée, but, as was typical in Paris, the space wasn't very large. No one was sitting yet, so we were all sort of crammed in, standing about.

Cigarette smoke filtered through the air, competing with whatever delights Chef Debord and Julia were working on in the kitchen. A waiter meandered through, offering a tray of glasses filled with champagne, Bordeaux, or Armagnac, and another was navigating through the little crowd with a platter of fried oysters, which I was pretty sure were the handiwork of my friend Julia Child. Sadly, I declined everything except a glass of champagne, figuring that at least wouldn't stain, as it was the same color as my frock.

When I saw former Inspecteur Devré come in, I can honestly say I didn't have even the slightest jolt of disappointment that he was not accompanied by his nephew. I hadn't expected him, anyway, for there would be no reason for Merveille to make an appearance here tonight—although I did see that Devré had a handsome, actually quite beautiful, man of his own age with him. They were clearly a couple in the same way my grand-père and Oncle Rafe were. Coming in behind them were Docteur Jackson, the former Bostonian who'd been a medical examiner here during the time Devré was at la Sûreté, and a stunningly gorgeous older woman, presumably his wife.

I met them all, receiving cheek kisses and even a perfume-scented hug from Madame Jackson—Lucie-Geneviève, who'd apparently been a famous courtesan as well as a murder suspect about fifty years ago. That was a story I definitely wanted to hear someday.

At last, Grand-père clapped his hands to gather everyone's attention. He and Oncle Rafe stood off to the side, beaming, and they once again welcomed everyone to their new place. Then, to the sound of applause, he used a wide, expansive gesture to suggest that everyone take their seats.

For tonight, the long banquette-style bench in front of the window was left open for sofa-like seating. Normally, smaller tables would be set perpendicularly in front of it, with chairs on the opposite sides of the tables. But for tonight, that arrangement was put aside. Instead, a single, large, circular table had been set in the middle of the space. There were ten chairs around it, and one of them was mine.

This was, as I understood it, the table for Grand-père, Oncle Rafe, and some of their old friends from the Resistance. I was just maneuvering into my seat, graciously helped by the grave and polite maître d' Monsieur Barbier, when I noticed the vase of flowers in the center of the table.

My knees gave out, and I plopped awkwardly the rest of the way into my chair as I stared at the perky, unassuming cornflower-blue flowers gracing the center of the table.

A chill rushed through me, and my stomach pitched.

I counted them. There were nine.

CHAPTER 6

I couldn't ask Grand-père or Oncle Rafe about the *bleuets*—for that was definitely what they were—and so I had to content myself with waiting until later.

The evening became a blur of food—*oh*, the *food*!—and non-stop boisterous conversation. The small place echoed with laughter, jokes shouted across the table, and joviality. When the first course came out of the kitchen, I very regretfully declined to be served.

But my messieurs (and, I think, Julia) would have none of that. Less than a minute after I shook my head and waved off the waiter, Monsieur Barbier hurried over to me. He was carrying an apron, which I recognized as Julia's.

I felt my face go hot and red, but everyone at the table insisted that I put it on.

"But of course you must, mademoiselle! You cannot be so strong-willed as to miss these creations of Chef Debord!" said Monsieur Hauet, an old friend of Oncle Rafe's, who'd taken the seat next to me.

I acquiesced and, under the watchful and encouraging eyes of everyone at the table, donned the apron. I felt rather foolish and a little like a child, but it did cover the entirety of the front of my precious Dior. As soon as the first course was at last set in front of me, I realized I was glad I'd done so . . . because it was *beautiful*.

Oeufs au melon . . . I couldn't imagine where the cantaloupe had come from in late March. But I could imagine Julia being in raptures in the kitchen, having such a fresh summer ingredient in her repertoire. The dish featured a small thin cup carved of melon. Nestled in the bottom of it was steamed spinach, and in the center was a gently poached egg. A scant amount of béarnaise sauce was drizzled over the top. I recognized by smell the finely chopped tarragon and mint that were scattered over the plate and lightly over the egg. As if to punctuate the dish, a tiny white flower sat on the edge of the plate, accompanied by a small sprig of tarragon and more tiny flakes of the same.

That was only the first course. I'm sure I don't need to describe how incredible it tasted. The eggs were followed by *langoustines*—very large prawn-like shellfish that actually looked like the crawfish I found in Belleville Lake, near where I grew up. They were served simply in a dish with a white wine–butter sauce dotted with a trio of blotches of a vibrant green pesto made from basil, chervil, and tarragon.

There was more: a light and delicate consommé, a small portion of *croustade de barbue Lagrené*—a lovely, elegant sole served atop a cheesy soufflé with a wine-butter sauce

The main course, however, had everyone murmuring and exclaiming quietly.

Chef Debord himself came out with Monsieur Barbier and the waiters as they brought trays with twenty-two plates, each covered by a smooth silver cloche. A plate was placed before every seat—ten at my table and four at each of the three booths. Then quickly, table by table, the cloches were removed in unison with great fanfare. An amazing smell filled my nose as I looked down at the pièce de résistance.

"And this, we have here a creation of my own, specially for Messieurs Saint-Léger and Fautrier," said chef proudly. *"Magret de canard Maison de Verre!"*

He went on to describe the dish as my fellow diners oohed and aahed over it. Apparently—as I later learned—a *magret* was the breast from a certain type of duck that was raised specifically to make *foie gras.* The breast of this particular duck, a moulard, is much thicker and juicier and more tender than a normal duck breast. In this case, the presentation was of very thin slices of duck breast, all quite pink, almost red, in the center. The breast had been prepared, as Chef explained, like a steak: seared with butter and seasonings and then sliced for serving. A rich brown sauce was drizzled over it.

From the exclamations of surprise and interest, I realized that this was a new approach to duck breast, and everyone was quite impressed by its simplicity and incredibly rich, juicy taste. Along with the duck were delicately steamed haricots verts and a little puff of mashed potatoes, lightly browned on top and dusted with minced chives. Several purple chive flowers and a sprig of tarragon garnished each plate.

It was divine. I was beginning to wonder whether I would burst the seams of my frock, but I couldn't stop enjoying the lovely meal.

But there was more—a small green salad dressed with vinegar and oil and topped with tiny chamomile flowers, which looked like minuscule daisies. I only recognized them because Grand-père grew them in his herb garden.

Next was a cheese tray and by then I was so full, I couldn't move, but, good grief, there was *dessert.* This delection was flambéed peaches in port, served over a mille-feuille with the flamed sauce and a dollop of crème fraîche and topped with three tiny candied flowers. I recognized violets and violas because my mother had grown them back home.

And, finally, I knew the end was in sight because they brought out the *digestifs.* I was dying for a cup of coffee, but that simply wasn't done in Paris after, say, 4:00 or 5:00 p.m. I pulled myself to my feet with a groan and excused myself from the table. I felt soft and sluggish, and I realized I was a little tipsy from the wine that had been refilling my glass since I sat down.

After freshening up—which included splashing a little cold water on my face—I popped into the kitchen, mainly so I could avoid having more food or drink pressed on me.

Julia was in her glory. Her face was shiny with perspiration, and her eyes sparkled with delight. She wore a proper chef's hat over her springy hair. Her apron was stained with food, and she couldn't stop smiling.

"Oh, *Tabs*! Wasn't it *wonderful*? Who would have *thought* to sear a duck breast like that—and a *magret*, at that! Debord is *brilliant*! Wait until I tell Chef Bugnard! And the croustade! Wasn't it just *divine*?" She went on like this for minutes, showing me everything she'd done and contributed to the meal, rattling off all the techniques she'd learned and experienced. Of course, most of it went over my head, so I just nodded and smiled and in the end gave her a big hug and smacking kiss on the cheek.

"Thank you for doing this for my messieurs," I told her.

She hugged me back, hard enough that I was afraid she'd squeeze the peaches flambée out of me. "Thank *you* for having them ask me!"

After we finished our mutual admiration moment, I sobered. "Listen, Julia, I noticed something. The flowers on my table, the circular table of ten . . . It's a vase of *nine cornflowers—bleuets—* with white roses."

Her eyes popped wide. "What?"

I nodded, agreeing with her shock. "And none of the other tables have the blue flowers on them. The other ones only have the roses."

"What do you think it means? It *can't* be a coincidence!"

"I'm sure it can't. I haven't been able to ask Grand-père or Oncle Rafe about it—it's been a madhouse out there. Speaking of which, I better go back out there." A sudden thrust of worry shot through me.

Without another word, I hurried off, berating myself for having left my gentlemen unattended for so long. To my relief, I found them chatting with Devré and his gentleman friend, along with Docteur Jackson and his wife, who appeared to be leaving. People were standing around talking, as well. The other two booths were empty; it appeared the guests there—including Monsieur Dior and *la* Madame Colette—had already gone. Not that I blamed them—it was nearly midnight, and we'd started at seven o'clock. The rest of my table, the seven remaining, were still sitting there with those nine bleuts in the middle, taunting me. They were taunting me because I couldn't wait to ask Grand-père or Oncle Rafe if there was any reason nine *bleuets* were in the center of our table.

"Come, come, sit with us, Mademoiselle Tabitha," said Monsieur Taban, another old friend of Grand-père's, patting the chair next to him. "You must hear about how Lussier here played the piano during the war!"

I sat. I had no choice, and I was feeling sleepy and slow from all the food and drink.

I don't know how long I sat chatting with Monsieur Taban and Madame Demailly and the others at the round table. Even as we conversed, my attention strayed to the vase of flowers in the center. I counted them two more times, just to make sure I hadn't imagined it. There were definitely nine *bleuets* in the center cluster, surrounded by small white roses. I had to tamp back my impatience to find out what, if anything, they meant.

At last, at *long* last, everyone began to rise, to say farewell. I was glad, for if *I* was exhausted, my messieurs must be even more so. People hugged me, kissed me—on cheeks, lips, the back of my hand—shook my hand, said au revoir and bonsoir, and promised to come back and to tell their friends about Maison de Verre . . . and more. It was all a blur, but at last it was only Grand-père and Oncle Rafe and me, besides the staff cleaning up. The space was quiet but for the faint clink of dishes in the kitchen.

"I'm *exhausted*, so I can't imagine how tired you must be, but what a night!" I exclaimed, pulling them into a three-person hug. I would ask about the cornflowers tomorrow; now I only wanted to celebrate their night—and get to bed. "It was wonderful!"

"It was a *triumph*!" Oncle Rafe declared. "Debord—*il est un génie*!"

"It was indeed," Grand-père said, kissing me on the forehead. His eyes danced; he didn't look tired at all. How was that possible? "And you, *ma mie*, you were magnificent. Everyone loved you. Everyone did! You shined like a beacon, *non*? You made Rafael and me so very proud."

I was blushing, and just about to reply that I hadn't done anything but eat and drink when the front door burst open. Madame Demailly staggered in.

"He is dead! Oh, good God, he is *dead*!" she cried, her eyes wild, as she staggered toward us. Blood stained the front of her coat, and I saw it on her gloves and hat, as well. "There! Out there!"

I bolted for the door, pushing past her.

The cold air shocked me without my coat on, but as earlier today, it was welcome. I looked around. The sidewalk was empty; no one was in sight. A taxi trundled down the road in the distance.

I walked a little way down the sidewalk, and as I turned to come back, Madame Demailly stumbled out the door, Oncle Rafe on her heels.

"I don't see—"

"There! He is *there*!" She pointed across the *rue* and to the left, and that's when I saw it: a shadowy lump on the ground, just beyond the circle of illumination from a streetlamp near an alley.

I bolted across the street, heedless of my heels and lack of a coat, kicking up slush behind me as I did. I was lucky I didn't slip and fall, but there was no ice, only melting snow.

The man had collapsed against the edge of a building, fallen to the ground in the shadows. Someone walking by would have certainly seen him, but from across the street or even in a car, it would otherwise have been easy to miss him.

His head sagged forward as he slumped, half lying against the brick wall. His hat was missing, but he still wore gloves.

I saw the blood—there was a lot of it, but it mingled with the slush and the dark snow and was more black than red. It didn't take an expert to see that he'd been cut across the side of the neck and throat. His head lolled forward. His gloved hands, wet with blood, looked as if they'd fallen away from trying to stem the flow from his throat.

I lifted his head with a gentle hand—ungloved, for I'd taken off my gloves to eat—and saw his face. My heart jolted, for I recognized him. He was an old man, well past seventy. He wore a bristly white mustache and had had dancing brown eyes. It was Paul Hauet, and he'd sat next to me during the dinner. A friend of Oncle Rafe's.

He'd only left the restaurant a short while ago. Five, ten minutes? Everyone's leaving had been prolonged, chaotic, and a blur, but his hadn't been very long ago. He couldn't have been here very long at all. I slipped my fingers under the cuff of a coat sleeve to touch the wrinkled, crepey skin beneath his glove. He was still warm, as I'd expected. No, he hadn't been dead very long at all.

Just then, Oncle Rafe got to my side, his shoes slapping in the wet mush, his bald head shining in the night.

"It's Monsieur Hauet," I said, looking up at him.

"What? *Non!*" Oncle Rafe said in an explosive sort of moan. "*Non! Ah, non.*" He knelt slowly and carefully next to me, then, heedless of the blood, took the still hand of his old friend. "Ah, Paul, *non, non* . . ." He glanced at me, and I saw the damp of tears in his old eyes.

"Who would do this?" he said angrily, looking up and down the empty street, as if prepared to bolt after the culprit, should they appear. "Who would do such a thing? To jump an old man, to cut his throat and to take what little he has, eh? Someone who would do that . . . Eh, they are the worst of fiends!" He dashed a hand over his eyes, and I reached over to cover his hand with mine. His fingers were cold and knobby, and now they were damp with blood.

"I'm so sorry. He seemed a very nice man, Oncle. I enjoyed sitting next to him at dinner. He had so many stories about you." I gave him a sad smile.

Neither of us had coats, gloves, or hats, but I wasn't about to leave Monsieur Hauet. Still, I felt Oncle Rafe trembling next to me. I wasn't certain whether it was from the cold or from grief or anger.

"I'll stay with him until the police arrive," I told him. "Go and tell Grand-père. I don't want him to come out here."

Oncle Rafe hesitated, then nodded. He and I were both cognizant of my grandfather's more rickety constitution. There was no need for him to be exposed to the chill, either. "Thank you, *chérie.*"

I helped him to his feet and watched as he walked across the *rue* slowly and painfully. Grand-père and Madame Demailly stood in the doorway of the restaurant, looking out at us.

I crouched back down, feeling the strain in my calves from the heels, but I didn't feel right about leaving Monsieur Hauet down there in the slush on his own, even though my gorgeous Dior was getting mud and ice along its hem. I realized that I was still wearing an apron—which had saved me from getting blood on the front of my frock, thank goodness. I untied the apron and pulled it up over my head.

"I'm so sorry, monsieur. Who did this to you?" I asked before laying the apron over Hauet's face and torso. "We'll find out," I added, unable to keep from using that pronoun. Whoever *we* was, it would include me, for, as Madame Vierca had said, death found me. It seemed to be my calling . . . my destiny.

And because of that, I had a connection and now felt an obligation to the dead man.

The sound of a police siren drew near. I rose to my feet, hardly aware of the chill except in my fingers, as the car rolled to a stop.

Two police agents in uniform climbed out of the car and approached. I didn't recognize either of them and assumed they'd come from the local station. A homicide investigator would soon arrive.

I heaved a sigh. Maybe I would be seeing Inspecteur Merveille tonight, after all.

CHAPTER 7

I had been inside with Grand-père, Oncle Rafe, Madame Demailly, and the cooking and serving staff for nearly fifteen minutes before the restaurant door opened. We were sitting at the large round table. The staff was still cleaning up in the kitchen. Everyone at the table but me was smoking cigarettes, and we each had a small glass of cognac. I had prevailed upon Julia to make some coffee, and I had dumped my cognac into it. I'd been cold from being outside for so long without a coat, and the chill had not left me even once I sat down.

Through the window, I'd seen the second car drive up to the scene, so I was not surprised when Inspecteur Merveille stepped over the threshold into Maison de Verre followed by a police agent.

He wasn't the sort of man every woman would find attractive; his features were a little uneven, with deep-set eyes and a very broad, square jaw, which was invariably clean-shaven. I'd never seen even the hint of a five o'clock shadow there, and I'd seen him at many different times of day. He had a strong, prominent nose and olive skin that proclaimed a Mediterranean heritage, along with very dark hair, which was always perfectly parted slightly to one side and combed into place. His shoulders were broad but in proportion to a lanky, toned build. I'd never seen him in anything but a suit coat and trousers, but one could assume.

Merveille's attention went to me first. For once, there was no admonishment in his gaze before it shifted to my messieurs as he strode over to us.

"Monsieur Saint-Léger. Monsieur Fautrier," he greeted them soberly. He glanced at me—"Mademoiselle"—then looked questioningly at Madame Demailly, obviously the only person he didn't know. "Madame."

She was close in age to my messieurs, as well—perhaps a bit younger, but still aged. Her pale skin was wrinkled around the corners of her eyes and mouth, and her chin and neck were soft with sagging skin. What little was left of her red lipstick had bled into the skin around her mouth. A layer of fine hair lay like down over her cheeks and chin. She had thick shockingly white hair that had been twisted into a chignon, and she wore sparkling dangling jet earrings that nearly brushed her shoulders. She'd taken off her blood-soaked coat but still wore the shoes and hat that were spotted with Monsieur Hauet's lifeblood.

There was a moment of silence when no one spoke, so I stepped in. "Madame Demailly found Monsieur Hauet," I told him. "They were both here first, along with all of us and a number of other people."

Merveille nodded as he removed his fedora, revealing perfectly combed dark hair even at two o'clock in the morning. His locks had had a trim since I'd seen him last, I couldn't help notice.

"I understand my uncle, too, was present. It was he who telephoned me, you see." His eyes, dark and gray like a churning sea, were as sober as always. There was no hint of warmth or familiarity—or, to be fair, the irritation they usually held when he realized I was once again involved with a murder.

"*Mais oui,* I called Guillaume first," Grand-père said when I looked at him in confusion. "I wanted him to come, but—"

"Ah, well, I suppose he will turn up, monsieur," said Merveille. He sounded even more grim than usual. "Now, if you please, Madame Demailly, tell me what has happened."

"We were all leaving, saying goodbye, and so on," she said. She twisted her hands in her lap, staring down at them, as she spoke. "I came outside—I think I was one of the last to leave, you see, and I said *au revoir* and then I began to cross the street—I live only a short distance east. It isn't a far walk, and the streets here—they are safe." She made a noise that was a cross between a laugh and a sob.

"I went only a few steps, and I saw Paul—Monsieur Hauet—down the block a bit. I called to him so we could walk together, but he did not answer. He—he was walking strangely. Staggering. I thought perhaps he'd had too much *vin*, eh? He stumbled and bumped into the building—and then he just . . ." Still looking down, she made a "whoosh" sound, and her hands moved, rising and then moving down quickly, to demonstrate his collapse. "Of course, I still only thought he had tripped." She looked up now, her eyes wide, blinking rapidly. "I didn't know . . . I didn't know . . ."

"*Oui*, madame, of course," said Merveille in a kind voice. "How could you have?"

"*Non*," she said, shaking her head. "I went to him. I was going to help him up. And then I s-saw the blood. I couldn't . . . I didn't know what to do. But of course I tried to help him up, tried to wipe away the blood. I used my scarf . . . I tried to *stop* it." Her hands fluttered at her own neck, then fell away. "But it—it was just coming and coming . . ." She swallowed hard. "And then he . . ." She shrugged and blinked rapidly. "He was gone."

"And did you see anyone else on the street, madame? Anyone, perhaps, running off or darting into an alley? A car driving away?"

Madame Demailly shook her head. "*Non*, Inspecteur. There was no one that I saw." She shivered and hugged herself, huddling into her chair.

"Madame, please . . . if you could think hard about it for me . . . Did you see Monsieur Hauet leave the restaurant? He was before you, *hein*?"

"*Oui*," she said quietly. "I didn't notice when he left. It was . . .

it was loud and busy, and we were all hugging and kissing, you see. It had been a long time since we were all together. It was very . . . messy." She gave a wan smile.

"Did you notice whether anyone was with him?"

"No, Inspecteur."

"And the direction he was walking . . . there on rue Las Cases . . . Do you know if is it where he lives? Or perhaps where he parked a car?"

"I don't know about a car, monsieur. And I . . . I do not know where he lived, Inspecteur. I am sorry."

"*Bien.* Thank you, madame." Merveille glanced at the police agent, who stood with a pad of paper and a pencil, assuring himself that the man was taking notes. That was typical of the *inspecteur*—he seemed to prefer to focus on the interviewee rather than have his attention divided by writing it all down himself.

It was an effective technique. I knew what it felt like to have those steady, cool gray eyes fastened on me as the questions came . . . sometimes rapidly, sometimes casually, easily, as if to lure one into ease and then pounce.

I also knew what it was like to see those gray eyes appear more blue, even lit with levity or easiness. Not soft, but not so hard.

I gritted my teeth. Boy oh boy, did I have it bad for the enigmatic detective.

Merveille glanced at me at that moment, and I felt my cheeks heat. Surely he couldn't read my mind.

"Mademoiselle?" he said, and I understood he was asking for my statement, as I had been the next person to see the dead body. I liked to think that he knew he'd get a clear and objective recitation from me—after all, this was not the first time he'd interrogated me over finding a dead body.

"Grand-père and Oncle Rafe and I were the only ones left here in the restaurant—except for Julia and the others in the kitchen. Madame Demailly rushed back in—she had left, of course, a few minutes earlier—saying that someone was dead. That 'he' was dead. At the time, I didn't know who he was. I ran across the street to . . . to look." My voice faltered a little under the steady regard of his gaze. I knew what he was thinking: *Why is this woman always finding dead bodies?*

I had a feeling he'd scoff if I told him what Madame Vierca had said.

I continued my story. "It was obvious he was dead. I only touched him in order to lift his head to see who he was. I didn't expect it to be someone who'd just left the restaurant. I just assumed it was a random person on the street. But I wanted to look, and . . . and of course I recognized him. He sat next to me at dinner." My eyes stung suddenly, and I blinked hard. "I did touch his wrist, also, to feel how warm the skin was, and it was clear he'd died very recently. Minutes before, I think. I didn't touch or move anything else."

"And you covered him then, mademoiselle? You left the body, came back in here, and found something to cover him?"

"Oh, no. I . . . I was wearing the apron, and I took it off right there. I didn't leave him until the agents arrived."

The flash of surprise and confusion in Merveille's eyes was mildly amusing and a little insulting. "You were cooking, mademoiselle?" The fact that he was moved to ask such an inane question suggested how surprised he was.

"No," I replied, then closed my mouth. It wasn't relevant why I had been wearing an apron, and I certainly didn't want to reveal that I'd had to don a bib like a child, Dior or not.

My answer hung there for a moment, but he didn't press. He made a quiet sound and then turned to Grand-père and Oncle Rafe. "Messieurs. I am very sorry for your loss, for it seems Monsieur Hauet was a friend of yours."

"*Oui.* And of your *oncle*'s, as well, Inspecteur," Grand-père said.

As if on cue, the restaurant door rattled, then opened, and former Inspecteur Devré walked in. He was carrying a walking stick and was followed by Docteur Jackson.

I felt rather than heard Merveille's suppressed sigh.

"Étienne. I am so very glad you are here," Devré said as he approached. "Thank you for coming."

"Of course," Merveille murmured. His jaw—how was it perfectly clean-shaven at two in the morning?—shifted a little, but his expression remained bland.

"Where is the body?" asked Docteur Jackson. He had been a celebrated pathologist for the police department when it was known as la Sûreté, having studied with the great Alexandre Lacassagne first in Lyon, then here in Paris. I understood that he and Devré had worked together on many cases. "Has it been taken away yet?"

Merveille shook his head and gestured to the police agent to take Jackson to the place where Hauet was. I wondered if Merveille had expected the retired pathologist to arrive with his great-uncle and had delayed sending for the morgue for that reason. He had a sort of resigned look about him suggesting that was the case.

"Now, what is it that has happened?" Devré said, taking a seat at the table. He was still a striking-looking man at eighty, or however old he was, with a very close and neatly trimmed mustache and goatee of iron gray. His nose was long and straight, and his brows equally long and straight, thick and emphatic, over his dark eyes. I saw no real family resemblance between him and Merveille except for the shape of their eyes. It was more their personalities and demeanors that suggested a familial relationship.

Other than a light shading of whiskers around his jaw, Devré appeared as carefully groomed as he had been at dinner, and as far as I could tell, he was still dressed in the same attire. He'd probably just arrived home when Grand-père called with the news. "Tell to me about what happened to poor Paul."

Merveille filled him in himself, probably in order to keep the discussion short and to the point. "I was just about to ask Monsieur Saint-Léger and Monsieur Fautrier whether they noticed Monsieur Hauet when he left." He lifted one brow just enough to pitch the question toward my messieurs.

"No, no, of course not," said Grand-père, with a wave of his hand. "It was, as Berthilde says"—he gestured to Madame Demailly—"loud and chaotic. I don't believe I saw anyone actually walk out the door. Rafe?"

Oncle Rafe considered for a moment. "It is possible I noticed Paul when he was leaving . . . It's the mustache of his, eh? That big white abomination that he never liked to trim," he said, with a sad laugh. "I waved and he looked back and that is all I saw of him. But was someone with him? That I cannot say for certain."

"Do you remember anyone who might have still been here after Monsieur Hauet left?" asked Merveille. This time he included his uncle in the question.

By now, I'd deduced that Merveille suspected—or at least wondered whether—someone might have left with Paul Hauet and cut his throat as they walked away. Or left ahead of him and lay in wait in order to attack him. The thought was jarring and terrifying. Everyone who'd been here tonight knew each other. They had all been friends. I'd gathered through the conversations at dinner that many of them worked together during the war to resist the Germans.

I was well aware that people killed people they knew—in fact, that was the case in the vast majority of homicides: the murderer was usually known to the victim. But still, all twenty men and women were over sixty (except, I thought, for Monsieur Dior), and most of them were significantly older than that. It was hard to imagine one of them having the strength or coordination to do such a thing—especially in the dark, after a long evening of eating and drinking.

It was harder to imagine that someone with whom I'd sat at the table and enjoyed fellowship had left with the intention of killing one of their dinner mates.

Devré's gaze was sharp and his words were thoughtful as he responded. "Of course, I have been thinking about only this, and speaking with Monsieur Jackson, as well. I do know that the four at that table, and at that table"—he gestured to the two booths next to where he'd been sitting—"had all gone before it got so very chaotic with the farewells, as you say. They were gone sometime before we rose to leave, and they left together, all as couples, you see, Étienne."

"And so you do not believe that *la madame* would stand by and watch *le monsieur* slit the throat of a man," Merveille said dryly. "Because the two of them left together."

"One of *les messieurs* was Christian Dior, and another guest was *la* Madame Colette and her friend, so, no, I do not think so," Devré responded. "And when we four left, there was no one in sight. No one lurking or loitering." He gave his nephew a meaningful look, which I took as a reminder that he was a former cop and was still very observant of his surroundings.

Merveille nodded. *"Bien."* He turned his attention back to my messieurs and Madame Demailly. "Do you know of any reason someone might have wished to harm Monsieur Hauet?" He included his uncle in the question as well.

"I cannot think of one," replied Grand-père, with a shrug. "Paul, he was an old man—as we all are, eh?—and he is only occupied with his antiques business. It is a stall at Mouffetard," he added when Merveille's brows lifted in question.

"You think this was no random event," Oncle Rafe said, his eyes sober beneath the slash of his brows.

Merveille gave an abbreviated nod in acknowledgment. "I think that when a man's throat is cut on the street and his wallet remains in his pocket and his fine pocket watch in his coat, one must conclude it was no random mugging."

I felt a little prickle over the backs of my shoulders. I hadn't looked through Monsieur Hauet's pockets, but if I had done so, I surely would have come to the same conclusion. Merveille glanced at me, as if expecting me to speak, but I did not.

"Poor Paul," said Madame Demailly quietly. "He was . . . Ah, I knew him for so long. We all did, *non*? We were so close at one time. Before, I might have had an idea, but now . . . It's been years since I've seen him. I do not know, Inspecteur."

"Ah, *oui*," said Grand-père sadly, stabbing out his cigarette. "And so now, les Neuf Bleuets . . . are nine no more, eh, Rafe?"

I jolted and barely suppressed a sound of surprise. Of course Merveille's attention snapped to me.

"Mademoiselle?"

"It's . . . nothing. It's only—" I stopped suddenly, staring at the vase of cornflowers and white roses in the center of the table.

All feeling drained from my body; I actually felt my face go white and my mouth dry up. I counted again, but it was obvious that there were now only eight *bleuets* in the vase.

One of them was missing.

CHAPTER 8

"Mademoiselle," Merveille said again, this time more sharply.

My brain felt as scrambled as the eggs Julia had taught me to make, but not nearly as fluffy. Instead, I felt heavy and confused, almost as if I were on a spinning carnival ride. Every hair on my body was vibrating.

The others gaped at me. Grand-père and Oncle Rafe wore identical expressions of shock and concern, but neither of them spoke up.

I started with the simplest thing. I gestured to the vase. "There are only eight flowers. There *were* nine . . . before. *Neuf bleuets.*"

Devré made a sound of interest. "Ah. *Intéressant.*" His attention flickered to my gentlemen. He didn't appear surprised as much as fascinated.

"Explain, if you please, monsieur," Merveille said in a clipped voice. He was looking at Grand-père.

"The Nine Bluets we were," Grand-père said. He was frowning at the vase of flowers, as if he didn't quite believe me. I noticed him reach over blindly to cover Oncle Rafe's hand with his paler one. "We were a secret group that was part of the Resistance here in Paris. Nine of us." He cast a glance at Devré. "You knew about it, *non*?"

"*Mais oui,*" he replied. "A bit. But that was not my . . . As you know, I was not involved in the group. That group," he added, with a bit of emphasis on *that.*

"We were all . . ." Oncle Rafe gestured to the table. "We sat here, all of us, tonight. With Tabitha, we made ten, you see? It was the first time in many years les Neuf Bleuets were together. You see, after the war, we . . . Eh, it was not so necessary for us to see each other. And I think . . ." He glanced at Madame Demailly and then at Grand-père. "I think that we needed to try to forget some of the things . . . to, eh, be relieved of those days, those memories." His expression had become drawn and tight, with deep lines at the corners of his mouth. His eyes clouded.

I didn't know many details of what my messieurs had done to help the Resistance during the Occupation. I knew they'd helped to hide Jedburgh soldiers coming through the city, and that Oncle Rafe had had something to do with a secret publication—a newspaper or pamphlet for those attempting to subvert the occupiers. There'd been a young woman named Andrée who worked at the police station and who used the copy machine there to make copies for them.

I also knew that Oncle Rafe was very black and white and judgmental about those who had collaborated and those who had resisted—and that he was of the mind that a Parisian, a Frenchman, had had to be one or the other. That there was no gray area between the two . . . and that he and Grand-père had some disagreement on that front. Likely that was because Grand-père, as a partner at a prestigious bank here in Paris, had had no choice but to work with—or at least pretend to work with—the Nazis.

That was the only subject the two of them truly disagreed on—deeply and savagely. I had seen them argue about it, and it was unsettling.

"*Oui*," said Madame Demailly. Her face was tight from the difficult memories. "It was good not to think about it all . . . about those who didn't survive. Those we helped, those who betrayed us . . ." Her voice turned hard, and her hands, surprisingly slender and soft for her age, curled on top of the table.

"You say there were nine flowers," Merveille said, abruptly turning the conversation back to me. "When did you notice this, mademoiselle?"

"I noticed there were nine of them when I first sat at the table," I replied. I really didn't want to get into the situation with Madame Vierca—at least not now, and not until I talked to my gentlemen about it.

"You counted the flowers?" He tilted his head, looking at me closely. "Did you know about les Neuf Bleuets?"

Damn it. How was he so intuitive about these things?

"I didn't know about the group, no," I told him honestly. "I just noticed that there were nine flowers . . . and now there are only eight."

"And so a flower, it has gone missing, and one of the nine it represented is dead." Merveille was emphasizing the obvious purposely, I was sure. "Do you have any idea when that flower might have gone missing, mademoiselle? And no one here . . . no one of you took it?" He swept his attention over the members of the Nine.

The three shook their heads. Merveille turned back to me.

I heaved a quiet sigh. "It was after dinner sometime. I know there were still nine flowers when we were sitting here after dinner, talking. So it must have gone missing . . . I guess when everyone was leaving," I added softly. The hair everywhere on my body rose again.

"You had a fascination with these flowers, mademoiselle." An implied question, and perhaps a little suspicion, was in Merveille's voice. "That you noticed this."

"I like flowers," I said lamely. I was *not* going to talk about Madame Vierca right now, no matter how hard he prodded. If it made sense to do so, I would tell him later.

But one thing was certain: I would be showing up on Madame Vierca's doorstep as soon as I possibly could.

"One of the flowers was *missing*?" Julia exclaimed.

She actually stopped what she was doing, which was beating something rapidly in a large copper bowl, to stare at me.

I nodded and shrugged. "I couldn't believe it, either. If I hadn't been so obsessed with the nine bluets, I probably wouldn't have noticed it, either."

"How do I *always* miss everything? Ye gods, there I was, back in the kitchen, *slaving* away, and all sorts of things are happening—like Madame Vierca's prediction coming true." Even though Julia had gone back to whipping whatever it was in the bowl, she managed to shudder without interrupting her rhythm. "Did you tell Merveille about it?"

I snorted. "Of course not. I didn't want to say anything in front of Grand-père and Oncle Rafe, considering how they reacted to her being around the other day—at least until I talked to them first. And, besides, can you imagine what Merveille would have said? He probably would have carted me off to the insane asylum or laughed himself silly. Although since I've never seen him do anything more than a wry little smile, *that* might be worth it. Anyway, I'm pretty sure he suspected something was up."

"So . . . are you *going* to tell the handsome and oh-so-serious inspector?"

"I haven't decided yet. Did *you* talk to Merveille last night?"

"Oh yes. He came into the kitchen and spoke to all of us. But we—Chef Debord and me and the two servers and Monsieur Barbier—were all busy in there during the time everyone was saying goodbye. None of us left the kitchen."

"Not even to go out back into the alley and smoke or to toss garbage?" I asked, well remembering from my first visit to Maison de Verre how the back of the restaurant opened into a narrow alley that led out to the street where Monsieur Hauet had been killed. It wouldn't have taken anyone very long to dart outside under the guise of having a smoke and do the deed.

"Merveille asked the exact same question," Julia told me, her eyes dancing as she gave me a *look*. "No one left. Not even to put garbage out; it was all taken out when we closed up. We were busy, but everyone was working together. I would have noticed if someone stepped away for long enough to kill M. Hauet."

I nodded, my internal sprite doing a happy little dance that I was thinking like a homicide detective.

"What did your grandfather say about Madame Vierca's prediction about the nine bluets and them dying?"

I heaved a sigh. "I haven't talked to him or Oncle Rafe yet. They were still sleeping when I left to come over here. I don't blame them. Last night was long and wonderful, and then it got really difficult and terrible. They had to be exhausted—physically and emotionally." I gestured to her bowl. "I can't believe *you're* up and at 'em after such a long night, too. Did you go to class this morning?"

"I knew class was going to be canceled because of one of those blackouts—and *Monsieur le Soufflé*, he must be attended to," Julia proclaimed, showing me the bowl. Inside was a mass of thick white peaks.

"What's that?" I peered, squinting. I felt as if I should know—after all, I *had* tried to make a soufflé once before—but I didn't want to guess and be wrong.

"Egg whites, of course. You've made a soufflé, haven't you, Tabs?"

"I prefer not to think about that incident," I said with a little shudder. "My egg whites never looked like that, and my soufflé went *pffft* like the *Hindenburg*."

"Were you beating the egg whites in a copper bowl? Were they at room temperature?" Julia asked me.

"No and no," I replied. "Actually, I don't remember if they were at room temperature. Maybe. But I don't have a copper bowl."

"Well," Julia said, and I could tell she was slipping into her lecture *en cuisine* mode. "If you don't have a copper bowl, then—don't ask me why, but egg whites cooperate *so* much better in a copper bowl!—you must add a bit of cream of tartar, and you have to use at least a stainless-steel bowl. Don't use glass or porcelain—it has something to do with how slippery the sides are, and it won't work.

"*And* you *have* to make sure the egg whites aren't too cold, *and* you have to make certain there isn't the tiniest *iota* of eggshell *or* the teeniest *drip* of egg yolk in them. And then they should whip up just beautifully, like these darling little mountain peaks." She lifted the balloon whisk out of the bowl. It was covered with frothy white, the tip pointed and curled over like the top of a soft-serve ice cream cone. "It looks just like a little pompadour, doesn't it?" She smiled at the whisk as if it was her own offspring and she'd combed its hair into place.

"I'll try to remember that," I said. It would be a lot easier if I could just eat Julia's soufflé instead of trying to make one myself. "What kind are you making?" I admit, I was hoping for chocolate.

"It's going to be *cheese*," she said on a gusty sigh, her eyes sparkling with lust. "Lots of *fromage*, but my delicious *monsieur* will still be light and airy and want to float away like a puffy *cloud*!"

I acknowledged to myself that cheese was just as good as chocolate when it came to a soufflé—or, really, any sort of food.

"Yum," I said, stopping short of expressing my strong desire to partake of the finished product. Julia fed me and my messieurs so often, I felt guilty about it. Instead, I turned my attention back to the bigger problem. "I'm sure it's no accident that the ninth flower is missing and one of the Nine Bluets is dead."

"Did the killer *take* one of the flowers? Did they think no one would notice, or did they *want* someone to notice?" Julia mused. She'd moved on to what I recognized as a charlotte baking dish—the sort of thing one used to cook soufflés, if they dared. The inside had been covered with butter and, it looked like, grated cheese. I'd never done that. . . .

"If they *wanted* someone to notice, *why*? Because it's a warning?" Julia looked at me. The light of humor and fun that had been dancing in her eyes was gone. Instead, there was worry and concern.

"That's what I'm trying to figure out," I said, pushing down the squiggle of fear in my belly. Maybe I shouldn't have left Grand-père and Oncle Rafe home alone, even though I'd told Bet and Blythe not to let anyone in the house except for Devré, Docteur Jackson, or Merveille. Those were the only people I knew for sure I could trust. I had also told the maids to call over to me at Julia's if someone else showed up and wanted to come in or if any sort of package was delivered. "But the biggest concern is, if the killer deliberately took the flower from the vase, that means he or she was there last night—and was probably sitting at the same table as me."

"I was afraid you were going to say that, because that's *exactly* what I was thinking," Julia said, still sober as she picked up a large bowl that had a lot of cheese in it, along with a silky béchamel sauce. (I'd muddled through making a béchamel sauce for the *croque-monsieurs* I'd somehow learned to cook.)

"But why would the killer want to make it obvious he or she was there?" she said. "That seems counterintuitive, because it gives the cops a limited number of suspects. Oh . . . but maybe one of the others took the flower just as a reminder of being part of the group."

"It would be nice if that turned out to be true," I said, unconvinced. "Because then I wouldn't have eaten dinner with a killer."

There was silence for a long moment, and I looked up to find Julia eyeing me. "What?"

She tilted her head to the other side. "You're going to dive right into this, aren't you? This investigation? You know what Merveille's going to say." She made a tsking sound, even as a smile played around the corners of her mouth.

"He's not going to be pleased," I agreed. "But Madame Vierca was right. People just keep getting murdered around me, and you have to admit, I've been able to help find justice for them."

"That may be the case, but I'm sure Merveille would argue that the authorities would get their man just as quickly with or without you help."

"Whose side are you on, anyway?" I said, laughing.

"Well, your side, *of course*," Julia said, spooning a glop of egg white into the bowl with the cheesy béchamel. She began to expertly flip and fold the white peaks into the sauce. "So, you might as well tell me about all your suspects, Tabs. As soon as I'm done *folding*—one must take care, you know—these little Alps into their bed of saucy *fromage*, I'm going to pop this little darling into the oven.

"Look how nicely the rest of the batter is letting my little peaks ease right in! They're so polite—it's almost like a *waltz*, the way they mingle together just so. Fold, turn, fold, turn," she said, smiling affectionately at her bowl as she turned it with each step. "Paul's going to *love* this."

I couldn't hold back a little giggle. Julia and the way she talked about food and cooking was amusing—but at the same time, so very descriptive. "You really ought to teach people how to cook, Julia," I told her. "You'd be a fantastic teacher."

"Funny you should say that," she said, looking over at me. "A friend of mine from the embassy—really, the wife of a friend of Paul's—just *asked* if I'd teach her how to *cook*! She says she has another friend who wants to learn. She's going to *pay* me! To teach her! I can't imagine anything else I'd rather do, Tabitha!"

"That's wonderful, Julia! I think you'll be perfect for it. And I think the first thing you ought to teach them is how to make eggs Florentine," I teased.

She burst out laughing. "Oh, Tabitha! You're so funny." She wagged her wooden spoon at me, still laughing. "*Terribly, terribly* funny. You haven't *told* anyone about that debacle, have you?"

"Of course not. I still want you to feed me sometimes, after all." I blew her a kiss as she continued to guffaw.

"All right. Tell me about your suspects, Tabs. I can listen while I peel parsnips and potatoes. I'm making soup, too." She slid the soufflé into the oven and immediately turned down the heat, then used a spoon to taste a sample from a pot of dried beans simmering on the stove.

"All right. There were ten of us at the table—the Nine Bluets and me. I don't think anyone from the booths did it, either—certainly not Devré or Jackson. Or Monsieur Dior and Madame Colette and those sitting with them. Definitely not."

"Right," Julia said. "And they all left early and in groups, right?"

"Exactly. So if someone from the dinner last night is the killer, and it has to do with the Nine Bluets, then I would think it would be someone at that table. Obviously, it's not me or Grand-père or Oncle Rafe. That leaves six, because Paul Hauet is the victim, not the killer. I'll go around the table and tell you what I know about each of them." I didn't have to think hard at all about who had been sitting where, for I'd spent most of last night doing just that instead of sleeping. There were dark circles the size of barges under my eyes to prove it.

"Monsieur Hauet sat next to me, and then there was Madame Munzel. She seemed the quietest of everyone at the table, so I don't have much of an impression of her, really. She mostly sat and smoked and ate and drank. I do know she runs a small brasserie with her brother and his wife, near Châtelet, I think she said. Her husband died in the Great War.

"And next to her was Monsieur Taban. He was very loud and funny and had a story about everything. Maybe that was why Madame Munzel was so quiet—she couldn't get a word in! He wears round glasses that sit crookedly on his nose—I kept wanting to reach over and straighten them out. He's an apartment measurer."

"What?" Julia frowned. "Is that what it sounds like?"

I nodded. "I've never heard of anything like that before, either. But apparently, because so many architectural plans have been destroyed or lost over the years, building owners and landlords need to know the square footage of the flats in order to set or change the rent."

"So that means Monsieur Taban must go into a lot of different buildings and homes," Julia said, her eyes filled with interest and calculation.

"Right. Measuring each and every room, drawing up crude maps and providing them to his employer. He talked a lot about buildings he was in, and the terrible things the Germans did to them when they were here.

"Next was Madame Demailly—the one who found the body and came back. She's probably the youngest of the group, but she's still got to be over seventy. From what I understand, she was a music and piano teacher. I think she gave—or maybe still does—lessons from her home. She kept telling Monsieur Taban to let someone else talk," I added with a smile. "But he didn't listen. He just kept going.

"Then there was Monsieur Sénac. He's very tall and has a beard. He looks closest in age to my grand-père and seems a little less spry than some of the others—although none of them are young! He's got a sort of sober personality, but he wasn't quiet like Madame Munzel. He . . . I think he drives a delivery truck or something like that.

"Okay, next was Monsieur Capron—I could tell he's done very well for himself, although I can't tell you what his occupation is or was. Some sort of office or professional business, I guess. I think maybe he's a real estate agent—they were talking about a house. He dressed in very nice clothing, and I'd say he had a sort of air about him—like Grand-père and Oncle Rafe. Confident and smooth. He's got money, is what I'm trying to say. And he has a pointed beard and a mustache that looks just like those villains in the old silent movies—with the long ends that they twist when they chortle evilly?" I said, demonstrating with an invisible mustache

"All right," Julia said, laughing. "Is that all of them? I lost count."

"There's one more. Monsieur Lussier. He's got a head of thick white hair—even more than Grand-père—and he also has a full beard and mustache. Santa Claus–like. Monsieur Lussier seemed pretty energetic when we were sitting at the table, and I'd say he's one of the younger of the nine. He did some sort of electrical work, I guess, but they also said he was a piano player during the war." I shrugged.

"So two women and four men," Julia mused. "All older—that's got to play into it, don't you think? Someone's got to be pretty steady on their feet to be agile enough to slice someone across the throat, right?"

"Yes." I had been thinking about that, too. "And whoever it was had to have had the knife with them, right? It wasn't like they went into the kitchen and grabbed one. So that means the murder was planned."

"Could they have taken a knife from the table?" Julia said.

"Hmm. I suppose that's possible," I replied. "But is a small table knife sharp enough and big enough to just—you know, *slice*?" I made the sort of gesture I imagined had been done, slicing through the air toward her. "I've been trying to picture it . . . the killer walking down the street toward Monsieur Hauet—and when they got close enough, just *swipe*? Just lash out and hope you get him across the side of the neck? As you're going past each other?"

"Trying to picture someone who's not very steady on their feet or arthritic or something doing that is difficult." Julia paused, her head tilted, as she tried to imagine the scene. "Did you notice whether any of them had a cane or walking stick?"

"Oh. Yes, actually there were several walking sticks, but I'm not sure whose was whose. They were all leaning up against the wall so they were out of the way of the servers. Wait a minute—are you thinking one of them might have had a blade hidden *inside* a cane? And that was where the weapon came from?" My precocious internal sprite, who loved the idea of hidden staircases and secret passages, fully approved of a walking stick with a camouflaged blade.

"Well, no, but that *would* explain where the knife came from, wouldn't it? I was only thinking about whether anyone needed a cane for balance or something—*especially* if they were going to lash out at someone with a knife." She set aside a third peeled parsnip and reached for one of the four potatoes.

I nodded, making another thoughtful humming sound. It was really helpful to be able to talk about these things that had been mushing around in my head since last night. Somehow, Julia—as she did in the kitchen—helped me to organize things into a recipe that made sense.

"There's another interesting thing . . . How did this person get to where they would be in position to cut Monsieur Hauet if he or she had left the party near the same time he did?" I said. "Do you see? To cut him in the front, they would have to be facing him somehow. Hard to do if you're coming up behind after him or walking with him. Even harder if they tried to cut him from behind."

"Or they could have left before him and laid in wait for him to pass by," Julia said. "*Or* . . . they just called after him to wait, and then when they caught up to him, *skiiitzch*!" She made the slicing motion and appropriate sound to go with it.

"Wait." I caught my breath, staring at her. My whole body had gone hot, then cold. "Oh my God, do you remember? Madame Vierca—she did that exact same motion yesterday. As if she *knew* someone was going to get sliced."

Julia stared at me, and I saw the comprehension in her eyes. "She did, didn't she?"

"Yes." I said, but I didn't know, really, what that meant or how it might help except to give credence and validity to Madame Vierca's visions or messages—or whatever she called them.

Julia and I were silent for a moment; then I spoke, picking up the thread of what we'd been talking about. "So anyone could have done it—anyone who left the restaurant either before or after Monsieur Hauet. They just called out to him to wait. So, the weapon could have been hidden inside a cane or walking stick. Or it could possibly have been taken from the table—"

Julia was shaking her head. "No, I don't think so, now that I think about it. We would have noticed if a knife was missing. They all fit in those flatware cases, and nothing seemed out of place or missing a piece. They're new, of course, so we'd know."

"That means whoever did it must have brought the knife with them, either in a cane or had it hidden on them somewhere. Which means . . ."

"Which means it *was* planned." Julia's eyes were wide with dismay. "Somehow knowing that makes it even worse."

Just then, the telephone rang. It was such a different sound from what I was used to back in Michigan that it always startled me, even though the telephone was on the lower floor of the Childs' apartment.

"Can you answer that, Tabs? I'm practically up to my ears in these potatoes . . . and I have to salt the beans a little more before I forget. They're going in the soup, you know. It might be Paul telling me what time he'll be home for lunch."

I hurried out of the kitchen and down the stairs to the parlor.

It wasn't Paul on the telephone; it was Blythe. "Mademoiselle, they are leaving! You should come, mademoiselle. You said to keep them safe, but now they are leaving!"

Damn. I slammed the phone down and bolted back upstairs to tell Julia, snatching up my coat, hat, and, handbag as I did so. "I'll keep you updated," I called as I bounded back down the stairs, unwilling to wait for the elevator.

"Don't go see Madame Vierca without me!" she shouted back.

I was just pushing my second arm through its coat sleeve when I burst outside. I could see Grand-père and Oncle Rafe coming out the front door of our house. Fortunately, with them being of a more advanced age, they were moving far more slowly than I was. It was simple for me to hurry across rue de l'Université and catch up to them as they trudged around the walkway to the portico on the side of the house where their Bentley waited.

"Ah, *chérie*, there you are," said Grand-père in a far more chipper voice than I'd expected. He looked wonderfully dapper this morning—recently shaved, with a dark bowler hat, shined boots, and a long, fluttering wool coat. A dark red scarf was tucked into the opening of his coat. "We wondered where you had gone off to."

"Where are you two going?" I asked, trying to keep from sounding accusing. I offered my cheek for a kiss and got a good whiff of Grand-père's aftershave and lotion. He smelled fresh and spicy.

"We are going to see an old house," Oncle Rafe told me with a smile. He'd placed a fedora over his bald head and was just as nicely dressed as Grand-père, with a gray muffler over a black wool coat. He, too, gave me a kiss on the cheek and a pat on the arm.

"A *house*?"

"Yes, yes, of course. Did you not hear us talking about it last night?" Grand-père asked. "It is a house that was owned by a friend's family for many years—since before the Great War, even. And it is empty now that the last of them have passed on. Philippe Capron told us it is now available. He is *l'agent immobilier* for the estate, you see."

"But you already have a house," I said, gesturing to the very one at which we stood. "And it's very beautiful and lovely, and—"

"Ah, of course we do," said Oncle Rafe, opening the passenger door to the Bentley so my grandfather could climb in. "But this place . . . it is special to us, and there are many memories from before. And so we thought we would take a little peek, eh?" He looked terribly dashing when he grinned at me.

"Do you think that's a good idea?" I said as Grand-père eased himself into the car.

"But what do you mean, Tabi?" he said, looking up at me from inside.

"Well . . . Paul Hauet was murdered last night, and—"

His expression sobered, and the delight drained from his eyes. "*Oui, oui,* it is a terrible tragedy. And we are going to see about the arrangements, *ma mie,*" he told me. "His funeral, of course. He hasn't any family anymore, you see, and so Rafe and I will do it. We are meeting with the priest after we visit the house."

I was still standing next to the open door of the Bentley. Oncle Rafe made an impatient sound and gave me a pointed look, as if to encourage me to move out of the way. But I wasn't ready to do that.

"That's very sweet of you to take care of those things for him," I said, doing my best to sound casual. "But don't you think you ought to stay around here for a little bit? A few days? Until things settle down?"

"Pourquoi?" Oncle Rafe frowned. "Stay around? Things to settle down?"

"Monsieur Hauet was *murdered,*" I said in a voice that, despite my attempt to remain casual, came out a little too high and tight. I took a deep breath and continued more calmly. "Aren't you worried that you might be in danger, too? Someone who was at the dinner last night had to have done it."

They both exploded with ridicule and denials.

"But of course that is not true!" cried Grand-père. "No one would do such a thing. *No one.*"

"Tabi, *ma chère,* you have been reading too many of the detective novels—of course, we understand, these last months have been so difficult for you, filled with all the horrible murders . . . but our dear Paul was sadly, terribly, and violently taken from us by no more than a cowardly street thief. There is no one who was there last night who would do such a terrible thing."

"And even if this fantasy is *true,* that someone there did it"—Grand-père scoffed and flapped his hand at the absurdity of the idea—"there is no reason to think *ton oncle* and I are in danger from them or from anyone! They are our *friends.*"

"You must understand, we all worked to *save* lives and to protect people during the war!" Oncle Rafe said earnestly. He took my arm and gently but firmly moved me away from the car door.

"But what about the flowers?" I demanded. "First, there were nine, and then there were eight. And don't forget what Madame Vierca said!"

The Bentley's door slammed closed on Grand-père's outraged exclamation.

Oncle Rafe turned to me. "I would not mention that woman in front of your grandfather," he said. "And what is it she has been telling you? You have spoken to her?" He frowned at me.

I spewed out a breath. I didn't *think* either of them had strictly forbidden me from talking to Madame Vierca—they had told *her* to go away. Even so, I decided not to answer. It didn't seem like the place and time to stand here under the portico and argue about it. If I could just get them to go back inside . . .

"Oncle Rafe, please. I think there might be more going on here than you—we—realize . . . Um," I said, grasping at my last straw, "what does Inspecteur Devré think?"

"Ah, that I do not know. I will talk to him later. And that nephew of his, *oui,* I believe he is doing his job. And he is good at it, eh? And so there is no reason for Maurice and me to stay locked up in our house." He reached for the driver's side door. "I am sorry, Tabitha, but we must leave now, or we will be late to meet Capron."

They were meeting Capron at an empty house?

Cold fear washed over me. Monsieur Capron was one of the

people who'd been around the table last night. He was the man I'd described to Julia as being affluent and who had the wide villain-like mustache and triangular beard. (To be clear, I didn't think he was a killer just because of his melodramatic mustache, but even so, I did not like the idea of my gentlemen meeting up with him—or anyone who'd been at the dinner last night—at some empty house.)

"I'll go with you," I said. "I'd like to see this house."

Oncle Rafe gave me a level look, and for a minute, I actually thought he might deny me. Then he sighed, rolled his eyes, and shrugged. "Very well, then, *chérie.* Perhaps you will, eh, comb your hair in the car? Before we meet with Capron?"

Ignoring his comment about my hair (I was sure it was kind of a mess, as I had run across the street without putting on my hat), I climbed into the back of the spacious and elegant vehicle and settled into the leather seat. Oncle Rafe said something to Grand-père in a low murmur that prompted another scoff from my relative—probably explaining why I was there and how crazy I was—and a moment later, we were off.

I checked to make certain I had my Swiss Army knife, and it was where I always kept it: in my skirt pocket. If I was going along with my messieurs to make sure they were safe, I needed as many tools at my disposal as possible. Not that a tool knife was a great weapon, but it had helped me out of more than a few difficult situations.

Almost twenty minutes later, when the Bentley pulled off to the side of rue Saint-Blaise (and I had refreshed my lipstick and tousled my hair into something presentable), I gaped at the neighborhood we were in. It was not at all what I'd expected. It was outside of the most exciting and modern parts of the city, over in the northeast edges of Paris.

"You're looking at a house *here*?" I said incredulously as I joined Grand-père and Oncle Rafe outside the Bentley. "It . . . Well, this area doesn't exactly look like your style."

They looked at me as one and began to laugh. "It is not for us to live here, *ma mie,*" said Grand-père. "But perhaps we might consider it for the investment—to make it into flats, *non*?—or perhaps a temporary hotel for the Americans who keep coming here, filling up our city, driving all around like the crazy ones?"

I gave him a wry look. If any particular nationality was known for crazy driving in Paris, it was the French. They seemed determined to somehow prove that an automobile had superior speed over any other vehicle. Even the police agents who directed traffic couldn't keep the cars from speeding.

"But the place, it is not on this street. It is there." Grand-père pointed toward a narrow passage that ran between two long rows of buildings. "Of course, we cannot drive in there, eh?"

Rue Riblette was a narrow lane, almost an alley. It was walled on one side with an allée of spindly trees and scraggly bushes on the other, and definitely no room for a motorized vehicle. We started down the little street, and I slowed my normally brisk pace so my companions wouldn't feel rushed.

The day was sunny, and although not exactly warm, it was mild enough that the last of the snow had mostly melted away. All that was left was a bit of slush along the edges of the buildings that lined the street.

Grand-père led the way down the lane, which didn't seem to go anywhere in particular. Nor did it seem the sort of place I wanted my elderly messieurs to be going, and definitely not alone. The entire area was too quiet, too empty, even a little eerie, I suppose is the word.

I was even more glad I'd invited myself to go along with them.

The pathway on which Grand-père was walking was made from horribly uneven cobblestones. He'd also waved off Oncle Rafe when he tried to take his arm.

I gave Oncle Rafe a look that expressed my dismay and exasperation at this entire escapade and hurried up next to my grandfather. Slipping my arm through his, I tucked up next to him, knowing he wouldn't be so ungentlemanly as to shrug off his granddaughter.

"This is going to be fun and interesting, Grand-père. I'm glad I came along. What is this place?" I asked, gesturing ahead as we made our way through the cobbled alley. I had glimpsed what seemed to be a small courtyard, with another small passage going off in a different direction.

"It is part of the Charonne village, you see. There are many of these such villages in Paris—where some little *rues* come together, and they make a little place of their own. And as you see, it is quiet and away from the rest of the busy city." By now we had come to a small intersection with another equally narrow lane called Cité Leclaire, and I'd felt Grand-père's step hitch only once. He gestured, and we turned onto Leclaire.

"I see," I replied.

It was just as he'd said: this seemed to be a sort of tucked-away little space where the lane rambled along, flanked by terra-cotta pots ready for spring and the iron posts called bollards installed in front of the buildings. The lane felt private and set apart from everything else, even though I could hear the buzz of city life in the distance. Some trees thrust up behind the walled courtyards we passed, with some straggly wintering grass around them and a few skeletal bushes waiting for spring.

Leclair ended abruptly, and there was a small square of cobbles and bricks, with buildings clustered around it. There were the familiar smells of cigarettes, coal, and woodsmoke, along with something cooking that I couldn't identify. The scent of baking bread reminded me that I hadn't had anything to eat at Julia's just now—very unusual—and that my single breakfast croissant was long forgotten. Laundry lines hung high above between the narrow gaps of the buildings, and as today was mild and sunny, there were shirts and trousers fluttering on some of them.

I imagined what it would be like during the summer—the people who lived here sitting or standing around, smoking, talking, drinking—maybe even sharing some cooking over a spit in this little cul-de-sac. Did they have little gardens at the backs of the houses? I thought yes, for there were walls behind them and along the alleys.

There weren't only houses, residences here. I picked out a tool repair shop, a small bakery, a locksmith.

It would have been a charming little space were it not for an air of abandonment and a lack of upkeep combined with the starkness of winter. I couldn't tell whether the stark loneliness was due to the season or whether no one actually lived here anymore.

"And there." Grand-père pointed with a gloved finger to the building directly to the right at the end of the road.

It was a plain house, a two-story residence, plastered in what had once been white but was now yellowish gray from age and lack of care. Definitely not Haussmann.

I didn't quite know what to say, for as I'd expected, this property was not at all something I'd imagined my very properly outfitted and wealthy messieurs to have an interest in.

"This Monsieur Gavril, he had a little repair shop there for many years. For the antiques, you see. He would buy from the scavengers, the ragpickers—or sometimes he even was the one who found the pieces—the antiques. He cleaned them, repaired them . . . and then he sold them to the dealers in the city, who then sold them for much more, eh?" Oncle Rafe's eyes glinted slyly as he smiled at me. I interpreted this as acknowledgment that he and Grand-père had acquired some of their fine pieces directly from Monsieur Gavril, not from the dealers at Drouot.

The house seemed to eye us with its vacant windows, dark and quiet, as we approached. I felt the same sort of tingling rush I'd experienced in the presence of Madame Vierca, especially when she'd touched me.

I almost balked and made them stop. Something was telling me not to continue, but I felt foolish about it—wouldn't anyone; for there was no actual *reason* to feel this impending dread—and remained silent. Still, I was on high alert, like Monsieur Oscar Wilde when there was the possibility of a treat being given him . . . although I did not feel as if what was in front of us would be as pleasant as a treat.

The front door was ajar.

"Ah, he is here already," said Grand-père with satisfaction—even as the tingling down my spine became stronger. He withdrew his arm from my grip.

"I'm not sure—" I said, but Oncle Rafe was pushing the door inward . . . into a dark, dank, cold interior.

"Philippe! We are here," called Oncle Rafe, far more jovially than the situation called for, at least in my opinion.

I pushed past both of them, propelled not by my curious internal sprite, but by some other primordial desire to protect.

There was no answer to Oncle Rafe's greeting. Everything was quiet and still. A nasty smell wafted from somewhere in the depths of the abandoned house, and I was pretty sure I didn't want to know what it was that stewed and rotted back there.

Dust motes, disturbed by our entrance, danced and swirled in the slim beam of sunlight that followed us inside. The room smelled stale and musty, with the hint of cigarette that, it seemed, clung to nearly every room in every building in Paris. It was colder in here than outside, and I suppressed a shiver that wasn't entirely due to the temperature.

"Philippe!" called Grand-père. "We are here."

I'd stopped only a few steps over the threshold, causing my messieurs to do the same. The three of us were in a room shrouded in shadows and populated with sheet-draped shapes that suggested chairs, tables, and other similar amenities long unused. An upright piano stood in the corner, its bench long gone. The fireplace was cold and dark and empty of anything except a pile of some indistinct material. A few old paintings hung on the wall, dusty and crooked, and there were old wires protruding from holes that indicated where lights had once been affixed to the walls or ceiling. There was a single bulb near the entrance, and two floor lamps that had not been swathed in sheets.

A rickety beam of sunshine fought its way through one of the dirty windows, leaving a jagged path over the sill and onto the floor and its worn rug. I thought I saw something skitter in the corner, and there was a definite quiet rustling somewhere in that direction. Neither rodents nor snakes bothered me; I just didn't like to come upon them unexpectedly.

"Perhaps he is not yet here," said Oncle Rafe.

"But the door was open, and we are the ones who are late," said Grand-père, looking at the old-fashioned pocket watch he still used. "Nearly fifteen minutes we are late." His reproach to me was unspoken but pointed nonetheless.

I heard a little click, then the sound of dissatisfaction from Oncle Rafe and realized he'd tried in vain to turn on a light in the room.

"Maybe we should wait outside," I said, still feeling that wild, trembly sensation, the prickling over my shoulders. "This place feels . . . well, kind of eerie to me, Grand-père. Creepy. As if it has a *presence.*"

He smiled down at me, but even in the faulty light, I could see a shadow in his eyes. "Ah, well, *ma mie,* this is indeed a place with many memories and many stories. And so, perhaps, some unhappy spirits linger, eh, Rafael?"

"Sadly, yes, *cher.* This was a place . . . Ah, it was a meeting point in the war, especially for les Neuf Bleuets. And a safe house, too. We met here often, Tabi. We hid people—Jews, spies, anyone who needed a place to hide. Why do you think it is so far away from everything? And . . ." He looked away, into the distance, into the shadows, and sighed. "There were bad things that came about. And so, yes, perhaps there are the spirits still lingering here. But what they are waiting or hoping for, I do not know."

I suggested again that we go back outside, but this idea fell on deaf ears. Instead, Grand-père pulled one of the sheets away, revealing a large armchair that even I, unschooled in antiques, could appreciate for its beauty and craftsmanship.

He sighed like a lover admiring his mate and ran a light hand over the curving arm. I got the sense that he wasn't only admiring the chair's beauty and age but was also caught up in some memory attached to it.

Oncle Rafe came to stand next to him, and I heard the low murmur of their voices. I couldn't discern the actual words, but

I sensed the two men were sharing a memory—perhaps a difficult or sad one. Their body language, the way they looked down at the chair, the quiet, sad laugh from Grand-père.

It was a moment that didn't include me, and so I stepped away and looked around.

Still a little unsteady, I tried to figure out why this house was giving me the willies. It was quiet and old and abandoned, but my reaction to it was so visceral I couldn't understand it.

"Philippe!" Oncle Rafe shouted again, startling me with the suddenness of it. "Where are you?"

"Perhaps he cannot hear us," said Grand-père. "If he is upstairs, eh?"

I'd noticed the narrow, rickety steps in the small hall beyond this front room. Farther back there appeared to be two other rooms with their doors hanging open. The smell coming from the depths of the building was stronger here.

"You're not climbing up there," I said firmly. "That stairway looks like it'll collapse at any moment."

"Bah," said Grand-père, starting in that direction. "There was a man living in this house until last month, Tabitha. Of course those stairs are not going to fall away."

"You don't know whether he *used* them," I countered, standing impertinently in the opening that led into the tiny corridor, blocking his way from entering. I didn't think he'd use his walking stick to poke me out of the way, but I wasn't completely sure. "For all you know, whoever it was just lived down here on this floor."

"But Philippe might be up there," said Oncle Rafe. "What if he has fallen and injured himself and cannot call back to us?"

I gave him a narrow-eyed look. "I'll go upstairs and look. You two can stay right here."

The two men exchanged covert looks while nodding in agreement. I suddenly had the impression this was what they'd intended all along. I'd been played.

I wondered why they wanted me out of the way.

"Fine," I said, giving them a narrow look back. "I'll go look for Monsieur Capron. Stay down here."

Sticking close to one of the walls, I climbed the steps carefully in case they collapsed in the middle. They creaked and groaned, but held as I slowly made my way up.

The staircase was dark and shadowy, but I could see some natural light spilling over the top step and beyond. From below, I heard the sounds of footsteps and movement from my messieurs.

I was just placing my foot on the top step when I heard the shouts from below.

"Mon Dieu!"

"*Le bon Dieu*! Ah, Philippe, *non*!"

I pivoted around on one foot and, heedless of my previous caution, bounded down the stairs.

"What is it?" I cried, although I already knew. I already *knew*.

Fortunately, the steps held even under the pressure of my stomping feet, and I made it to the floor—actually, I jumped down, missing the last three steps.

Grand-père and Oncle Rafe were in a tiny room that served as a kitchen and bathroom. I didn't take the time to notice any details other than the dingy white tub that sat in the corner, for the still figure on the floor understandably snagged my attention.

It was Philippe Capron.

CHAPTER 9

Monsieur Capron had not gone easily to his death.

It turned out that the terrible smell I'd noticed wafting from the rear of the house was coming from him. Body fluids had pooled on the floor and stained his clothing. He'd also vomited, and the remains were caked around his mouth and on his gloved hands. I barely managed to keep from vomiting myself. I pulled my scarf up over my nose and mouth to help muffle the stench and saw that Oncle Rafe and Grand-père, standing at a distance, had done the same.

I assumed it was poison that had killed Monsieur Capron—something that had caused the entire body to violently reject it, trying to rid itself of the contaminant. I had no idea what the toxicant might have been, but having seen several people who'd died from cyanide, I was certain this was not the case here. He had clearly been in distress for an extended period of time, finally collapsing facedown on the floor in a curled-up heap that suggested he'd suffered great pain and anguish. Cyanide worked more quickly and without quite as much expulsion of bodily fluids.

The fact that everything had started to dry—the vomit and the other expelled fluids—suggested Capron had been here for at least a little while. Maybe an hour or so.

"Philippe," Grand-père said sadly. "Ah, what has happened to you?"

"He seemed fine, only just fine, last night," Oncle Rafe said.

Both of them seemed to be in a state of denial, and for the moment, I decided to leave it that way.

I looked down at Philippe Capron, wishing I could force myself to examine his body and look through his pockets. But I couldn't—mainly because it was a terrible, malodorous, messy scene. And even though it seemed that Capron had just collapsed here in the throes of agony and there was likely no trace of the killer, I suspected Merveille would want to see everything undisturbed.

"We should cover him," Grand-père said, looking around the kitchen for something.

"I'm sorry, but I think *l'inspecteur* would want to see everything left undisturbed. I'll call for a constable," I said, turning to my messieurs. I knew there was no chance of there being a working telephone in this building. And the little courtyard had shown no signs of life or of a public phone booth, so I'd have to go out to the street where we'd parked to find help. "Why don't the two of you wait in the Bentley?"

"No, we will *not*," replied Grand-père. "We wait with Philippe. We will not leave him . . . this way . . . alone. At least we can do that."

Oncle Rafe nodded in solidarity, leaving me no choice but to abandon them as I went off to find a telephone or someone who could flag down a police agent. I didn't like the idea of leaving them unattended, with a killer seemingly hunting members of the Neuf Bleuets, but I had no choice.

So I ran across the empty square, through the walled alley, over the cobblestones, out onto the street where we'd parked.

I didn't see any public telephones, but fortunately, the first shop I found on rue Saint-Blaise had a telephone. I made the call to the 36—the nickname for the *police judiciaire* due to its address on Île de la Cité—to leave word for Merveille, then asked the shop owner, a leather maker, to contact the local police office in order to send an agent, as well.

By the time I got back to the abandoned house, I was out of breath and sweaty, but I could see that my messieurs were safe. They'd moved the two chairs that were at the postage stamp–sized kitchen table and were seated in them near the entrance to the room. Monsieur Capron was nearby but slightly out of their line of sight. I could understand why they'd positioned themselves that way.

"Tabitha," Grand-père said, his face gray and tense.

"What is it?" I said, sudden fear striking my heart at his grave demeanor.

"It is possible . . . eh, it is *likely* . . ." he corrected himself, glancing at Oncle Rafe, who nodded in encouragement, "that you are correct . . . about—eh, about all of this." He gestured sharply, impatiently. "Two of les Neuf Bleuets gone within twenty-four hours . . . both of them murdered. And so violently."

I released the breath I'd been holding. "I'm sorry, Grand-père. Oncle. I know they were friends of yours, and that it's difficult enough to think of them being gone—and in such horrible ways. But it does appear that someone is trying to . . . to . . ."

"Eliminate," Oncle Rafe said quietly.

I nodded, a lump in my throat. "Eliminate members of les Neuf Bleuets."

"And you believe we may be in danger, as well," Oncle Rafe said, his eyes serious.

"What else am I to believe? You gathered the group together—for the first time in years—and the first death happened shortly after. The second one happens just as you arrive to meet with the victim."

"But . . . you are not suggesting *we* are being *framed* for such a thing!" Grand-père exclaimed.

"No, of course not. Neither of you could have killed Monsieur Hauet. But the fact that you have been present when both victims were found . . . it makes me afraid for you."

"Eh, perhaps, but we are no foolish youngsters," Oncle Rafe replied. He now wore a set expression I'd never seen on his face. It was hard and certain and bespoke of great capability. Even violence.

"No," I replied, suppressing a shiver. After all, I didn't know exactly what he'd done during the war. Either war, for that matter. He'd have been in his forties during the Great War. "No, you are not."

I looked back down at Capron, lying there so pitifully. By now, I'd become a little more used to the smell and even the horrible sight.

I edged closer, crouching a little, careful to avoid the pools of vomit and other waste on the worn wooden floor. I began to circle the body from a prudent distance, looking for anything that might be helpful or of interest.

The room we were in, the kitchen, was at the back of the house, and it possessed a dirty but curtainless window that allowed a filtered beam of light to spill in. It was only because of this added illumination that I saw what was crushed beneath one of Capron's arms on the far side of his body from the doorway.

I drew in a sharp breath and eased a little closer, holding the muffler tighter over my nostrils while trying not to gag.

It was a flower. Hardly noticeable, nearly completely covered by the inert body . . . but there was enough visible for me to recognize the delicate crinkled petals of a *bleuet.*

I dared not move Capron, even to lift his arm to make sure. But I didn't need to.

"Grand-père. Oncle." My quiet voice drew their attention immediately, and I beckoned for them to come around and join me. "Do you see?"

Grand-père didn't attempt to kneel, but Oncle Rafe crouched a little next to me, placing a hand on my shoulder for balance.

I heard their twin catches of breath when they realized what they saw.

"*Mon Dieu,*" murmured Oncle Rafe, pushing gently off my shoulder to stand shakily.

"There seems to be no doubt that whatever is happening, it's related to the Nine Bluets," I said.

"*Oui,*" was all Grand-père said. His face was dead white, almost gray, and for a moment, I was afraid he'd collapse. But then a bit of color flooded back. "Is it because of us, Rafe, do you think? Because we drew everyone back together again?"

"*Non, non, cher,*" said Oncle Rafe, rubbing the center of Grand-père's back. "We are not to blame for whoever is committing these atrocities. Don't think it, Reece, even for a moment."

They sank back into their chairs, appearing deflated and weary. I left them speaking quietly to each other going back to the front of the house in order to flag down the police agent and Merveille whenever they arrived.

I took the opportunity to examine the outside of the house. There was no snow to conveniently leave footprints in, not even a bit of slush, but I looked anyway, because it seemed to me that if a *bleuet* had been left with Monsieur Capron as a sort of sign, it could very well have been left by the killer. If I was working with the assumption that the murderer had taken the ninth bluet last night, then he or she must have been the one to leave it today.

That meant the killer might have come earlier this morning to see the house with Monsieur Capron, who was the estate agent and would surely be showing the property to other people besides my messieurs. If so, the killer could have poisoned him at that time . . . then stayed to watch as their victim died a horrible death. How long did it take arsenic to work?

I shivered. What sort of person could stand by and watch what had been such a horrific and painful death? And that person, whoever it was, had sat with me and my gentlemen at dinner—laughing, joking, eating . . . all the while plotting and planning such heinous crimes.

I was lost in thought, still poking around the outside of the house, when I heard the sounds of people approaching.

Merveille had arrived with the police agents.

He greeted me, as he always did, with a simple, uninflected "Mademoiselle."

"Inspecteur." My response was just as cool and unemotional and down to business. I was proud of myself for not doing a quick mental audit of my appearance. Who cared what my hair looked like and whether my lipstick was still in place? "This way."

I'd watched Merveille at far too many crime scenes in the last three months, but it never felt tedious or boring. I found it interesting, and perhaps even comforting, because I knew he was very good at what he did.

He was never rushed. He never spoke or even made any sort of sounds of interest or curiosity. As I'd seen him do every time before, he walked into the room, just over the threshold, and stopped. He scanned the space, taking it all in.

Only then did he remove his hat, handing it to a nearby agent. He moved closer to the body, taking his time, his attention never wavering from the victim. I saw no hesitation or even any reaction when he drew near the horrific and malodorous scene, which led me to wonder how many examples of this sort of malevolent violence had Merveille been forced to confront so stoically.

What did that do to a person, looking at, getting close to, taking *on* these examples of the worst actions of human beings day after day? Was that why he never smiled, never showed a hint of weakness or even emotion?

I'd seen more than my share of death and violence recently, but Monsieur Capron's body was the most devastating example of them all.

I remained silent but vigilant, standing next to my seated messieurs, as Merveille did his examination. When he moved around to the back of the body, where I'd seen the crushed *bleuet*, he glanced up toward me, ever so briefly that I might have imagined it.

But I knew I hadn't.

Once he was finished looking at the body, Merveille rose and gestured for one of the agents to cover the monsieur. Then he approached the three of us.

"Monsieur Saint-Léger. Monsieur Fautrier." He nodded at me, but as I'd already been greeted, he obviously didn't feel the need to do so again. "Will you tell me what happened, if you please?"

Grand-père explained how we had all come to be here. When he finished, Merveille looked at Oncle Rafe and then me, as if to ask whether we had anything to add.

Neither of us did.

"Were you aware of anyone else who intended to look at the property with or without Monsieur Capron?" asked Merveille. "Anyone who mentioned it last night at the dinner?"

"We all talked about it," Oncle Rafe said. "All of us. Everyone expressed some interest in visiting this old place. It . . . has many memories. But I don't recall anyone in particular making a specific plan to do so."

"Nor do I," replied Grand-père. "It was, as you have been told, Inspecteur, very loud and chaotic." He offered a wan smile.

"Did anyone hear you make your plans to meet Monsieur Capron today at—What time was it?"

"We intended to meet him at noon, but we were delayed," Grand-père said, sliding a pointed glance toward me.

"I didn't want them to come alone," I said. "And, apparently, I had good reason. These two deaths are clearly related to the Nine Bluets. You saw the flower."

Merveille inclined his head in acknowledgment, then asked again, "And who might have known you intended to meet Monsieur Capron today at noon?"

Grand-père and Oncle Rafe exchanged glances and shrugged. "Anyone might have heard," said Grand-père.

Merveille nodded once more. He might have been about to speak again, but just then he looked up sharply, behind me. His expression changed so very slightly, and I thought I heard a quiet noise from the back of his throat . . . a barely perceptible grunt or groan. I turned.

Inspecteur Devré had arrived.

I quickly looked back at Merveille, but his face was blank of expression other than polite welcome to his uncle. I wondered whether Merveille had contacted Devré or whether his uncle had somehow learned of this new development and came along of his own volition. I had the sense my second option was the correct one.

I wondered how Merveille felt trying to do his job while under the watchful eye of a man who was not only his uncle but a legend in police investigation. Perhaps he appreciated having a second set of very experienced eyes, and an intelligent mind. But I suspected I wouldn't want to be in his position, with someone assessing every move I made.

I remained silent during the inspecteur's brief recap to his uncle of what happened and how we all came to be here. Devré listened carefully, then went over to Monsieur Capron's body lifting the sheet to look beneath it.

I was only mildly surprised when Merveille left the room. Either he felt the need to put some space between himself and his great-uncle, or he saw no reason not to continue with his own investigation while Devré satisfied himself. After all, he certainly didn't need his uncle's guidance or direction.

I found myself following Merveille out of the kitchen and out to the front of the house. Though he still wore his coat, he was gloveless and hatless, and his trim dark brown hair remained, as always, miraculously unmussed and smoothly combed, even though there was a lift of a breeze. The long coat flapped gently just below his knees as he stood, hands in his pockets, looking at the house and its surroundings.

"Mademoiselle," he said when he saw me. He didn't smile, but he didn't look forbidding, either; and for once, I didn't detect the irony or irritation he usually emitted when I found myself embroiled in a murder investigation. Maybe he was getting used to it—or at least accepting the fact that I had no control over these things that happened.

"Have you ever heard of Madame Vierca?" I asked. I'm not sure why I chose that way to start our conversation, but that's what came out. I blame my little imp—she likes to stir things up.

His brows lifted a little. "The medium. *Oui, bien sûr.* She is quite . . . known . . . to us at the 36. Why do you ask?"

I had not expected this sort of mild, benign response, so I was taken by surprise, and it took me a moment to regroup. "I . . . Well, she . . . approached me."

"I see." The calm, steady regard from his gray eyes—today they seemed a little more blue than usual—made me feel self-conscious, and I despised myself for it. I wasn't a young, naive schoolgirl with her first crush.

Yes, what I felt for Merveille was a crush; no doubt about it. But I was thirty years old, and I shouldn't be this loopy over a man—especially one otherwise engaged. Literally. And especially when I had a nice distraction like Jean-Luc.

I regrouped yet again. "First, she visited my grand-père and Oncle Rafe, and they wanted nothing to do with her. And then she approached me when I was out with—when I was out at a café the other night. She was rather insistent and very intense."

He remained silent. He was so much better at that than I was. I supposed it was an investigative technique—to keep quiet and let the other person feel the need to fill the void and keep talking. So I did.

"She claimed she had a vision and that Grand-père and Oncle Rafe are in danger. And then she said, 'The bluets are losing their blooms. They are dying.' "

I was sure I saw a flicker of interest, rather than skepticism, in his eyes. "When was this that she claims she had this vision, mademoiselle?"

"It was the day before yesterday—the day before the dinner. And also yesterday morning she said almost the same thing again when Julia—Madame Child—and I went to see her."

This last confession prompted a reaction. "You went *to* her? To see her? In rue des Grands-Degrés? Ah, but it was the morning, *non*? Not the evening?"

"Yes. We went in the morning. Why is that important?"

He shook his head; grimaced, really. "Mademoiselle, there are places I would not suggest any young woman go—*ever*, but especially after dark. And that is one of them."

I didn't react visibly, but inside, I couldn't help but agree. If rue des Grands-Degrés had felt eerie and strange to me at eleven o'clock in the morning, how much more so would it feel when the sun was low or even gone?

"Please do not go there alone again, mademoiselle. And by alone," he added firmly, "I mean without some—eh, some gentleman—to accompany you. As formidable as Madame Child is, I do not think she is equipped to fight off a street thief—or worse."

I noticed he didn't mention that *I* was formidable.

"And so what happened when you saw Madame Vierca at her place?" he asked when I didn't respond.

"She did a reading. One for me and one for Julia. She said—she said that death comes to me. It comes not *for* me, but *to* me. So, you see, it's *not* my fault this keeps happening." I gestured to the world at large.

I swore there was a flash of humor there in his gaze just for an instant. But then it was gone, and those stormy-sea eyes became sober and serious and now irritated. "And so you think this gives you the permission, then, mademoiselle? To poke around the bodies? To insert yourself into the investigations—just because a medium has said it?"

"To be fair, Inspecteur Merveille, I haven't been poking anywhere," I said, my hackles going up—hadn't we been just in a little bit of a truce, an easy exchange of thoughts, and now he had to get all prickly? "I simply came here today with my messieurs in order to make sure they would be safe in case—Are you *scoffing* at me?" I couldn't control my outrage.

"No, no, mademoiselle, no. Forgive me, please," he said. His mouth had twitched—I had *seen* it—and now it had flattened into sobriety again. "It is only that I was envisioning Monsieur Saint-Léger and Monsieur Fautrier gallantly stepping aside in order to allow you to defend them from a murderer. With, perhaps, your Swiss Army knife."

I tried to keep a straight face, but I failed. My lips twitched, and I laughed, shaking my head. Our eyes caught and held, and I felt a huge rush of warmth bolt through me before I jerked my gaze away. "They saw through my machinations," I said, my hilarity ebbing even as my cheeks throbbed with heat. "But they let me come with them, anyway."

"Yes, of course, mademoiselle. Ah," he said, looking over. Devré had emerged from the house, along with the gentlemen of our conversation. Behind them came two men carrying Monsieur Capron's shrouded body on a stretcher.

"What kind of poison do you think it was?" I asked quickly, trying to take advantage of our camaraderie.

Merveille swiveled his attention back to me. "Arsenic perhaps. It is often messy like that. Or there was once a murder with the lily of the valley flowers and leaves . . . It can have a similar effect. We will see."

He'd actually answered a question! I didn't want to break the spell and follow up with another one, even though I was dying to ask how long it took arsenic to work and how he thought it might have been administered. I had my own ideas, of course, but I didn't know enough about poisons to have a theory yet. And I hadn't known lily of the valley was poisonous—but even so, where would someone get such a thing in March?

But then again . . . where would someone get cornflowers—*bleuets*—in March? Obviously, there were resources, for my messieurs had obviously obtained them.

"Mademoiselle," he said hurriedly, for the other men were approaching, "if you decide you must speak to Madame Vierca again—and I do not recommend it, you understand—but if you do, I would ask . . . I would ask that you allow me to accompany you there."

I blinked in surprise. "Of—of course," was all I could say. "When would you be available to go?"

He sighed, looking at me as if pained. "And so I was correct. You intend to visit her again."

"I think it's relevant," I replied tartly. "If she's seeing visions or premonitions, maybe she knows something that can help."

He didn't respond other than by giving me a steady look, for Devré and my messieurs approached. Merveille stepped away for a murmured conversation with his uncle.

"We are free to go, Tabitha," Oncle Rafe said. His attention went from me to Merveille and back again. "Do you want to stay?"

"No," I said firmly. "There's no need to stay."

We started to go off, but Merveille turned and caught my eye. "Mademoiselle?"

I knew what he was asking: when was I going to see Madame Vierca? But his schedule was far fuller and more important than mine. I shrugged and spread my hands.

"I will telephone, then," he said and turned abruptly.

"What was that, eh, *chérie*?" demanded Grand-père. "Are you making a date with the inscrutable and compelling inspecteur?" Fortunately, he'd waited until we were out of earshot—at least I hoped we were out of earshot; Merveille had eyes like a hawk and so he probably had hearing like an owl as well.

"Not the sort of date you're thinking of," I replied a little testily. I wished people would stop trying to poke into my love life, such as it was. That was probably why I told them the truth. "We're going to see Madame Vierca."

This pronouncement had both of them stumbling to a halt in the middle of the alley.

"What is this?" Oncle Rafe exclaimed.

"You are not!" cried Grand-père, leaning heavily on his walking stick.

I looked at them and saw more fear than outrage in their expressions. My own ire eased. I slipped a hand around an arm of each of them and said, "I'll tell you about it when we get back home and can sit down. Please, just wait until we can speak calmly about it, all right?"

CHAPTER 10

I told my messieurs everything.

To my surprise, they were the most upset about the fact that Julia and I had gone to see Madame Vierca alone.

I calmed their fears by confirming that if I went back, Merveille would be accompanying me. Even so, I wondered why it was so dangerous for me—a woman—to go there, but not for Madame Vierca to *live* there.

We'd settled in the salon, of course, upon returning home. The appointment with the priest to make arrangements for Monsieur Hauet's funeral had been postponed. Bet (or Blythe) had brought up a tray of coffee and three small chocolate croissants. In honor of Philippe Capron, Oncle Rafe poured servings from a very old and distinguished bottle of Armagnac.

Oscar Wilde was on the floor, transferring his attention eagerly from person to person as each of us lifted something to eat or drink. He'd already been greeted with a treat from me as well as Oncle Rafe, so I knew he wasn't starving.

Madame X eyed me from the top of the bar credenza. I think she was still mad that I'd even had a whiff of a thought about bringing Lupin into the house.

"So now it's your turn to tell me what you think," I said, giving my messieurs a quelling look. We'd toasted Monsieur Capron and downed the cognac, and now it was back to the matter at hand. "Madame Vierca's premonition was right—the bluets are dying. Literally. Why would one of the group be killing off other members? And why now, after so many years have passed since the war?"

"It is not so many years, Tabi," Oncle Rafe said gravely. "It is only five years, and you know that the scars, they have not truly begun to heal. You have seen that in your own experience. We are still raw and wounded, and there are still those who accuse and blame." He stabbed out his dark, spicy cigarette with vehemence.

"*Oui*," agreed Grand-père. "And sometimes, *hein*, the memories—they stew and lurk, and then they come out."

"All right. So *who* is killing off the Nine Bluets? And by the way, since you seem to agree with me about that, I hope you will agree not to go anywhere or let anyone in this house unless I'm with you, or Inspecteur Devré or Merveille."

They looked at each other, grumbling; then Grand-père shrugged. "I suppose we must take the precautions, eh, Rafael?"

Oncle Rafe nodded and withdrew a pistol from behind the cushion on his chair. "Oui, *voici ma précaution*."

I sighed. "That's not going to help if someone poisons your wine or your coffee."

"We will be careful, Tabi, this I promise you. We are not such old doddering fools that we cannot take care of ourselves," Grand-père said proudly.

I managed not to scoff at this ridiculous pronouncement. Instead, I allowed fear and worry into my eyes and voice. "Please be careful. I love both of you so much, and if anything happened to you, I'd be devastated. Please, just . . . don't go anywhere or do anything without someone to watch over you."

"But we must speak with the priest," said Grand-père, but kindly. "We were going to meet him after the house, but then Philippe . . ." He shook his head. "We are hoping to go tomorrow, and we will be very careful."

"No one will hurt us at a church," Oncle Rafe told me gravely.

It was all I could do not to roll my eyes. Surely, they weren't that naive. Maybe they thought *I* was.

However, seeing that this was a losing battle for the moment, I returned the conversation to the subject at hand. "You must have some idea who might be holding a grudge against the rest of you. Or who would be capable of doing these things—slitting Monsieur Hauet's throat and poisoning Monsieur Capron so horribly. Who of the group is capable of such terrible things?"

Once again, they looked at each other, but this time it was for a long moment—as if they were somehow exchanging a silent conversation.

"You see, Tabi, *chérie*, the war . . . it makes *anyone* capable of doing something terrible. Things one might not believe one could stomach, that one could do . . . well, they are done." Oncle Rafe spoke in a low, grave voice. "And so, to be honest, I believe any one of les Neuf Bleuets is capable. The things we did . . ." His gaze went somewhere far away. "The things we *had* to do. They were difficult and dark, and sometimes, they were horrible. And at times, the things we had to do—they were good. So very good." A small smile flickered over his lips even as he stared into nothing.

We subsided into silence.

I didn't know what to say. I was trapped between empathizing with their difficult memories and being frustrated that no matter what I asked or how I asked it, the answer was vague and nebulous and filled with "But you don't understand how it was in the war, Tabitha." It was probably because they didn't really *want* to relive those times. I couldn't blame them.

The sudden buzz of the doorbell below startled me into action.

"Are you expecting anyone?" I asked, shooting to my feet.

Grand-père and Oncle Rafe looked at each other and gave those annoying Gallic shrugs that meant more of "What does it matter?" than "I don't know."

I bounded down the stairs just as Blythe (or Bet) reached the door. "I'll get it," I told her with a smile. I thanked her again for being so vigilant now and earlier today, and then I looked through the peephole.

"Julia!" I flung the door open. "Thank God it's you!"

She seemed surprised that I was so delighted to see her. "Ye gods, we only saw each other this morning, Tabs." She laughed, then gestured with the very large basket she carried. It contained something emitting a wonderful smell, and my stomach gurgled with interest. (The small chocolate croissant hadn't done much to assuage my hunger pains.)

"I brought you and your messieurs a bit of something absolutely *scrumptious*!" Her announcement came in a singsong voice of delight.

"Well don't just stand there, bring it in," I said, laughing. The rush of pleasure that came over me wasn't just due to the fact that I'd soon be eating something—as she put it—*scrumptious*—but because my fear that someone had come in search of my messieurs was put to rest.

But just as I was closing the door behind her, I noticed someone standing near the street. They were looking at me and our eyes caught.

The person—I couldn't tell much about them, bundled up as they were—beckoned to me quickly and covertly with a hand at their waist.

"I'll be right there, Julia," I said, ducking out the door before she could speak. I was coatless, but I didn't want to take the time to change that.

I approached the person. When I drew near, I was able to tell that it was an old, *very* old, gnarled little man. He had to be ninety if he was a day. His coat was worn but buttoned up neatly, and his head was wrapped in a plaid muffler, as if he had a toothache. The only reason I was reasonably sure he was a man was because of the thick spread of silver and gray whiskers that went from jaw nearly to his eyes. The criss-crossing of wrinkles over his face resembled a screen door, and he smelled strongly of cigarette smoke. He looked familiar, but I couldn't place where I might have met him.

"Can I help you?" I was digging in my skirt pocket in case I had a few francs in there. He might just be hoping for a handout, and I didn't mind sharing what I had.

"M'selle Knight, yes?" he said in a gravelly voice. He saw me digging in my pocket and held up a hand to stop me. "*Non, non,* I don't need none of that. Marie sent me."

"Marie?" For a moment, I was stymied; then all at once it hit me. The reason he looked familiar was because he was the spitting image of Marie des Quatre Saisons. "You must be her brother."

"*Non*!" he said, as if I'd gravely insulted him. "I'm her papa, you know."

Marie's *father*? I supposed that made sense age-wise. "She sent you? Why? Does she want more of my grand-père's herbs?" We often gave or sold to Madame Marie some of the tarragon, chervil, lavender, and other herbs that were grown in the greenhouse over the portico.

"*Non, non.* She said as how the ragpicker saw something last night." He leaned closer to me, and I nearly fainted because I don't think he'd brushed his few remaining teeth for some time, and the residual of that lack, combined with a *lot* of stale cigarette smoke and coffee, did not a fine perfume make.

"Last night? Do you mean about the murder on rue Las Cases? In front of Maison de Verre?"

"*Oui, oui, bien sûr,*" he said, again sounding as if I should already have known. "The *kittzzch*!" He made the sound and gesture of slitting someone's throat.

"The ragpicker saw something," I repeated. I knew what a ragpicker was . . . sort of. I didn't think there were that many of them left in the city, but I knew they were the people who came out during the night and scavenged the streets and sewers for anything that had any value and could be sold or used: rags, paper, metal, glass, crockery, fabric, half-smoked cigarettes . . . anything.

"That's right. He won't talk to *les flics,*" he went on. "But Marie, she said he'd likely talk to you, m'selle."

"All right," I said. "What is this ragpicker's name, and where might I find him?"

"Ah . . . well, that's a fine question, and I think you'd have to go about to rue Zacharie. It's where he dosses, 'at's what my Marie said, and she would know, eh." He nodded sagely. "She knows it all."

"Right." I had no idea where rue Zacharie was. Probably not in a very nice area of town. I assumed "dossing" meant sleeping or living. "What is his name? The ragpicker?"

"Keep-on-Smiling," he said.

I blinked. "Right. I will. I'll try. But can you tell me his name?"

"Keep-on-Smiling," he said again, a little more vehemently.

I frowned, trying to understand what he was saying. But it still didn't make sense. I smiled, hoping that would satisfy, and asked once more, "How will I know which ragpicker to ask for in rue Zacharie? What's he known as?"

"*Sacré bleu, dame,* I told you. Keep-on-Smiling!"

"The ragpicker's name is Keep-on-Smiling?"

"Isn't that what I said?" He looked at me as if I were an imbecile.

"Right. Sorry," I replied, wondering how on earth I was supposed to know that was a name. "All right. Thank you, then . . . er . . . What is your name?"

I braced myself, waiting for something strange, but he just said, "It's being Martin."

"Thank you very much, Martin," I said again. "Can I give you something for your troubles?" My pockets were empty of funds, but I could run into the house and grab something.

"*Non, non,*" he said, waving a hand wrapped in cloth instead of a mitten. "Marie, she takes care of me, and I just watch the birds while she's gone. Nice to get out a bit, though, eh?" He looked up, gesturing to the clear blue sky and the welcome sunlight.

"Yes, it is," I said, realizing that even though I'd been standing out here for a few minutes, I wasn't really cold. It might be actually getting near to spring. Finally. "Thank you again, Monsieur Martin, and thank Madame Marie for me. Tell her I'll bring some thyme and rosemary for her tomorrow."

When I turned to go back into the house, I saw that Julia had been standing there in the doorway, watching me.

"What was that all about?" she asked in a low voice, glancing up the stairs toward the salon.

I told her quickly, and her eyes widened. "Are you *going*?" she demanded.

"I think I'm going to have to at least look into it," I said.

"Tabi? What is it?" Oncle Rafe was standing at the top of the stairs, looking down at us. Oscar Wilde joined him and sat on the step below, eyeing us eagerly. He knew just as well as anyone that when Julia arrived, it meant *food.* "Ah, Madame Child! You are here! How nice to see you! You were *un miracle en cuisine* last night!"

"Julia brought us over something to eat and . . ."

"And Bet is heating it up. We'll bring it up in a few minutes," Julia said. "I know it's late for luncheon . . ."

"Ah, but we didn't eat," Oncle Rafe told her. "And so we are quite ready for anything you have brought us, Madame Child! And then we will tell you all about the new tragedy."

"What new tragedy?" Julia gave me an appalled look, and I grimaced.

"I didn't have the chance to tell you." So as we went into the kitchen, I filled her in on the trip to the empty house and finding Monsieur Capron.

"How terrible," she said. "What an awful thing . . . to die like that, alone and in such a terrible way."

"It was. And Grand-père and Oncle Rafe were quite upset—but at least now they believe me when I tell them there's something going on related to the Nine Bluets."

"Well, let's hope Merveille and Devré can figure things out soon. What's this, Tabs? Did someone send you *flowers*?" Julia had noticed the vase on the half table in the foyer. It contained a dozen roses, tied with a shiny pink ribbon.

I smiled. "Yes, they're from Jean-Luc. They were here when we got home today, and I've hardly had the chance to enjoy them."

She snatched up the card that sat next to the spray of red roses—perhaps a cliché choice, but then again, Frenchmen were consummate romantics. "'Lupin continues to evade my efforts to return him to you, and so I send these as a poor substitute for your heroic alley cat. When may I see you again? Jean-Luc.' Aw." Julia looked at me with puppy-dog eyes. "When *are* you going to see him again?"

"I don't know. Probably not until this whole mess is figured out," I said. "I'm not leaving my gentlemen unattended."

"You could always invite him over here," Julia suggested, her eyes dancing.

"And be subjected to questions from Grand-père and Oncle Rafe about why we're here instead of rolling around in a bed somewhere?" I said, laughing. "You know they would say it."

Julia was laughing, too. "Probably. I swear, all these French people think about are food, wine, and sex!"

By now, Bet (I didn't know how Julia knew which twin it was who'd helped her in the kitchen; maybe she'd just *asked*) had finished making up the tray to be put in the dumbwaiter. Julia's pot of soup was on it, along with a fresh loaf of bread. There was also another bundle wrapped in a cloth.

"It smells *magnificent*!" cried Grand-père when we got upstairs and opened the dumbwaiter. "You are the most generous of women, Madame Child. I am certain we owe your Monsieur Child some great favor, for you are always sharing your meals with us so generously."

"Oh, it's nothing," Julia said, her cheeks turning pink with pleasure. "Paul slipped home to have the soufflé I was making earlier, but he's busy with an exhibit opening tonight at one of the galleries, and he's required to eat with his colleagues for supper. He complains about it, but sometimes a man has to do what a man has to do!" She laughed, a booming, delighted guffaw, as she settled into a chair. Then she sobered quickly. "I'm very sorry to hear about your friend Philippe Capron," she said, reaching over to pat Grand-père's veiny hand.

"Ah, *oui*, it is a tragedy," Oncle Rafe said. "A terrible tragedy, these things that are happening. Maurice and I . . . ah, we cannot believe it. We cannot take it in."

"Now, what is it you have brought for us today, Madame Child?" Grand-père was practically sniffing the air like an eager rabbit.

"It's only a pot of vichyssoise, made with parsnips, potatoes, and purple runner beans," Julia said, looking proud and humble at the same time.

My grand-père's expression faltered and Oncle Rafe stiffened, but they quickly recovered. "Ah, well, thank you, madame. That will be lovely," said Grand-père after a moment. He smiled at her.

"There's also a sweet bread with walnuts," Julia added, glancing at me with a question in her eyes. I shrugged. I had no idea why my messieurs had reacted that way. "And Bet sent up a baguette, as well."

"Merci beaucoup, madame," said Oncle Rafe.

Julia busied herself serving the soup and bread, and I assisted. I didn't know why my messieurs had had such a tempered, almost pained response to her offerings. It was very much not like them at all. I supposed it was just that they were feeling unsettled and grieved over what had happened to their friends.

"Will you tell us about what les Neuf Bleuets did during the war?" Julia asked once we were all settled with soup and bread, as well as coffee. "Maybe there's some clue in there."

"Eh, perhaps." Grand-père didn't sound as if he wanted to think so, but I knew he'd come around to the fact that even if he didn't want to believe it, there was really no other explanation. "It is really Rafael's story to tell, eh, *cher*? I came in rather late."

"You *had* to stay out of it," Oncle Rafe said, "in order to be useful. And safe. You see, of course, the Germans wanted control of the banks, and so Maurice had to . . . eh, well, he had to work with them. *Appear* to work with them. To collaborate." He shrugged in that offhand way that was meant to be insouciant, but I knew it was forced.

This had come up before—the fact that Grand-père had had to dance in the gray area between collaborating with the occupiers and finding ways to resist. Oncle Rafe, on the other hand, was far more black and white about it all. It had been—and still was, on occasion—a source of stress and strife between them.

"You see," Oncle Rafe said, a little sad smile twitching his mustache and beard as he glanced at Grand-père, "when the war was just on the cusp of beginning . . . in thirty-nine, I was . . . shall we say, I was expressing my displeasure with the capitalistic society. With the—"

"Ah, say it! You were running wild, Rafael. And at your age . . ." Grand-père scoffed, then gave him an affectionate smile. "You were practically an anarchist."

"I never was an anarchist," Oncle Rafe retorted.

"A communist, then?" Grand-père said in a gentle challenge, a smile tugging his lips.

"*Non*! Not that, either. I was . . . experimenting and exploring—"

"You were lost. Because you had walked away from . . ." Grand-père glanced at me and sighed. "From this. From us." He spread his hands. "From me."

"It wasn't only me," Oncle Rafe responded, giving him a wry look. "*We* were not happy, you and I. You were the stuffy, the haughty, the bourgeois—"

"And you wanted to break the bonds of society, to stretch the rules, to . . ."

"To be free. To *live*."

They lapsed into silence as Julia and I gawked at each other. I'd had no idea Oncle Rafe and Grand-père had had, I guess, a breakup—and a long one, it sounded. I'd just assumed they'd been together forever—or at least since my grandmother had left to live with my mother and father in America after the first war.

"Go on, Oncle Rafe," I said in a low voice. "It was nineteen thirty-nine, and you were doing your own thing."

"*Oui*. I painted and wrote poetry. I frequented the flophouses and the brothels, and . . ."

"Slept with anything that moved," Grand-père interjected wryly.

"And you did not?" Oncle Rafe gave him a quelling look. "Don't think I didn't know about the Mansour."

Grand-père's fair cheeks pinkened a little. "You and I—we were not together then."

"No, we were not. And so then the Germans came," Oncle Rafe said, returning to a matter-of-fact tone. However, his expression was grave. "And everything happened. All of the bad things, the *very* bad things—the Jews had to hide or leave so they weren't sent away to the camps, the travel was restricted, the food was gone—you understand, there was *nothing* to be had to eat in those days. We waited in lines for hours just for a loaf of bread, for a sausage. People ate the rats and the pigeons.

"The Nazis, they lived in our houses and drank or ruined our wine and destroyed our homes . . . took our businesses . . . It happened so quickly, and the government, the Third Republic, it just *fell.* They only just gave up, gave in—*surrendered*!—and voted themselves into nothing. Into meaninglessness. They gave in to the Germans, castrated themselves—and all of us. And Pétain—" His voice choked off with fury, and Grand-père reached over, closing his wrinkled, veiny hand over Oncle Rafe's darker one. I saw him squeeze it bracingly.

"We will not talk about him or the travesty, the *atrocity*, that was the supposed French government in Vichy," Grand-père said, glancing down at the bowl of soup. Grimaced. "Forgive me, Madame Child—it is not your soup that pains me. It is quite delicious and most soothing. Very creamy and herby. But it is only the name of it—the vichyssoise—that gives me and many of us Frenchmen the sad reminder of that monstrosity in Vichy. The dull ache over the memory of the ones that gave us away—gave control away. They gave our nationality away. Our pride."

Julia winced and looked at me. I grimaced in return. But neither of us could have known a simple chowder would cause such pain.

"But we were still here, and we were *les Français*! We were not going to stand aside. And so there were some of us who made our own network . . . our own group," Oncle Rafe said, picking up the tale again. He paused, sampled the soup, and smiled, nodded, then went on. "One had to take care when asking around . . . You see, one had to be circumspect when feeling out a friend or acquaintance about whether they were strong enough, brave enough, *willing* to resist. To join us. Whether they could be trusted.

"It happened so fast, you see, and the authorities—the government—giving up, surrendering!—that they made it seem as if it was the right thing to do. The only way to protect our nation. But we knew it was *not.* We, the French, we knew it *could not stand.*

"And so we had to find a way to help. We hid those who were Jewish—as I said, often in that very house we visited today. It was a safe house, and Monsieur Gavril allowed us to use it. We helped the Jews to get out of the city, out of the Free Zone, out of the country. To do that, we had to have the *Ausweis*"—he spat the German word as if it soiled his mouth—"the papers that allowed one to freely go about the country. And the ID cards.

"There was a girl. Andrée was her name. She worked at the *police judiciaire*, and she would steal blank ID cards whenever she could, and they would get sent through the networks to be made into false identification. You see, you could go nowhere in France without your papers," Oncle Rafe said, his eyes cool and remote, as if he were reliving those days. "And Andrée, she had a typewriter in her office, and she could even make the copies on the Roneo.

"And so she would type up the information very early in the morning, before her bosses arrived, and she would make as many copies as she dared of these papers with the news and warnings and intelligence that we needed to have. And she would give them to her brother, and they would be distributed. She was so very smart, so very brave—she would even take the ribbon from the typewriter where she did this so that no one would know what it was she had typed."

"Why was she not part of les Neuf Bleuets?" I asked. "This Andrée?"

"*Eh.* It was because she was in her own network, you see? With her brother and some other friends—It was best to keep the connections small, eh? But this Andrée . . . she became famous for her bravery. No, les Neuf Bleuets . . . we were our own small network. Our own group. It was best, you see, to have the small networks, where very few people knew even fewer people who were of *la Résistance.* Because the fewer people you knew, the fewer names that could be tortured out of you."

I suppressed a shudder.

Silence fell.

It was incredible for me to imagine living in a place that had been my home, my city, my nation . . . and for it to suddenly no longer be mine. To be owned, controlled, *ruled* by some other entity.

"There was a time once," Oncle Rafe went on, a wry little smile twitching his mustache, "that we were very excited over the arrival of some one thousand ID cards from England—blank ones that had been counterfeited and printed there and they were coming to us via a courier so that we could create the papers needed to help the Jews and the young men—ah, yes, I will tell you about that, the young men, if you do not know.

"But the ID cards from England . . . when they arrived, we saw that we could not use them, for they had been printed on such very good, firm stock from Bristol . . . and the ones we had here were printed on the very flimsy and the very cheap papers, and so no one would believe they were real." He shook his head sadly. "It was a shame, and so then, of course, the English ones had to be burned so that no one would be found with them."

"And what about the young men?" I asked. I couldn't help but think about Merveille—as I had done many times but had never dared to ask—what had he done during the war? I wasn't certain I wanted to know. Where had he been? What had he been doing?

He was a police officer—had he been one then? Surely, he had, for he was an inspector now, and it was only five years after the war. Even with his great-uncle's reputation, it would take some time for a man to work his way from police agent to inspector.

The police had been collaborators with the Germans, helping to round up Jews to send them off on trains to the concentration camps, helping the occupiers to control and repress and arrest—even torture—their fellow Parisians. That was why, even now, there was an inherent dislike and mistrust of the authorities, especially from those who'd remained here during the Occupation. It was partly why I had been successful in helping Merveille to solve the murders in which I'd become involved—people would talk to me because I was a woman, I was natively fluent in the language, and, most of all, I was *not* the authorities.

That was why, I suspected, Madame Marie had wanted me to know about Keep-on-Smiling, the ragpicker.

"*Oui,* the young men." Grand-père took up the story. "There was a decree in February of nineteen forty-three. *Le service du travail obligatoire,* it was called. This law meant that every man who was under the age of forty-six must go to Germany and do their industrial work for them. To work in the factories or on the farms, or anywhere the Nazis wished."

I caught my breath. I'd had no idea. "That . . . why, that is nothing more than *slavery.*"

"*Bien sûr, chérie,*" agreed Grand-père with a fierce light in his eyes. "And that is when so many more of these secret groups were suddenly created. They formed overnight, in order to help these young men escape from France before they were sent away."

"And that is when Maurice became involved," Oncle Rafe said, smiling at him.

"That is when you came to me," Grand-père said, wearing his own soft smile. "You came to me and asked if the bank's couriers could somehow help to transport information, ID cards, and more. You see, we still had great freedom to send and receive packets, papers, money, for, as we know, the money, it makes the world work. And so you came to me quite bravely, *hein,* Rafael. You were desperate, and you came to me."

Oncle Rafe's cheeks had gone a bit dusky. "I didn't want to, of course. I saw no reason to see you again, to be confronted by your wealth and power . . ."

"To be assaulted by the memories, *non?* To return, hat in hand, and ask for me to use that power and wealth you so despised."

They looked at each other, nodding, lost in the past. I glanced at Julia again, feeling as if this was a private moment at which I shouldn't be present.

"And yet you took the risk," Grand-père said after a moment.

"And I learned that you had not been sitting quietly and doing nothing," Oncle Rafe said soberly. "That you had been careful, but that you had been resisting all along."

"And so I joined les Neuf Bleuets," Grand-père said, looking at me. "No one could know who I was, you see. It was too risky, and so Rafe, he was the go-between. I was an unnamed member of the nine."

"Did the others of the nine know who everyone was in the group?" I asked slowly as a thought—just a wisp of one—caught at the back of my mind, then disappeared like the remnant of a dream.

"Not at first. Not until later. Much later. Not until . . . ," Oncle Rafe said with another of those private looks at Grand-père, "not until after the war was over did they even know of Reece's identity."

"Do you mean the Nine Bluets didn't know who the other eight were until the war was over?" Julia said incredulously.

"That is so," Oncle Rafe replied. "I was only one of the group, and in fact, I did not start it myself. I was asked in by Paul Hauet. It was he and Renald Lussier who started it, and then Hauet asked me, and Lussier asked another, and so it grew in a sort of spokelike, weblike fashion. You see? Hauet and Lussier were the center, and I was a spoke, and so was Ruth Munzel and Louis Sénac, and then each of them extended their spokes to include Robert Taban and Berthilde Demailly. And I asked Reece, and then he suggested Capron, who knew of many empty houses and unique spaces that could be used to hide people and things. And so we were nine."

"Can you think of any reason one of the nine would want to harm the rest of you? Anything? Did someone close to a member of the Nine die, and somehow the killer thinks it was the fault of the Neuf Bleuets?" I asked.

"There were people who died, Tabi. Many of them. Most tortured to death. Some sent off to the camps, never to be heard from again. Some left to rot in prisons until they no longer had the will to live. But I cannot think of anything for which the Nine could be blamed," Oncle Rafe said.

I was just about to speak again—probably simply to express my frustration over not getting anywhere—when the bell at the front door rang. I bolted to my feet, along with Oscar Wilde, who was galvanized by the possibility of a new arrival who might give him a morsel of a treat. He barked wildly and dashed to the top of the steps.

"I'll get it," I called to Bet and Blythe as I bounded down the stairs. I slowed when I got to the bottom, however, because it occurred to me that I was supposed to be protecting my messieurs from a killer—a killer who'd used a knife to slice his victim's throat. I couldn't just throw the front door open without having some sort of defense.

But when I looked through the sidelight, my heart gave a little lurch. It was Merveille.

CHAPTER 11

I opened the door, ignoring the cacophony of barking from the excited Monsieur Wilde, and saw that Devré was also there, standing slightly behind and to the side of his great-nephew.

"Come in," I said, stepping back for them.

To my surprise, Devré greeted me like his own granddaughter—with an embrace and a kiss on the cheek. He smelled of tobacco and something spicy and fresh. I did not look at Merveille, and I felt the heat rise in my cheeks. It would be a cold day in hell before the nephew followed his uncle's conduct.

"Grand-père and Oncle Rafe are upstairs," I said, probably unnecessarily, as that was the only place they ever were when they were home. "Oscar Wilde, *silence*!" My voice cracked a little with that bottled-up frustration.

"Ah, no, mademoiselle—*le petit monsieur* is all right," Devré said with a quiet smile as he started up the stairs. "I will give him a tiny biscuit, and he will settle down—most probably in my lap."

Merveille didn't immediately follow his uncle, and that left both of us alone in the foyer.

"If you still intend to speak with Madame Vierca, I will go with you now." He'd removed his hat and was holding it in ungloved hands. "Oncle Guillaume will stay with them." He glanced toward the stairs. "They will be safe with him."

"Yes, I'm sure they will. Oncle Rafe has a pistol under his seat cushion," I confessed with a little grimace. "Now is fine." I resisted the urge to reach up and check my hair or to look in the mirror that hung over the mezzaluna table where my flowers stood in their vase. "But there's somewhere else I need to go, as well."

Merveille suppressed a sigh and waited for me to continue.

I explained about the ragpicker. "I don't know what he saw, but I think it's at least worth talking to him. And he'd be more likely to talk to me, I think," I added hesitantly.

His expression didn't change, but I knew he understood my meaning. Whether he agreed with me was a different matter. "And where is this ragpicker? He is called Keep-on-Smiling, you say?"

"Monsieur Martin said to look for him in rue Zacharie, but I don't know where that is. I've never heard of that street, but I haven't had the chance to look at my map."

He was frowning. "I don't know it, either." I could tell he didn't like not knowing, that it irritated him more than he wanted to let on. "Oncle Guillaume will surely be able to tell us."

I heard a burst of laughter from Julia upstairs, and Merveille looked at me. "I didn't know that Madame Child was here."

"She brought some soup. I'm sure there's enough for you and the other inspecteur if you'd like some."

I think he tried to hide the delight and relief that flared in his eyes, but it was hard to tell. I was certain he was very glad to have had the offer, and I wondered whether he'd even had anything for breakfast, let alone lunch. After all, he'd been up late last night with Paul Hauet's murder and had surely been following up on that this morning—and then he would have gotten the message from me about Philippe Capron and been busy ever since. I was more than a little surprised he'd found his way here, presumably to accompany me to meet with Madame Vierca.

I gestured for Merveille to go upstairs; then I went to get soup bowls and utensils for him and Devré.

"Rue Zacharie, you say?" Devré was saying as I appeared at the top of the stairs. "Ah, but I have not heard it called that in many years."

"It is now known as rue Xavier-Privas," Oncle Rafe said as I began to dish up soup for our guests. "It was changed back in twenty-nine, I believe."

Merveille made a sound of comprehension. "Ah, *oui,* of course. I know the street as Xavier."

"What is it you want there? It is not a nice place for a young woman, Tabitha." Oncle Rafe's eyes were fixed steadily on me, warning and concern in them, as he blindly stroked Monsieur Wilde.

"Inspecteur Merveille is going with me," I said and steadfastly ignored Julia's gaze, for I knew what I would see: morbid delight.

"It's near Saint-Séverin," said Devré, giving me a big smile as I set a bowl of soup in front of him. I'd been careful not to call it vichyssoise. "Nearly to the quai. Zacharie—Xavier, if you wish—ends very near the river, just across from the *île.* It is a place with the most interesting of reputations, and the strangest of happenings," he went on, his gaze and expression sober. Then his eyes lit up. "Ah, Madame Child, I must tell you—have heard so many times from my nephew about your expertise *en cuisine,* and now for two days in a row, I am to partake myself. I am honored and very grateful."

Julia beamed and thanked him for his kindness.

"You will not go at night, when it is dark, even with the good inspecteur, Tabitha, do you hear me?" Oncle Rafe said flatly, holding Oscar Wilde firmly so that he wouldn't launch himself toward the temptation of Devré's soup. "The street was once known as rue des Maléfices . . . and for good reason."

Witchcraft Street? I felt a little shiver in my belly.

"Maléfices? It is appropriate, the name, *oui,* but I have never heard it called that," said Devré, looking up from his soup. He sounded curious and intrigued rather than contentious. "If so, it is an apt name."

"It is so," Oncle Rafe said. There was an inscrutable look on his face as he settled into his chair and lit one of his skinny dark cigarettes. "There was once a man I met who had a map of our beloved Paname. A very, very old hand-drawn map . . . I cannot tell you how old, but it was the oldest piece of paper I have seen not in a museum."

"Paname?" Julia asked, frowning.

"Paris. It is a little nickname for Paris," Grand-père told her with a smile. "There are those who think it came about because of the Panama scandal in ninety-two, although it could also be due to the panama hats that were so popular when we were young, eh, Guillaume?" He winked at Devré, who chuckled but didn't speak, for he clearly didn't want to be interrupted while eating his soup.

"Tell us about this map, Oncle," I urged even as I glanced at the clock. It was nearly five, and the sun would be gone in an hour or two. Merveille must have noticed, for he caught my eye and gave a brief nod that indicated he'd be ready to leave after he finished his small meal—of which he was efficiently partaking.

"Well, there isn't much to tell. It was an Englishman by the name of Garrett who showed me the map—I might even have been there, in Maléfices, myself at the time when he did. I cannot quite remember . . . Those days of mine were filled with many adventures and activities on those dark streets, and they all blur together, you see." Oncle Rafe spread his hands languidly.

"This map of the Sorbonne, he claimed it was drawn by the old scholars at the Irish College—which is how, I suppose, this Monsieur Garrett came to have it. But on this map, I saw it quite clearly—this street you are speaking of was marked as rue des Maléfices." He shrugged. "I don't know that I ever saw the man again. He was rather like the Old Man Who Appears After Midnight—he was there, he completed his task, and then he was gone."

"Ah. *Bien entendu.* The Old Man Who Appears After Midnight," Devré said, nodding sagely.

Grand-père murmured his assent as well, also nodding as he poured a stream of golden cognac into a snifter.

I looked from one of the old men to the other, and then the other, mystified and fascinated. "Who is that—this man who appears after midnight?"

Grand-père sat back in his seat and put his long, elegant nose into the snifter and inhaled. For a moment, I thought he wasn't going to answer me—that none of them were. Then he spoke.

"There is no simple answer, Tabitha, about the Old Man Who Appears After Midnight—just as there are no real answers about the building in rue de Bievré that disappeared after a gypsy put a curse on it, or the watchmaker with the very special watch that ticks back and forth between time, so that he never ages.

"You see," he said, smiling a little, "Paris—she is such an old, *old* city. She has still the road that leads directly to Rome, if you choose to take it. And she has many, many other secrets from over the centuries. Do you know, it is strange. Here we have not so many of the lingering ghosts that are found in the other cities—London or Vienna or Prague. Instead of haunted houses or eerie, possessed spaces, we have the spirits, the tales and truths, the strange and inexplicable and fantastic that live here in our Paris.

"Her streets are old, *ancient*, the walls and bricks—they hold these spirits and their essences within them. These traditions, this knowledge—they are instilled into the space and the dirt. I do not try to understand, to explain why strange things happen here in certain parts of this city. I simply accept."

That was not the least bit of an answer to my question. I glanced at Julia, who was looking as confused and mildly frustrated as I felt. She caught my eye and shrugged. Sometimes I thought my messieurs liked to be mysterious just for fun.

"The Old Man Who Appears After Midnight," Oncle Rafe said in a mild voice, with a little wry smile toward Grand-père, "is simply that: a man who shows himself usually in a public house or dive and always after midnight. He is simply, suddenly, just *there*. Most often he is noticed during a disagreement or discussion or mild altercation.

"He will speak one or two brief sentences, but they will be

truths. They will often give direction or advice that those involved in the disagreement will ignore at their own peril. And then, suddenly, one notices his glass is empty, and he has gone." He spread his hands, as if it was the most common thing in the world.

"Have you ever seen him—the Old Man Who Appears After Midnight?" I asked, skepticism lacing my voice.

Oncle Rafe looked at Grand-père, who looked at Devré, who looked back at Oncle Rafe and Grand-père . . . and they each *nodded.*

"You've seen him," I said. "All of you?"

The three nodded again.

"Were you all together when you did? Was it at the same time?" I was skeptical but curiously fascinated, as well.

They each shook their head, wearing expressions that could only be described as matter of fact.

I opened my mouth to speak, to probe further, but Merveille rose. "Mademoiselle, it grows late."

I nodded and stood, but not without giving my grand-père and Oncle Rafe a searching, skeptical look. Then I said, "Julia, we're going to see Madame Vierca, as well. You said you wanted to come when I went again."

"Oh. No, no, I can't go now," Julia said, waving her hand at us. "You go on ahead, Tabs."

Absolutely no one in the room was fooled as to why she "couldn't" go with us, except maybe—*hopefully*—Merveille.

"All right. You'll stay with them until we return, Inspecteur?" I was speaking to Devré but obviously referring to my messieurs.

He nodded gravely. "But of course. And we will talk much about the old times, and perhaps I will even find a clue amongst these reminiscences." He glanced at his nephew and added, "You will take care of the lovely mademoiselle and of yourself, Étienne."

Merveille inclined his head as he pulled on his coat, then gestured for me to precede him down the stairs.

"Are you sure they'll be all right?" I asked, suddenly very aware that even though he was a decorated police officer and detective, Devré was long retired and was just as aged as my messieurs.

Merveille had retrieved my coat from where it hung in the foyer next to the half table, and helped me into it.

"We will not be gone long, mademoiselle," he said with a glance up the stairs. "And besides that, I have arranged for Agent Richot to stand guard. Perhaps you wouldn't mind if he came inside and sat in the kitchen? Surely your grand-père won't mind."

"Of course not," I said, relief flooding me.

Moments later, after this was arranged and the young, earnest police agent was settled with a pot of coffee and the remnants of Julia's soup—along with strict instructions—Merveille and I were on our way.

As rue Zacharie—Xavier—was slightly closer in proximity to rue de l'Université than Madame Vierca's place, that was to be our first stop, in search of the ragpicker. That was also logical, for Keep-on-Smiling would likely start his nightly work of scavenging as soon as the sun set.

I'd never ridden in a car with Merveille before, so this was a first—climbing into the front seat of the dark, nondescript sedan and having him close the door once I'd drawn my feet and legs inside. Always the gentlemen, these Frenchmen were. We didn't speak much, which wasn't a surprise, as my companion was a man of few words. I was acutely aware of how close we sat in the car and how the small interior concentrated the pleasing scent clinging to his hair and clothing: pine and, I thought, vetiver.

The sky was still clear and blue, but the sun was lowering, and by the time we found parking off rue Saint-Jacques, the shadows were already growing long. We walked along Saint-Séverin, a narrow street that connected rue Saint-Jacques and boulevard Saint-Michel and where the church of the same name had been in existence since the thirteenth century. Once past the cloisters and edifice of the parish church for the Sorbonne, we walked only another half block before we came to rue Xavier-Privas.

"So this is Witchcraft Street," I said as we turned into it—north, toward the river.

I felt awkward and uncomfortable—and yet safe—being alone with Merveille, walking these narrow streets in this old, storied, mysterious part of the city. I couldn't seem to decide whether to relax and enjoy myself or whether I should be on guard.

I wished Julia had come with us; she would have been a good buffer and helped ease the strange tension I was feeling—a tension that could be attributed to my unresolved feelings about the man with me or the strange stories I'd heard about the so-called rue des Maléfices.

"So says your oncle," Merveille replied. "I have never heard that name, as I said, but I have always accepted there is something different about this place."

"You've been here before?" I paused, looking at him in surprise.

"*Bien entendu.* There are not many streets in this city I have not been in," he replied.

"Is it dangerous?" I asked, looking down the narrow pathway of the *rue.*

Xavier-Privas—aka rue Zacharie, aka rue des Maléfices—definitely had a disquieting feel about it. Even more so than where Madame Vierca lived, although both of these small, crooked lanes near the river were only some blocks apart.

Rue Xavier was very, very narrow, with no sidewalks. Every structure was built right up into the cobbled street, their irregular facades creating random nooks and alcoves, extrusions and intrusions. The lane doglegged off to the left, or east, about two blocks down, giving the impression of a dead end. The street was so narrow there weren't even the black iron bollards—the random posts set into the ground to provide a barrier between motor and pedestrian traffic.

The road street's surface was cobblestone, and I don't think a car would have been able to drive down without great care, perhaps not at all without scraping the buildings in some areas. These masonry edifices were tall and long, with narrow doorways jutting out or set into little nooks and an occasional window or cornice. There were also two little extrusions in the road, creating a tiny square-like area about halfway down. I saw one abandoned cart parked there and no one to pull it.

It was like walking down an irregular lane between two brick walls that stretched three or four stories high and blocked out most of the light. The street was dim and shadowy, though it was just approaching six o'clock.

It was also quiet, with very little activity. I saw someone ahead of us go into a building and a dog dart across the street. There were no bicycles or carts but the one, no pedestrians, no telephone booths, nothing but an allée of quiet and still. I didn't even smell anything cooking, although there was smoke in the air and other odors far less pleasant.

An overwhelming sense of disquiet pervaded the space, and I shivered, wondering what it would be like at night, when the shadows were even longer and the gas lamps that hung over the street on wrought-iron arms projecting from the buildings were the only source of light. The few windows at street level had bars on them, and they were as dark and empty as dead eyes.

There was definitely a "feel" to this street . . . something I couldn't define. It wasn't frightening, it was just *strong*. Intense.

"Dangerous, mademoiselle?" Merveille said. He'd taken a moment to respond, as if he, too, had been caught up in the atmosphere of the place. "It is more strange than dangerous, I think. Despite the warning of Monsieur Fautrier, you need not worry."

"I find strange rather interesting," I said.

"And danger interesting, as well, hmm, mademoiselle?" His voice was mild, and I glanced over, wondering if there was a hint of a smile in there, as well.

"I don't seek out danger," I retorted, my lips twitching a little. "It finds *me*." I knew he believed otherwise, and based on my recent experiences with the other murders in which I'd been involved, I couldn't really blame him.

He made a skeptical sound but didn't speak.

"Monsieur Martin didn't say where to find Keep-on-Smiling," I said as we went on. "I suppose we could find a—a pub or someplace and go in and ask."

"Bien." He was walking in the middle of the street, and I noticed he shortened his strides so that we stayed together. As his assurances suggested, he gave off no impression of discomfort or nerves; even so, his keen gray eyes never seemed to stop moving—scanning and examining the street.

He gestured for us to stop at the first door that had a soft glow of illumination behind it, which indicated there was some sort of life and occupancy within. An old, mostly unreadable sign, its only discernible letters being *P, i, g, n,* was bolted to the brick wall next to the entrance. But the door opened easily, and we stepped inside. We were swallowed up by a close, low-ceilinged space, engulfed by the smell of stale beer and wine and the remnants of tobacco smoke that painted the interior.

It was here that we encountered the first real sign of activity on rue Xavier-Privas, for there were about a dozen people inside the pub. They sat, drank, talked, smoked, and seemed wholly unconcerned by our arrival. This lack of a reaction eased the last bit of apprehension I'd been harboring.

Gas lamps bolted onto the walls flickered, and there were ugly stains from decades—possibly centuries—of their smoke behind and above the sconces. Slender black trails of kerosene leaked from beneath them onto walls that had once been creamy-white plaster but were now dingy and dull, cracked, and flaking. A poster that had once been glued to one of them had mostly been torn away. Its remnants were faded, and the image was obliterated.

I realized right away that the floor was nothing more than wide, loose planks laid over the ground—probably directly on the dirt. They shifted a little, lifting and thumping down quietly as we stepped on them. I found myself looking down so I didn't catch a foot on the edge of one of the planks and trip.

A tiny rectangle of a bar counter sat directly across from the door, and the wall behind it—instead of being filled with shelves of glasses and bottles—was unrelieved, unadorned brick. The single person behind the counter eyed us with neither malevolence nor interest as we made our way closer. The last bit of a smoldering cigarette was clamped between her—it had taken me a moment to realize the shapeless figure with a square face was a woman—lips, and a thick stream of smoke trailed from it.

Most of the stools lined up along the bar were occupied, and there were more seats along two other long counters affixed to the walls, beneath the sconces. A few tiny tables, hardly larger than upended wire spools, were scattered in the room with more stools and a few rickety chairs, also occupied by a smattering of patrons.

I noticed with mild surprise that those patrons seemed to come from various levels of society: some were dressed in mean, worn clothing; others in simple peasantlike garb; others in work clothes; and still others in more Bohemian sort of wear—loose straight trousers, scarves, berets. It was a fascinating array of patrons, and they made me feel less conspicuous in my nice wool overcoat and fashionable skirt and blouse.

"Bonjour, mademoiselle," said Merveille to the bartendress, removing his hat as he gestured me toward an empty stool at the counter. I noticed that at some point, he'd loosened his tie and unbuttoned the top of his shirt, perhaps trying to also be as inconspicuous as possible.

I added my own friendly greeting to the woman behind the bar as I slid onto the stool, controlling the desire to wipe off the surface first. I didn't want to come across as rude, so I sat and hoped nothing would stain or stick to the back of my coat.

Merveille stood behind and to the side of me, for the seats on either side of mine were occupied. "*Un jaune,* if you please, and whatever the mademoiselle wishes," he said, placing his hat on the counter.

I wasn't certain what a "yellow" was in regards to a drink, but I thought it was safe to say, "I'll have the same."

I'd had to tamp back a little spurt of impatience, realizing that my American upbringing, although slightly moderated since I'd come to live here in France—not to mention my internal sprite—would have encouraged me to immediately ask the bartender about Keep-on-Smiling. Instead, Merveille had subtly reminded me that the French way was not to barge in and leap right to the point (unless one was a police investigator, of course), but to politely greet and, if appropriate, avail oneself of the offerings in the establishment at hand.

And so I curbed my impatience as the bartender, whose name I realized was Pignolette after someone called for her at the other end of the counter, set two tall glasses in front of us. She was efficient in her movements, even as she stopped to light a cigarette to replace the one that had been dangling from her lips a moment ago while she yanked a bottle from beneath the counter, all in one fluid motion.

Her lipstick was faded, but I could see the red stain at the edges of her mouth. She was a solid woman of forty or so, with a thick head of hair pulled back into a tight bun. Not a tendril escaped from its moorings, and her brows were neat, shapely arcs over hooded dark eyes that seemed to constantly be moving. Pignolette wore clothing that could have belonged to a male relative: a loose sweater over a button shirt with trousers belted at a waist that was gathered in bunches because it was too big.

She uncorked the bottle labeled Ricard, which she'd pulled from beneath the counter, and poured about an ounce of the clear greenish liquid into each of the tall glasses. I eyed it cautiously, because there was a whole lot of empty glass above the liquor and I wondered what else was going in there. I was glad I hadn't reached for the one nearest me when Pignolette brought out a clay pitcher and began to pour something into each glass.

Water. *Huh.*

She diluted the liquor with four or five times more water than the Ricard, and as I watched, the spirit turned a cloudy yellowish sort of color.

"*Santé,*" Merveille said, reaching past me to snag one of the glasses, then lifting it to drink.

I followed suit, still cautious, and sipped the concoction.

It was . . . interesting. There were all sorts of unusual aromatic flavors—most of which I couldn't identify, although I suspected Julia would have been able to. I learned later that I was tasting anise and fennel, along with licorice and herbs like thyme, rosemary, and tarragon.

"What is this called?" I asked, half turning on my stool. Merveille was standing much nearer than I'd realized, and my skirt-covered knees bumped into his legs, and my eyes were suddenly right at the level of his mouth. Which was, I realized, a very nice mouth.

I quickly took another sip of the aperitif to wet my suddenly dry throat and eased my head and torso back a little so I could look him in the eye—and put a little space between us.

"Why, this is pastis," he said. "You are here in Paris nearly a year, and you have not tasted anisette?" He didn't seem to be uncomfortable, standing so near that I could feel the warmth of his body and the brush of his sleeve against mine. I had the urge to shrug out of my coat, for I was getting warm.

"Not until now," I replied, taking another sip of the drink. It was starting to grow on me, this strange-looking yet refreshing beverage. Its new color explained the term "*yellow*" when he'd ordered it. "It's good. Different, but good."

He nodded, as if pleased that I liked it. "It has an interesting story, this drink. It is a very young type of distillation—less than twenty years old. It was invented to replace the absinthe after that—the green fairy, as absinthe was called—was prohibited for being too hallucinatory, too dangerous.

"You see, unlike in America, where every spirit and even the wine and the beer was prohibited, it was only the absinthe that was outlawed here. And so then a Monsieur Paul Ricard, who lived in the South, concocted this new type of liquor called anisette. It became very popular there, in Provence and Marseilles, and the other places near the sea.

"And then the war came, and the Vichy decided such a potent drink—it has over forty percent alcohol—was counter to the values of *their* country"—he sneered a little at the pronoun—"and it was banned. It is not even one year now since it has been made legal again, although it had not been so long since I had partaken."

Good heavens. Was there a sly glint in his normally steely eyes? Or was the *pastis*—which was definitely potent; thank goodness it had been greatly diluted—affecting me so quickly?

"Do you mean you, Inspecteur—the ever so proper policeman—were drinking *banned* spirits during the war?" I asked, allowing a tiny bit of flirtation into my voice. I couldn't help it—the tension of the last two days, the proximity of one of the most attractive men I'd ever known, this sort of adventure on which we'd embarked, the drink—all combined in a way that made my little imp sassier than usual.

He shrugged nonchalantly and gave me a sidewise look. The corners of his mouth were soft but not quite smiling. "I became quite fond of an *apéro* with pastis when I was in Marseilles. Monsieur Ricard was a friend of Marguerite's family, and so I got to know him, as well."

The casual mention of Marguerite—Merveille's fiancée—was like a dash of cold water over me. He didn't seem to notice (how would he, anyway?) and continued. "Not only has Paul Ricard created a new liqueur, but he used his knowledge to help *la Résistance*. And so when I partake of this, I remember that he was a French patriot, as well." He lifted the glass in a little toast.

"How did he help the Resistance?" I managed to ask, sipping once more.

"He discovered how to distill cherries and plums into a sort of petrol replacement and provided it to the Resistance to use for their vehicles. He was no fan of the Vichy," Merveille went on with a faint smile, obviously enjoying his memories of those days with Marguerite, I thought sourly. "And he would ride about on his horse, shouting how he felt about Pétain and his government—but the specifics of what he said, they are not fit for a young woman's ears."

I scoffed and rolled my eyes. "My ears have heard plenty, and I've yet to be shocked over any of it," I retorted. "After all, I worked in a bomber plant. There weren't very many delicacies there."

"Ah, that is probably so, mademoiselle, but still, I am the very proper and the very correct inspecteur—with a certain 'off-putting demeanor,' as you have once pointed out to me, eh? And so I cannot allow myself to be so gauche as to repeat these things in your hearing."

There was a definite crinkling at the corners of his eyes, and the slightest twitch at the corner of his mouth. That only made him more devastatingly attractive to me, and I had to look away for fear my own eyes would broadcast this reaction.

If only I would stop stumbling over dead bodies, I wouldn't have any reason to be around him.

Then he moved close to my ear. The warmth of his mouth and the breath of his words made my skin prickle as he murmured, "I think you may ask Mademoiselle Pignolette about the ragpicker now. It is better if you do so, not I."

I nodded, relieved, when he moved back to stand well behind me again. "Mademoiselle." I gave Pignolette a little wave, and she came over almost immediately. "Do you know the ragpicker called Keep-on-Smiling?" I gave her a friendly smile and was once again grateful that my French was so perfect that I sounded like a native.

Pignolette's perfectly arched brows lifted and danced. "Oui, mademoiselle." Instead of expanding on this answer, she drew deeply on her current cigarette and looked at me.

"Do you know where I can find him?" I hesitated, then decided not to add any further explanation. Most people preferred not to be involved in murder investigations.

Her attention slid to my drink. It was only half gone, but the implication was that I should have another if I wanted information.

I knew I could not handle imbibing another pastis, so I hesitated. Then I threw caution to the wind and nodded, tapping the glass to indicate a refill. There was no requirement for me to drink it, after all.

Mademoiselle flashed me a smile, then retrieved the bottle of Ricard and splashed another ounce or so into my glass. She lifted her brow and gestured toward Merveille, but he demurred with a little smile, continuing to hold his glass out of her reach.

Once the water was added, Pignolette tucked the bottle and pitcher away and said to me, "Keep-on-Smiling, eh? *Bien sûr,* the ragpicker, he comes in here sometimes. But at this time of day, you are more likely to find him dossing with the Butterfly at the Salève."

I had no clear idea what she was talking about, but I felt Merveille shift behind me and assumed he did.

"Merci, mademoiselle," he said. "If the ragpicker comes in here, would you give him the message that the good mademoiselle wishes only to speak with him?" He gestured to me with one hand as he withdrew another hand from his pocket. He set a generous number of francs on the counter and picked up his hat.

"I will do that, monsieur," replied Pignolette, sliding the coins off the surface and away. "And you, monsieur—Lancelin, he has slept for you, has he?"

"*Mm, oui,*" was Merveille's assent. He set his hat in place and looked at me, but I was already sliding off the stool. "You are finished, mademoiselle?" He gestured to my very full glass of the cloudy yellow drink.

"Oui, merci beaucoup," I said to the bartendress.

I was relieved to be back outside, even though it was nearly full dark. The sun, once dipping below the horizon, takes the rest of her glow with her very quickly.

Even so, the cool fresh air was a pleasure after the close, thick space of the pub, and it also helped to clear my head a little. I was slightly buzzed, not even approaching tipsy, but if we had stayed much longer, I'm sure that would have changed.

"This way, mademoiselle," Merveille said, continuing along

the *rue* in the direction we'd been walking. "We are going to a place called the Salève."

"You know it?"

"I have been there."

"What is it? And what is the butterfly?"

He flashed me a look, and I noticed that even though he remained in the street instead of on the sidewalk, he walked closer to me than he had done before it got dark. "The Butterfly is a man who has a butterfly tattoo on his forehead, coming up from his nose and between his brows. The Salève is a place where tattoos are made and where, sometimes, a person can pay for a pallet to sleep."

I almost asked him if he knew the Salève because *he* had a tattoo, but managed to squash the urge. I couldn't imagine the neatly trimmed, always clean-shaven, buttoned-up, and necktied Merveille sporting an anchor or ribbony "Mom" image etched on his bicep . . . or "Marguerite."

"Who is this Lancelin that Pignolette asked you about . . . if he had 'slept for you'? Whatever does that mean, anyway? To sleep *for* someone?"

Merveille cast me another inscrutable glance from beneath the brim of his hat. "That is a complicated story, mademoiselle, which perhaps I will relate to you at a later time. We are nearly there." He gestured ahead to a dark doorway that bowed away, back into the depths of the building in which it was set.

I didn't know what to expect from a tattoo parlor on a lane that had once been known as Witchcraft Street, so I wasn't surprised when we went in and it was dark, dingy, and filled with a low hum of human activity from the smattering of people within.

Along with the smell of stale beer, earthy wine, and old tobacco, there was another strange and pungent scent that caught me at the back of the throat. I swallowed back the little tickle, the clinging, spicy sensation that gathered there. When I did so, I smelled and tasted an essence that was sweet and thick and fermented.

"Hashish," Merveille murmured to me, his voice close to my ear again.

I scanned the space, unsure how to proceed, for unlike at Pignolette's, there seemed to be no central bar counter or table. Pairs of eyes gleamed in the low light, turned toward us—some of them bored, some sleepy, some interested, some hopeless. The bodies in which those eyes were suspended were slumped, propped, or reclined on chairs, cushions, or the floor. Bowls of varying sizes sat near these watchers, with their wisps of smoke weaving into the air. Wine and beer bottles, and an occasional crust of bread, lay scattered in the area.

Conversation continued among the patrons after brief looks in our direction. They ignored our presence, continuing to go about their business of socializing over a shared smoke or floating gently in a haze of hashish.

"I don't see anyone getting a tattoo," I said quietly, thinking how dark it was in here and how difficult it would be for anyone to see what they were doing with a needle.

"Ah, *oui,* that is in the back room." He nodded and looked toward the back left wall of the space, where I saw a dark rectangle that indicated an opening or doorway.

I realized I'd edged closer to Merveille. I wasn't exactly apprehensive or frightened; it was just that the establishment felt so foreign and its occupants so forlorn, to me that I didn't know how to act or whom to approach with my question.

"It is there we might find someone who can tell us where Keep-on-Smiling is." To my shock and surprise, Merveille took my hand in his and began to gently tug me along with him toward that back entrance.

I was wearing gloves, and his grip was firm enough to keep my hand from slipping free but loose enough that it was clearly nothing more than a convenient way to propel me in the direction he wished to go. Even so, the feel of his strong bare fingers around mine gave me a sense of security I hadn't realized I'd wanted.

We navigated around slumped and sprawled patrons, bowls

and pipes, bottles and bags, cushions and blankets. I even saw a dog curled up next to his or her master on a blanket. He looked up and curled his lip in silent warning as we passed by.

No one spoke to us as we made our way to the dark rectangle on the back wall. The rectangle turned out to be a blanket hanging over a doorway. When Merveille pushed it aside, I found us stepping into a different world.

CHAPTER 12

When I say "different world," I don't mean that it was like a parlor or salon; it was just that there was more light—a lot more light—and better furnishings . . . and it didn't smell so strongly of hashish. There were long tables and chairs. A number of people lounged around drinking and talking. One man with large, soft muscles and pelts of hair growing on both his chest and back sat in the center with his shirt missing. Next to him was a table holding two gas lamps and a scrawny, weasellike man, who squinted at the needle he was driving into the shirtless man's skin. I wondered when, if ever, that needle had been disinfected—or at least cleaned—and shuddered a little.

I recognized the bulky man called the Butterfly almost immediately. As described, there was a massive blue *papillon* tattooed in the center of his forehead, its wings wide open over his brows. His head was bald, and there was a deep, vertical crease that ran from the bridge of his nose up his forehead—like the body of the butterfly—and onto the top of his head.

"We'd like to speak with Keep-on-Smiling," Merveille said, his voice carrying through the space without being a shout. "Does anyone know where he is?"

Someone grunted, and another person murmured, and then a skinny, bearded person wearing a faded red beret stood. He'd been sitting on a chair, watching the ink being driven into the bare shoulder of the shirtless, hairy man.

"What's it to you?" said the skinny man in the beret. His grizzled beard flowed down over the front of his dingy brown shirt and the black vest he wore over it.

"Are you Keep-on-Smiling?" Merveille said. He'd dropped my hand as soon as we walked through the blanket covered doorway.

"Depends," replied the man, hands on hips as he eyed my companion. A musty sort of smell mixed with tobacco wafted from his direction.

I nudged Merveille's arm in a silent suggestion that he let me do the talking. We already knew the ragpicker wasn't willing to speak to a police agent, and it was impossible for Merveille not to look and act like a police agent.

"Madame Marie told me you might have seen something last night, when the man was killed on Las Cases," I said. "He was a friend of my grand-père, and I want to help find who did it." I walked a little closer to him, putting space between me and Merveille. "My grandfather is very upset about it."

"'S throat was *kiittzch*," said the man I believed to be Keep-on-Smiling. He made the motion to go along with the sound and bugged out his eyes for emphasis.

"It was," I agreed.

The Butterfly; the shirtless, very hirsute man; and the tattoo artist—along with the others in the room—seemed to have lost interest in our conversation. Maybe it was because a man getting his throat slit on the street wasn't an unusual enough event for them to care. Or maybe they'd already talked all about it, having gotten the details from Keep-on-Smiling.

The man in the beret eyed me curiously, looking me up and down, as if trying to decide whether to talk. "And that?"

It took me a second to realize "that" was a reference to Merveille. I shrugged. "He's like a barnacle on a ship's hull. Can't get it off no matter how hard I try." I have no idea where that came from; the words just flowed out, as if someone else was speaking for me.

But apparently, it was the right approach. Keep-on-Smiling grinned, displaying tobacco-stained teeth and a gap where one of them had fallen or been knocked out.

He looked down over his torso and grunted as if in surprise, then pawed his long beard aside. I drew in my breath sharply when I saw the wilted, crushed blue flower sticking out of a buttonhole in his vest. It was a *bleuet*—and I suspected it was the flower that had been missing from the vase last night.

I didn't look over to see whether Merveille had noticed. Instead, I edged even farther away from him in an effort to continue to gain the ragpicker's confidence. "Where did you find the flower?"

I had had a momentary flash of disappointment because it was no surprise that a bluet had been found near Monsieur Hauet's body—since there'd also been one by Monsieur Capron. Where else would the killer get a bluet than from the vase on the dinner table at Maison de Verre? It had to be from there.

"By him. Was by him. On the ground." Keep-on-Smiling gestured to the bloom in his buttonhole.

"Did you see anything else that could help?"

"Isn't what I see, 's what I found," said Keep-on-Smiling.

Of course. His profession required him to be constantly searching the streets and walkways for anything of value.

"Nothing from his pockets. Nothing. Not a thief." He shook his head emphatically, raising his hands in negation.

I nodded. That made sense, and I believed him. Merveille had said Hauet's wallet and watch were still on his person, so the ragpicker hadn't gone through Hauet's pockets.

"What did you find that was near the dead man?" I pressed.

Keep-on-Smiling looked at me in the very same manner Pignolette had done when I asked for information. I had another moment of realizing: *Of course.* If he found something of value, he'd want compensation for it. That was how he made his living, simple as it was.

I had neglected to bring a handbag on this little adventure, for the very good reason that I didn't want to be tempted to be checking my face with the compact I kept in there, or refreshing my mascara or perfume, or fixing my hair. In my coat pocket, however, I had tucked a small coin purse, and in my skirt pocket I had my ever-present Swiss Army knife. And in a moment of weakness, I'd also slipped a tube of lipstick in with the coin purse, even though I had no intention of using it. After all, I didn't have a mirror.

The little purse contained both coins and paper currency, and it bulged temptingly. When I lifted the purse, Keep-on-Smiling's gaze went there and lingered with interest.

"Whatever else you found, I'll buy from you," I said.

Keep-on-Smiling nodded, but covered the beard-shrouded flower with his hand as if to indicate that, at least, wasn't for sale. Then his attention slid to one of the long tables at the side of the room that apparently served as a bar counter, then back to me. "Mighty thirsty."

"So am I," I replied, and still ignoring Merveille, started toward the counter with Keep-on-Smiling.

I'd read enough Sam Spade and Philip Marlowe to know that a detective had to lubricate their informants—usually with money, sometimes with booze, and often with both. Hercule Poirot and Nancy Drew didn't normally have to resort to such base tactics, but on the gritty, dark streets of Paris—especially *here* in this strange, disquieting lane—I could expect no less.

Admittedly, I might not have been so blasé about it had I not known I had a safety net in the form of my carbuncle-like police inspector companion. I didn't spare Merveille a glance as I approached the counter with Keep-on-Smiling and took a seat.

The ragpicker's beverage of choice was probably the only option available at this fine establishment: a thin red wine the color of a dull garnet. Feeling game, I acknowledged an order for two glasses, even though it was doubtful I'd be brave enough to partake of mine.

"What happened last night?" I asked as the drinks appeared in front of us. Their vessels were of a dubious level of cleanliness, but the wine smelled surprisingly good. I supposed it was true what I'd heard said: you couldn't get a bad glass of wine anywhere in France . . . unless you were a Nazi.

Keep-on-Smiling had produced the small, crushed stub of a cigarette, fishing it from the depths of one of his pockets. He gestured with it toward me, but I shook my head and spread my hands. I didn't have a light. The ragpicker looked surprised—who didn't smoke in this day and age?—that I didn't have a light *or* a full pack of cigarettes (I suspected he was hoping to replace the stub he'd probably picked up on the ground with a whole cigarette).

He was obviously disgruntled as he turned to the bartender for a light.

The bartender—a dark-skinned whip of a man whose scarf-wrapped head nearly brushed the top of the low ceiling—shoved a flickering candle in our direction. Apparently, that was his form of lighter. And apparently, I had to pay for the privilege of using that too, as well as the wines, based on the number of francs he named.

"Did you see what happened last night?" I asked, beginning to wonder how much longer I was going to have to play this game.

"Saw him fall down. All the blood. Bad news." Keep-on-Smiling shook his head.

"Did you see anyone else? Anyone running away? Anyone who might have done it?" Now we were getting places.

"Only the woman."

"The woman?" I sat up straight. Something prickled down my spine.

"Was by him, then ran away."

"Where did she go? What direction?" I forgot myself and took a drink of the wine. It wasn't half bad, and I assured myself that alcohol killed germs, so even if the glass wasn't the cleanest, I was probably not going to die.

"Across the street. The big window."

"Oh." I deflated. "That was Madame Demailly. She came and told us about what happened."

He drew on the tiny stub of cigarette, sucking audibly to get the last remnant of tobacco from the smoke. "Was there. Left. I was there."

"Did you see anyone else? Maybe someone running away?"

"No one."

"What else did you see?" He hadn't told me anything I didn't already know, and he'd cost me five francs for a thin but palatable wine and a light for his cigarette.

Keep-on-Smiling took a gulp of wine and set the suddenly empty glass on the counter, giving me a presumptive look.

Gritting my teeth, I kept my expression blank as I dug out another coin and set it on the bar, gesturing for the slender, whip-sharp man behind to refill it. If Keep-on-Smiling didn't give me anything else after this, I was leaving. I still wanted to see Madame Vierca, and it was getting late.

Once his wine was refilled, the ragpicker gave me a look. Then he began to dig in the very deep pocket of his vest. He extricated a number of items, setting them on the bar, as if to display them for me.

There was another cigarette butt. This had a lipstick stain on it and was slightly longer than the previous one he'd been smoking, confirming that he'd been hoping for me to replace the smaller one with a fresh cigarette.

A mildew-stained handkerchief, trimmed in black embroidery, joined the cigarette butt. A man's leather glove, which was probably an unusually valuable find. A broken shoelace. Two bottle caps. A crumpled and stained flyer for a jazz club. And a business card for Philippe Capron, property agent, on sturdy cardstock.

I looked at the array of treasures on the counter, then glanced at the man working behind it. He didn't seem particularly upset by the filthy, street-worn objects that had been introduced onto the surface where he served drinks, which confirmed my suspicion that sanitation was not high on his list of priorities.

I focused again on the items. Most of them could have been dropped on the street in that area at any time, the exception being Philippe Capron's business card. That was no surprise, for obviously Monsieur Capron had been talking about Monsieur Gavril's empty house at the dinner and had probably distributed his contact information to everyone. So either the killer or the victim could have had the card on hand.

Then I stilled as realization struck me.

I needed to know whether Paul Hauet had been found with Capron's card on him. If so, then the card found near his body must have been dropped by the killer. And if we—Merveille, I mean—could determine which of the others had Capron's card, perhaps that could help identify the killer. If Capron had given out his card to everyone, and the killer had dropped theirs, then they wouldn't be in possession of the card and wouldn't be able to produce one. Capron was dead, so he wasn't giving out any more business cards.

It was flimsy, barely circumstantial, but it was something. After all, I didn't have one single good suspect.

I nudged the card with my finger. I'd taken off my gloves, and so I felt the stickiness of the counter. *Ugh.* "How much for this?"

The ragpicker held up five fingers. I managed to control my reaction. Five francs for a used business card? The man knew he had me right where he wanted me.

Then he pushed the handkerchief in my direction. This was worth an additional ten francs, according to him.

I gave him a steely look and shook my head. I didn't need the handkerchief. I just wanted the business card.

"Together," he said insistently. "They together."

"Are you saying you found those together? The card and the handkerchief?"

Keep-on-Smiling nodded. His eyes, though bloodshot, gleamed.

"I don't think so," I said, pushing the handkerchief away. It was obvious the two hadn't been found together—or if they had, they hadn't come from the same source—for the business card was very nearly pristine, and the handkerchief had clearly been in the elements for some time. It was stained and smelled of dirt and mildew and was not the sort of thing one would put in one's pocket for a fancy dinner party—or *ever*, unless you were a scavenger.

"I'll take this," I said, picking up the business card. I turned it over for the first time and saw the scritch of pencil writing. *Ten o'clock, Tues.*

A little shiver went up my spine. So Capron had written the time of his appointment with whoever had had this card—quite possibly the killer. Merveille was going to be very pleased. Maybe the circumstantial would become even more solid.

"Five francs," I said and placed the coin on the counter.

Keep-on-Smiling was not smiling, but he also knew when to cut his losses. The coin disappeared into his pocket as quickly as his other treasures.

I was just about to rise from my stool when I felt a familiar presence behind me. . . . Then he brushed up next to me. "Ask him about the knife," Merveille said in my ear, then moved on and away so quickly I could almost have imagined him.

But my skin was still prickling from where Merveille had touched me, so I knew I hadn't imagined it. I eyed Keep-on-Smiling, who, although he'd put everything back in his pocket, had picked up his glass of wine and was finishing it far more slowly than he had the first one. I supposed he realized his gravy train had ended.

But maybe not.

I beckoned to the bartender and said, "Another, please," and indicated the ragpicker.

Keep-on-Smiling's eyes bolted wide, and he drained his glass, then slammed it onto the counter as if there was no time to lose before I changed my mind—and so that he would get a full pour in an empty glass. The bartender moved to refill the vessel, but I put out my hand to hold him off.

"The knife. Where's the knife you found?" I said, channeling Philip Marlowe and Sam Spade with what I hoped were piercing narrowed eyes and cool demand.

Keep-on-Smiling's eagerness evaporated and he hunched back and away. "No knife I saw."

I pulled out my change purse and made a show of opening it up. I withdrew twenty francs and set the bill on the counter with my finger firmly pressing down on it. "You found a knife by the dead man."

I had no idea whether that was true, but I trusted Merveille, and he'd told me to ask.

Keep-on-Smiling's attention darted from me to the franc note to the empty wineglass and around the room, then back again.

"There was a knife, wasn't there? You picked it up when the woman ran away to tell us about the dead man," I said, keeping my voice low. Maybe he didn't want anyone to hear.

I wondered if this was how a real detective interrogated suspects or witnesses: making it up, throwing darts at anything, and hoping they stuck somehow. I used my finger to shift the franc note back and forth on the counter, drawing his attention to it.

I guessed twenty francs was a lot more than what the ragpicker was used to getting in a night. And I'd already paid him five, plus lubricated him up with two—soon to be three—glasses of wine *and* gave him a light for his cigarette stub.

"I'll pay you twenty francs for it, but if the police find out you have it, they'll just take it as evidence, and you won't have anything to show for it," I said, still keeping my voice low. It was an effort, because in order to do so, I had to move closer to Keep-on-Smiling so he could hear me, and his lack of personal grooming was very evident.

He winced, hunching his shoulders a little more, then said, "Come with," as he looked around nervously.

I slid off the stool and took up the twenty francs. "It's yours if you produce the knife," I said, stuffing it into my pocket. "But not until."

Keep-on-Smiling looked sadly at the wineglass, shrugged and hunched yet again, and started to walk away. The bartender looked at me in question, and I nodded at the empty glass. As soon as it was refilled—after all, I'd promised—I paid with five more francs, took the glass, and went after Keep-on-Smiling.

The ragpicker had started off toward the back of the room,

opposite from where I'd come in. There was another door back there, and he paused and waited for me as I weaved my way around tables and stools toward him. No one seemed to notice or care about my presence, maybe because I wasn't the only female in the space. I didn't look around to see where Merveille was; I knew he was paying attention.

The door opened into a tiny space that could hardly be called a courtyard and led into the drabbest, darkest alley I'd ever seen. I'd be able to walk through, but I was pretty sure one of my elbows would brush the grimy brick wall. There were cigarettes smoked down to the butt littering the ground and a few piles of something that looked and smelled unpleasant, but nothing else to be seen—not even a cat—except for mud scraped over the cobbles. The only light was from the dark gray of the sky far above and a faint glow spilling from a window in the next building.

"Do you have the knife?" I wasn't exactly nervous being out here alone with Keep-on-Smiling, but he was aware that I had a bulging coin purse, and he might very well be in possession of a knife. Maybe I should have been a little apprehensive, but I wasn't. Whether it was due to my trust in Merveille or myself—meaning my assessment of the ragpicker's character, not to mention the fact that I had taken up my own tool knife in hand—I was more determined than nervous.

Keep-on-Smiling looked around, still hunching his shoulders, so that he looked like a nervous turtle pushing its head out from its shell, and dug in his pocket.

He pulled out a rag-swathed object of about four inches long that I was pretty sure was going to be the blade in question.

It was definitely a knife. Whether it had been the one that killed Monsieur Hauet? Very possibly.

Keep-on-Smiling unrolled it carefully, his hands shaking a little. The cloth stuck to the blade, which suggested that it hadn't been unwrapped since he found it last night, and that the blood had not been fully wiped clean. I handed Keep-on-Smiling the glass of wine and took the cloth-wrapped bundle, stepping closer to that small bit of light from the window so I could examine it.

It was a small knife—less than four inches long, including blade and handle; hardly more than a letter opener—but it could definitely do the job. You didn't need much length or width to slice a carotid—just a sharp blade. Even in the dim light, I could see the faint streaks of blood, now a rusty brown.

I tested the edge of the blade. It was sharp enough to leave a faint line of blood on my thumb with hardly any pressure. Yes, this would do the job easily.

"Where did you find it?" I said, wrapping it up again and sliding it into my pocket. Keep-on-Smiling made a noise of protest, but I withdrew the twenty-franc note and held it up. "I'm not going to stiff you. Tell me where you found it."

"Behind," he said, his eyes fixed on the money like a cat eyeing a mouse.

"Behind the dead man? Behind what?"

He shook his head. "Behind." He made motions with his hands that were completely ambiguous. "Behind things."

My brain scrambled around, trying to figure out what he meant. The body had been found half a block from the entrance to an alley, but not that close to it. Still, if I were going to hide a murder weapon, I'd stash it somewhere dark and unobtrusive—like in an alley. "Behind what sort of things? A trash can? A stoop? A car?" I had to tamp down my frustration and force myself to sound patient. For whatever reason, communication was a severe weakness of the man.

"Yes, yes." His head bobbed. "Bags. Trash."

"Behind a bag of trash—in the alley or near a house?"

He was eyeing the money with such desperation I could almost hear it. "Yes. Alley. Dark."

I gave him the money. That was all, I thought, I would get from him. Maybe Merveille would be able to take Keep-on-Smiling over to the scene, and he could show him where he had found the knife.

The twenty-franc bill disappeared into Keep-on-Smiling's pocket, and the wine followed, down his gullet.

"Are you sure you didn't see anyone else on the street when the man was killed? Anyone nearby?"

"The woman," he said.

"Besides her," I replied

"The woman," he said again and finished his wine.

"What was she doing?" I asked.

"By him. Looking. Touching."

I nodded. "Yes. She was trying to help him. Anyone else at all?"

He shook his head, looking sadly at the empty glass.

But I was at the end of my patiencc and over my budget. "Thank you," I said and turned to go back inside.

I opened the door and nearly ran into Merveille.

"I got the knife," I said. "Let's go."

I was ready to get the heck out of there. But as we started back through what I thought of as the tattoo room, I noticed a very large man standing on a low table. It was a wonder his weight didn't collapse it, especially since he seemed very drunk.

He was shirtless, displaying rolls and bulges of muscle and fat, along with a myriad of tattoos on his arms, pectorals, and shoulders. But his torso wasn't what caught my eye. It was the fact that his trousers had been rolled up to past both of his knees, and each of his knees had a tattoo on it.

One was a woman's face and one was a man's face, and they were facing each other—as if they were looking at each other from one knee to the other. It was a strange enough display that I paused to look as the man stood there, making the huge muscles in his legs move so that the faces seemed to jump and converse with each other. The audience laughed and crowed, shouting comments and jests as the large man continued to perform while drinking greedily from a bottle of wine.

"He is recounting the story of Vladimir and his Ill-Fated Knees," Merveille said.

"The what?"

He made a slight gesture with his head. "It's another story of a strange occurrence that happened once near rue des Maléfices," he said with a little smile.

"Another story that is very long and complicated that you might deign to tell me sometime?" I said dryly as we began to make our way out of the Salève.

"Perhaps," he replied, flashing me a look that was pretty close to being a smile. "Now," he went on, "to Madame Vierca's? It is only a short walk, maybe seven or eight minutes, to Grands-Degrés."

"Yes, of course. But don't you want to see the knife?" I asked as we walked through the front room of the Salève, where the smell of hashish still hung in the air.

"But of course—when there is better light. How much did the ragpicker take you for?"

"Twenty francs for the knife, five for a business card that belonged to Monsieur Capron, and another fifteen for wine," I said. "Oh, and another two for a light for his cigarette! Will the 36 reimburse me?"

He laughed. Merveille actually let go and really *laughed.* And oh, my . . . his rugged face was transformed into a carefree, easy expression that made him wildly attractive—at least to me. My belly dropped and my throat went dry. *Merde.* I looked away.

"I think not," he replied, still chuckling as he replaced the hat he'd been holding while we were inside. "But perhaps the police department could buy you dinner as a thank-you, eh?"

"I'm not even sure it's the murder weapon," I countered, easing back from the idea of having dinner with him—even though my internal sprite was doing cartwheels. She didn't understand the rule about not poaching on another woman's man—not that I thought Merveille would be susceptible to being poached.

"We will see," Merveille replied.

Instead of walking back in the direction of Merveille's car, we had continued on rue Xavier-Privas in the direction of the river. I noticed that the tiny lane had come alive now that the sun had set. There was much more activity—mostly people walking about in pairs or trios, smoking, drinking from wine bottles. I even saw—I'm pretty sure I saw—a prostitute and her john doing something very explicit in the shadows of a door's alcove. They certainly sounded like they were doing something explicit.

I kept my focus straight ahead and down so I wouldn't trip on the uneven stone sidewalk, and also so I didn't have to acknowledge to my companion what we'd probably both seen and heard.

By the time we reached the quai Saint-Michel and turned east, I had recovered and my blush had receded.

"We can walk along the quai or along Bûcherie," Merveille said.

I knew rue de la Bûcherie, one of the oldest streets in Paris. It was filled with restaurants, art galleries, and other little shops and was a popular area for students from the Sorbonne to hang out.

"But perhaps you might find it interesting to take the path to the quai de Montebello, near au Double," he went on before I responded. "That is where this Lancelin, about whom you're so curious, might be found." He cast me a sidewise glance. Though his eyes were shadowed by the brim of his fedora, I could see the little quirk at the corner of his mouth.

Maybe the pastis had softened him up.

"All right," I said, even though walking along the river at night seemed like something lovers would do.

It was nearly March, and although the weather was not quite balmy, neither was it the frigid, cutting cold we'd had in December and January. It was dry and calm; not even cold enough that my breath left clouds in the air.

I was comfortable enough in my wool coat, hat, and gloves even near the water, which always had a chill breeze wafting from it. The sky was mostly clear, and I could see the sparkle of stars, a portion of moon, and a few wisps of clouds sliding over those celestial bodies.

Paris sparkles at night, the lights she is so famous for illuminating buildings all along the Seine. Now that we were on the quai and away from the narrow, shadow-shrouded lanes of

Quartier Latin, I could see those golden lights opening up in front of me. To the west, the tour Eiffel rose like a glowing wishbone in the distance. Boats cruised along the river below, and Notre-Dame was just there—just across the way. You could hardly tell that a narrow stretch of river separated us from the famed cathedral. As her bells rang out the hour of seven o'clock, I discovered we'd spent much more time at the Salève than I'd realized.

When we reached the Pont au Double, one of the bridges that leads from the Left Bank to the Île de la Cité, Merveille walked toward it instead of continuing along straight to our destination.

There, sitting just at the corner of the bridge and the quai, were two men. A nearby streetlamp bathed them in a soft glow. The two were clearly persons who, if they didn't actually live on the street, definitely lived in very simple and mean circumstances—likely similar to those of Keep-on-Smiling.

As we drew closer, I saw that the men were identical twins in their forties or thereabouts. It was difficult to tell for sure in the evening light.

"Bonsoir, Monsieur Frédéric, bonsoir, Monsieur Lancelin," Merveille said. "I did not expect to see you here so late tonight, so it is a pleasure. This is Mademoiselle Knight."

The two men sat in folding chairs with many blankets and coverings over their laps and shoulders. One of them had a walking stick near his legs. Even in the shadows, I could see that his eyes were closed. He appeared to be sleeping—perhaps even dreaming, for he wore a sort of beatific expression. His eyes didn't open and his expression didn't change, despite Merveille's greeting.

"Eh, it is our *ami, monsieur le flic*," said the other man, who was smoking a cigarette. He smiled and nodded at me. "Bonsoir, mademoiselle. It is a lovely evening for March, *non*?"

"It is," I replied. "I begin to think that spring might actually arrive, after all."

The man gave a little laugh. "Spring always comes no matter

how long and hard the winter, and for that, we can be grateful. And how are you, monsieur?"

"I have had no problems, Monsieur Frédéric," replied Merveille. "Please thank your brother once again for sleeping for me."

He withdrew a hand from one of his pockets and passed a small packet to Monsieur Frédéric. The other man took it without looking and slipped it into the depths beneath the blankets on his lap.

"I will do that, of course, monsieur," replied Frédéric.

"And you—you have had no problems, the two of you?" Merveille asked. "From anyone?"

"No, no, of course not." Monsieur Frédéric smiled—this time as beatifically as his brother, even though his eyes were open. "Everyone is very kind, and they look out for us. But thank you."

"Bonsoir," said Merveille, touching the brim of his fedora.

"Bonsoir, messieurs," I said, wholly mystified by the entire exchange. The other brother—Monsieur Lancelin—had made no response or even shown any indication he was aware of our presence—during our brief interaction. I wondered if he was deaf, but if so, why would Merveille have greeted him verbally?

We continued on our way to Madame Vierca's. I was brimming with questions, but I decided to hold back. Merveille would know I was dying of curiosity, and since he'd pried the subject wide open by bringing me to the two brothers, I knew he would tell me eventually.

For now, I wanted to focus on what was going to happen when we spoke to Madame Vierca.

Rue des Grands-Degrés was the same narrow, quiet street Julia and I had visited yesterday. We passed a man walking his dog—the latter barked excitedly at us—and a woman hurrying along on the opposite side of the lane, shoulders hunched and head down. A couple of men stood near the corner, smoking, and although they eyed us as we walked past, there was no other interaction.

Still, as we passed farther along the street, a sense of disquiet, of *something* prickled over the backs of my shoulders. Not quite the same as when I'd come here before; that was nerves, I think, and anticipation. This time, I felt as if someone was watching or following me.

I even turned once to look behind us, but the only person in sight was the man with his dog at the far end of the block, walking in the opposite direction.

Merveille glanced over at me, and I shook my head in negation. There was nothing to tell him.

We arrived at the same green door Julia and I had visited . . . I could hardly believe it had only been yesterday morning. It felt so much longer.

"It's *open,*" I said, lowering the hand I'd intended to use to ring the bell.

The battered green door was, indeed, slightly ajar. The hair on the back of my neck lifted, and I looked at Merveille.

"Ring the bell," he said. His expression was cool, and I sensed he'd gone on full alert.

I rang. We waited. I rang again . . . , and we waited a bit longer.

"I think we should go in," I said, suddenly very worried. "Maybe something's wrong."

He made a noise that I took to be one of agreement, and I pushed at the door. It fell open a little more, and I could see into the hallway that led to the room where Madame Vierca had met us. It was impossible to see very much, for the single light bulb hanging in the hall was not lit and the only light was from a streetlamp a short distance behind us.

A faint, very faint, glow sat at the end of the hall, where the door to Madame Vierca's sitting room was. As before, the door was closed and the strip of light emitted from where the bottom didn't quite reach the floor.

Merveille, who'd produced a flashlight from some deep pocket, followed close behind me as I picked my way down the hall. I was grateful for the small beam of light he trained over the rug-covered floor, but at the same time I was annoyed with myself for not bringing my pocketbook after all—for I had recently acquired a small flashlight that I'd taken to keeping in my handbag for occasions such as this. I bet Philip Marlowe never forgot his flashlight.

As we made our way down the hall, my heart pounded with dread. It felt as if every hair on my body was standing at attention. The smells of woodsmoke and cigarette were much fainter than they had been yesterday, and it was still cold and dank in the hall.

When we reached the door, I hesitated, and Merveille put a gentle hand on my arm as if to hold me back. I admit it—I didn't mind. I had a feeling I wasn't going to like what we found, and it was fine with me if he went in first.

He turned off the flashlight and tucked it back in his pocket, then knocked on the door. "Madame? Madame Vierca, are you in there?"

"It's Tabitha Knight," I added, pitching my voice toward the door, in case the woman was hiding from some real or perceived danger. I was glad Merveille hadn't announced himself as the police. "I'd like to speak to you again, madame."

We waited for a long while, but there was no sound of movement or activity in the room. I wondered what or who was behind all of the other tightly closed doors on this hallway. Whoever—if anyone—was there made no attempt to find out what we were doing. The doors remained closed, and the building was silent and still. The only sound was the distant barking of a dog. The smell of yesterday's cooking cabbage had faded, and there was nothing in the air but cold, damp air, and mildew.

"We should go in," I said again. "The front door was ajar—something could be wrong." My heart was pounding. Maybe the killer had realized Madame Vierca knew about the bluets dying. He or she might have come here to silence her or to find out what else she knew . . . or both.

Merveille reached for the doorknob and turned it, then pushed gently. The door creaked, then grated in its frame as it moved. The fact that it was unlocked made me even more certain something bad was going to be behind that door.

"Madame Vierca? It's Mademoiselle Knight who is with me. Are you there?"

Silence.

Merveille glanced at me, but it was too dark to read his expression. I suspected it was something like a mixture of exasperation and concern—the exasperation toward me for getting him into this situation and concern for Madame Vierca.

"Stay back a moment, mademoiselle," he said, then pushed open the door.

CHAPTER 13

Standing back a little, I peered around Merveille as he stood in the open doorway, obviously assessing the situation.

Only one of the many lamps in the room was on, but it gave off enough light for me to see that, at first glance, the place appeared no different from the way it had been yesterday—with the exception of the absence of the thick, cloying scent and the stuffiness that had made Julia and me feel hot and murky. There was the faint smell of smoke—not from a cigarette, but from burning wood or a fireplace.

I followed Merveille inside as he once more called out for Madame Vierca. I turned on another lamp and looked around. Nothing seemed disturbed, and there was no sign of the room's occupant. I saw the burgundy paisley shawl she'd been wearing yesterday. It was draped over the chair she'd sat in when talking to Julia and me.

Merveille had made his way in a circuitous manner across the room to the other door, which I guessed led to madame's bedroom or perhaps a bathroom, although I didn't really think a place like this had much in the way of en suite plumbing. In fact, that might have been where one of those doors on the hallway led: to a tub and toilet for the entire building.

I started to follow him, but my attention was caught by the table in front of the sofa where Julia and I had sat across from Madame Vierca. There were three tarot cards lying on the table, faceup in a neat row, as if she'd been doing a reading, but the rest of the deck was missing.

I stood over the cards, looking at the pictures and words on them. A deep and ugly shiver slithered down my spine as I read them across:

Le Diable: The Devil. The picture was of a crude and frightening looking demonic character with wings and wearing armor. He had two minions below him, with rope bound around their necks.

Le Roy d'Épée: King of Swords. A king, dressed in full royal regalia with a wide-brimmed hat, brandished a red broadsword and a scepter as he sat on a throne.

The third one wasn't labeled, but I didn't need a caption to recognize *la Morte.* Death. The skeletal depiction of the lurking Grim Reaper was horrible. He carried a scythe as he walked over the bodies of his victims.

I was no expert on tarot cards, but I did not like what any of this implied.

"Mademoiselle."

I looked up to see Merveille standing in the open doorway to the other room. I rolled my eyes over his continued formality (why he couldn't call me Tabitha, as I'd suggested more than once that he do, was beyond me) and went over to join him.

"She is not here," he said.

The last bit of tension I'd been holding slid away. I had half expected to find Madame Vierca's body somewhere in the flat, and contrary to what others might think about my propensity for stumbling over corpses, I was very relieved to be wrong.

As expected, this door led to a bedroom, but in this case, the place was a mess compared to the sitting area. Merveille hadn't yet turned on any lights in the room, but I could see that the bed was unmade, its coverings tangled and sagging off on one side. A pillow had fallen to the floor. Several articles of clothing were strewn over a chair, the dressing table, the floor, and spilled from an open wardrobe. This room smelled more strongly of woodsmoke, along with stale cigarettes and that same musky scent, which by now I had come to realize was probably madame's perfume combined with some sort of incense.

"Either she's messy or she went somewhere in a hurry," I said, stepping inside the room.

I turned on the nearest lamp and looked around, trying to determine whether the messiness was due to the act of fleeing or was simply procrastination and a bit of laziness. If Madame Vierca had taken off quickly and unexpectedly, one had to wonder why—and whether it was related to the visions she'd been having about the Nine Bluets killer.

"Or she was taken," Merveille said.

I looked over in surprise, and he gestured to a glass that was lying on its side on the floor. The red wine it contained had spilled, seeping into the rug.

"She probably would have cleaned it up if it were an accident," I murmured. "Unless she was leaving in a hurry . . . but at least she probably would have put a rag over it so as not to ruin the rug. Maybe." I sighed. "If she was in a hurry, she might not have noticed it. It's hard to say."

"Exactement."

I went farther into the room, now looking for anything that might suggest an answer. As I scanned the scene, it occurred to me that Merveille might have called me over because I was a woman and it was a bedroom with female accoutrements. Perhaps he thought—and I had to admit I agreed if that was the case—that I might more readily identify something important . . . something that could help answer the question whether Madame Vierca had left of her own volition or not. I wasn't even certain whether or why that was important to know, but in a murder investigation, everything must be taken into account.

Either way, I think we were in agreement that she had gone in a hurry.

It was the dressing table that drew my attention. The dressing table's chair was only partially pushed into its place in front of the mirror hanging above it. A sweater had been tossed away and landed on the surface, covering some of the grooming items that were there. When I picked it up, I realized it was the source of the strong woodsmoke smell, and set it aside.

There are certain things a woman would take with her, I reasoned as I stood at the table, even if she was in a hurry—a hairbrush or comb being one of them. And, most likely, lipstick as well. Hand or face lotion. Madame Vierca had obviously been a beautiful woman when she was younger, and I would guess that even at her age, she had certain cosmetics that she used in an attempt to preserve that beauty.

Still wearing my gloves, I poked around the contents of the drawers and also the items scattered over the top of the dressing table. There was no hairbrush or comb, which to me was a definite sign she'd had the time to pack up her things.

I discovered a tube of well-used lipstick stuck in a drawer, near the back, which suggested it wasn't one she was currently using. I also found a compact with powder, as well as other makeup and some decorative hair combs, but there was no hand lotion or face cream, and although I couldn't be certain she had them, I leaned toward the opinion that she had.

After all, she was a Parisian and a woman. Vanity and style were instilled in us.

"Mademoiselle."

The tone of Merveille's voice had me spinning from where I'd taken a seat at the dressing table. He stood in the doorway to the main room, which he had wandered back into.

"What is it?" I didn't wait for an answer. I rose so quickly, I bumped my knee on the dressing table. Fortunately, my heavy coat acted as a buffer, and although the impact was a jolt and caused the table to rattle, it didn't hurt.

When I came back into the sitting room, he gestured me to a chair that was tucked in the corner opposite the bedroom door. A small table with a reading lamp sat next to it, along with a pair of eyeglasses, a little leather book that looked like a diary or appointment book, and a deck of Tarot cards—presumably the deck to which *Death, the Devil,* and *King of Swords* belonged to.

Right next to all of that was a familiar flower lying on the table.

"I believe we have found your missing *bleuet,* mademoiselle."

"My missing bluet?" I went to the table to examine it more closely. It was definitely a real flower and was showing signs of wilting. As far as I could tell, the stem was about the same length as the stems in the vase at Maison de Verre would have been.

"The one missing from the vase on the table last night. It is here."

"But that can't be . . . it's not . . ." I shook my head, regrouped. "There was one with Monsieur Hauet's body. That had to have been the flower taken from the vase."

His eyes narrowed, growing cool with displeasure. "I did not see a flower with Hauet's body."

"No, you did not," I said smoothly, "because Keep-on-Smiling took it."

He made a sound of irritation, then poked at the deck of cards. "But he did not sell it to you along with the knife and the card, mademoiselle?"

"If he had, I would have told you," I replied evenly.

"*Bien sûr,*" he admitted. "And he took nothing from his pockets?"

"He said he is not a thief, and I believed him."

Merveille made a sound of agreement—or at least acceptance. He looked down at the table. "Would a medium leave her tarot cards behind?"

"I wouldn't think so, except . . . maybe she intended to send a message." I showed him the trio of cards on the other table, realizing as I did so that they faced the sofa, not the chair where Madame Vierca had been seated. I'd had my cards read a few times at the county fair back home, and the Tarot reader had always laid out the cards facing them, not toward the person who was getting the reading.

I explained this and finished by saying, "Maybe she was leaving us—me, I mean—a message. She told me to come back."

Merveille made another little sound that could have been agreement or disbelief. "Perhaps, mademoiselle," was all he said. But I noticed he stared at the three cards for a long moment.

We looked around a little more, but there was nothing else that seemed important. I hovered by the tarot cards, feeling the compelling urge to take them with me. It felt a little like a violation. . . . Admittedly, this entire trespass into Madame Vierca's rooms *was* a violation.

Still, we hadn't technically broken in, for the door had been ajar, and I believe that when a medium is predicting death and she seems to have disappeared, it could be a sign of danger . . . or worse, so it had been the right thing to do—checking it out. Besides, I was in the presence of a police officer, and he'd clearly had concern for Madame's safety.

So I readily justified our entering Madame Vierca's rooms. I couldn't quite justify taking the cards with me. As I understood it, they were personal to the medium who used them.

"Mademoiselle." Merveille sounded slightly impatient. He stood at the door, the fedora back on his head.

I gave the three cards one last look, then followed him out.

We didn't walk along the quai back to Merveille's car; instead we took rue de la Bûcherie. By now, it was after eight o'clock and night had fallen heavily.

We weren't the only pedestrians; not by far. Bûcherie, which means "lumber," was the lane where, during medieval times, the lowest grades of meat were salted and boiled to preserve them, then passed off to the poorest residents of Paris to eat. Now there were restaurants, cafés, and a music hall spilling with drinkers, diners, and smokers, lovers, friends, and students, for we were right in the heart of the Sorbonne. It was almost another world between this little street of activity and the two smaller lanes we'd visited tonight—even though they were all in the same quarter.

The delicious smells of what was cooking wafted through the air, reminding me that Julia's soup had been hours earlier, and it had, after all, only been soup with a little bread. Certainly not a hearty meal. But I wasn't about to mention anything to Merveille, despite his half-joking suggestion that the 36 might be willing to spring for dinner.

We turned onto rue Xavier once more, that narrow, strange street known by three different names, passing the Salève and then Pignolette's dive bar. All the while, I found myself wanting to look over my shoulder. Maybe it was just the street itself, knowing its old name—rue des Maléfices—and the fact that it was nighttime, and dark and eerie, that caused me to feel that prickling over the backs of my shoulders. I had the sense, again, that someone was watching us.

But when I did turn to glance behind us, I saw nothing.

If Merveille noticed, he didn't mention it. He kept on scanning the area in front of us as we walked down the center of the cobbled lane.

All at once, two beams of light shot through the darkness. They were coming from behind us, and I heard the rumble of an engine, the unmistakable sound of tires thunking over stones.

Merveille and I both glanced behind at the same time and saw the vehicle bearing down on us in this very narrow lane, and fast. Much too fast. He swore and grabbed my arm, and we started to run. There was nowhere to go, and the end of the block was too far away for us to make it.

The lights blazed behind us, the motor roared, the sound filling my ears as I ran as fast as I could, the feel of Merveille's fingers tight around my arm as he helped pull me with him. His legs were longer, and I couldn't keep up, so he hauled me up and onward when I stumbled.

Suddenly, he dodged to the side, yanking me with him, and

all at once I was slammed up against the building by the force of his body.

The vehicle—a big one—roared past, so close I felt the heat of its engine and the sharp gust of air that came with it. I also felt the heat and strength of the man pressing up against me. The heaving of his chest against my cheek was damp with perspiration, as I, too, panted with exertion and relief. I realized I was gripping his coat with trembling fingers and my knees were about to give away.

That had been close. Very close. Neither of us moved for a long moment.

Then "*Je suis désolé, mademoiselle.*" Still a little out of breath, he stepped back, but my fingers were still curled into his lapels, so he didn't move very far away. His voice was low and a little unsteady. "You are not hurt?"

I forced myself to release him, but we were still standing very close. Probably closer than we'd ever been . . . except when he had been taking my fingerprints in his office, and he'd been very nearly embracing me from behind.

Why I thought of such a thing at that moment, I don't know.

Well, of course, in retrospect I know why. It was a *moment.* We were both still out of breath, still shaken from nearly being killed—or at least severely injured—and emotions were high. And he was standing ever so close to me.

The roaring in my ears subsided. "I'm not hurt. Thank you," I said, still using the wall to keep myself upright. I was afraid if I stepped away from it, my knees would buckle. "I think y-you must have saved m-my life." The emotion—shock, relief; the realization that I'd really truly almost died—made my voice waver. I blinked back tears and hoped he didn't notice.

"You are not hurt, from the wall? I did not mean to be so . . . rough." He eased back a little more, and although it was pretty dark, I felt the way his eyes traced over me, as if to make sure I really was uninjured.

"I'm not hurt. Thank you." I had bumped my head, and my

shoulder had hit the bricks rather hard, but I saw no reason to mention those minor discomforts.

I realized only then that we were in the indentation of a cornice that jutted from one of the buildings, and that his quick thinking and movements had propelled us into that safe nook, where we were protected from the vehicle as it whizzed by. My stomach rolled with nausea as I realized how close I'd come to dying.

He looked at me for another moment, then, holding up a hand for me to wait, edged out into the middle of the passage. Despite the roar of the vehicle on a road that probably rarely had them, there seemed to be no reaction from whoever might be around. No peeking out of doors or windows, no calling out to ensure someone's safety. Just . . . nothing.

Obviously determining that it was safe, Merveille beckoned me to join him. I geared myself up and told my knees to stop wobbling, and I stepped out into the road, still a little nervous.

I had nearly been run down by a car back in December, when a killer tried to sideswipe me while I was riding my bicycle. It was only because I'd stopped to look at the alley cat I was eventually going to sort of adopt and name Lupin that I was only bumped and bruised from being knocked off my bike.

That had been scary, but this incident was even worse. Tonight, I'd been trapped, running in vain for my life as the truck bore down on us, with absolutely nowhere to go. When I'd been knocked off my bicycle, it had happened so quickly and without warning, I hadn't had the time to be terrified.

"Thank you," I said again.

He shook his head, and only then did I realize he'd lost his fedora. And for the first time in my experience, his hair was rumpled and tufted out at the edges. "We were very lucky."

"It was deliberate, wasn't it?" I said, looking around for his hat. I could hardly imagine Merveille going on without it. I stepped away, peering back in the direction from which we'd run for our lives.

He glanced at me. "What is it, mademoiselle?"

"Your hat . . . it's gone."

"And so is yours," he replied in a surprisingly casual and unruffled manner. "I fear they've both been crushed and are certainly ruined from the slush."

I didn't see anything that resembled either of our hats, so I turned back to him. "It was deliberate," I said again.

He heaved a sigh as we started walking. "As it is not the first time you have nearly been flattened by an automobile, I suppose you would be the judge. Alas, there was no alley cat to save your life tonight."

"Only a quick-thinking police inspector," I said before I could stop myself, and immediately regretted it with every fiber of my being. But even though my face was hot, I went on. "If you hadn't—"

"Stop, mademoiselle. It is enough. *Ce n'était rien.*" He didn't sound angry as much as embarrassed, which I didn't blame him—for I had sounded like a swooning debutante in a Georgette Heyer novel.

I lapsed into silence and turned my thoughts to something other than the man beside me—specifically, why someone would have tried to run us down. Definitely deliberately.

There was no doubt in my mind, and I had felt it—something—before it happened. I'd felt someone watching me ever since we got to Madame Vierca's place. Had someone seen us go inside and realized we were investigating the murders?

"Ah," Merveille said suddenly, and I looked over. We were just about to turn back onto Saint-Séverin, and there was a delivery truck sitting there, its lights still on. From the way it had been parked, it looked as if someone had left it in a hurry. The driver's door hung open, and the truck had crunched into one of the bollards, which presumably was the reason it had to be abandoned.

I hadn't heard the sound of the crash, but granted, I'd been distracted and it probably would have been more of a thump than a crash at that distance. Still . . . whoever had piloted that vehicle toward us had wanted to make a quick getaway.

I waited while Merveille poked around inside the truck, obviously looking for anything that might identify the driver. I had the suspicion that whoever came after us had merely taken advantage of an opportunity and probably stole or borrowed the vehicle—for these streets were too narrow for someone to have been following us on wheels all the way from Madame Vierca's. Besides, we would have noticed, I think, if a vehicle had been coming along behind for blocks.

I voiced this opinion to Merveille when he emerged from inside the cab of the truck.

"I think you are right," he said affably. "The truck, it belongs to a company by the quai and was probably parked nearby for the night. Are you hungry, mademoiselle? I could eat . . . and I would also like a very strong drink. It has been a difficult day."

I blinked at this sudden change of topic, which included the surprising invitation. "Julia's soup was an awful long time ago," was all I said.

"You do not mind stopping? You're not in a rush to get home?" he asked, sounding hesitant now. "For . . . something?"

"I'm hungry and still pretty shaky," I admitted, even as I both dreaded and anticipated sitting tête-à-tête with him in a tiny restaurant or brasserie. "Besides, didn't you say the 36 would buy me dinner?"

He laughed, not as hard as he had before, but enough that his expression softened and his eyes glinted. "Ah, *oui,* mademoiselle, you are correct. So there is a little brasserie I like to go to, if you will, not far from Solférino. They make a very good roasted pork with mustard and turnips, and they also have some of the Kentucky bourbon whisky."

I agreed without hesitation, and we found his car and drove to the little restaurant—which was only a few blocks from Maison de Verre and therefore only a few more blocks from rue de l'Université.

It was, as most eateries in Paris were, tiny, crowded, smoky, and dimly lit. We were seated in a corner near the front window, and a small fire danced in a hearth next to me. The heat was a welcome comfort as it crept over my back, for I was still shaken and a little out of sorts from our near-death experience. Two cats—a white one splotched with fur the color of whisky, and the other tiger striped—surveyed the room from their perches on a credenza.

I wasn't about to eat without washing my hands and refreshing myself after the questionable cleanliness of every place we'd been tonight, and so both of us availed ourselves of the washroom before settling at the table.

I declined the bourbon whisky in favor of a red wine, which caused Merveille to give me a questioning look as the waiter walked away. "Another bad experience, mademoiselle?"

I chuckled, shaking my head. He was referring to the fact that I'd once told him I didn't drink gin or smoke cigarettes, because I'd had a bad experience with each of them, but fortunately not at the same time. "No. I just don't have the taste for it."

The crinkles at the corners of his eyes smoothed as he looked at the chalkboard menu hanging on the wall. "I recommend the pork, but the chicken would be fine as well, I am certain. I have never had a poor meal here."

We ordered, and before an awkward silence could fall, I plunged in.

"I have the knife from Keep-on-Smiling, but I don't suppose we should look at it now, here, at the table. It's still a little bloody," I said. "And there was also a business card for Monsieur Capron, with the time of an appointment written on the back of it. It was for this morning. The ragpicker found it on the sidewalk."

Merveille's brows lifted. "I see. That is interesting."

"If we—you, I mean—could determine who else has an appointment card from Capron—or, more importantly, who *doesn't*—that could help identify the killer. Did Monsieur Hauet have one in his pockets? If not, the killer must have dropped it. From what I understand, everyone was talking about going to see the house, so Capron was handing out his cards like candy."

"And it is possible the killer went ahead and made an appointment, there in the hearing of everyone else, and then arrived in the morning for that appointment and went on to poison Monsieur Capron?" he asked drily. "I am not certain the killer would be so obvious about it, mademoiselle."

"He's leaving *flowers* with the dead bodies. If that's not obvious, I don't know what is," I retorted as the waiter set down our drinks and a loaf of bread, placing the latter directly on the table. Bread is not served in bowls or baskets in France; it's put right on the tablecloth—a habit I had found off-putting at first. But in good restaurants, every table is covered with a cloth, which is changed between sittings.

The waiter also delivered two small bowls of a brothy soup with lots of hearty greens floating in it and a bit of cheese grated over the top. I suppressed a delighted moan. The soup smelled like heaven and I really was very hungry.

"It is possible the killer did drop the card," he conceded as he waited for me to tear off a piece of bread.

"Did you interview all of the suspects today?" I asked. "Monsieur Lussier and Taban and Sénac and Madame Munzel and Madame Demailly?"

"Yes, of course I have spoken to all of them." He glanced up at me from enjoying the soup, his gray eyes steady and knowing. "And I do not intend to review my notes or impressions with you, mademoiselle, no matter how nicely you might ask, so please do not."

I rolled my eyes. "I know. It's a police investigation, I need to stay out of it, et cetera, et cetera. But, as I've pointed out before, I can be helpful. If I hadn't talked to Keep-on-Smiling, you wouldn't know about the knife, the business card, *or* the flower by Paul Hauet's body. He wasn't going to talk to *les flics*. A civilian *can* be helpful."

He gestured in agreement with his crust of bread, then

swiped it through what was left of the broth. "I do not deny that you came upon the information perhaps more quickly than I, with my badge, could have done, but I would have acquired it at some point."

I scoffed. "I'm not so certain of that."

"And besides—it was I who told *you* to ask about the knife," he reminded me, pushing the empty soup bowl aside.

I had no response to that excellent point, so I changed the subject. "I'm worried about Madame Vierca. Do you think something happened to her?"

"Sadly, I think it is possible. I will make some inquiries, have one of the agents investigate. Madame is well known to us at the 36." The way he said it was a combination of exasperation and resignation. "The soup is good, *non*?"

"Very good. I didn't realize how hungry I was." I took up another spoonful, sipped my wine, then said, "So are you going to tell me about Monsieur Lancelin and this thing about sleeping for a person?"

"Ah." His expression eased; he probably thought I was going to interrogate him more about the murder investigation. I intended to, but I thought it would be a good idea to let him relax a little first. I couldn't help but notice how relaxed and almost boyish he looked, with his usually neat hair curling up a little on the ends, and one little tuft flipping out near his temple.

"*Oui.* You see, Monsieur Lancelin, he is known as the Sleeper, because he can 'sleep' for a person, and in doing so, he is able to take their pain away and heal them."

He said this all so matter-of-factly that I could only stare at him and blink.

"I . . . don't understand." I mean, I sort of understood what he was saying, but I wanted more details.

He gave me a little smile and settled back in his seat, sipping the whisky. "Those who have injuries or pain in their bones or muscles or the like—they can wait in line to speak with Monsieur Lancelin. His brother, Frédéric, is, I suppose one would call it, his manager, for Lancelin has no ability to move his legs or arms. If a person waits to speak with him, Frédéric will take his brother's hands and put them on the place of the pain on the person—the leg, the arm, the back—and Lancelin will . . . I suppose the way to describe it is, he will remember the pain, the location, the person."

"And he heals them with his touch?" I was torn between skepticism and fascination; mostly fascination, as Merveille did not strike me as the sort of person to be taken in by quackery or shysters.

"*Non,* at least not at that moment. After Lancelin feels the person's pain and memorizes it, Frédéric will enter a time and day in his appointment book—perhaps a day or two later, and the hour—and during that allotted time, Lancelin will sleep for the benefit of the injured person . . . and take on the pain, and the person can be healed. Is very often healed," he added, with a look that suggested he was one of those who'd been the recipient of this . . . doctoring.

"He *sleeps* for them?" I still didn't understand.

Merveille shrugged, spreading his hands. "There is no other way to describe it, and no one really knows what it is he does. When he sleeps with a person's pain or injury as . . . I suppose, his *intention,* perhaps his dream? . . . then the healing occurs."

"Even if the person isn't there?"

"The person is never there when he sleeps for them."

The waiter arrived with our entrées. I had taken my companion's advice and ordered the roast pork, which came bathed in a dark, fragrant sauce speckled with chopped herbs: rosemary, parsley, and thyme. Turnips, potatoes, and onions mingled in the sauce, and there was a bit of something that looked like toasted breadcrumbs sprinkled on top. It looked and smelled divine.

"And so you have been healed by this . . . Sleeper," I said.

Merveille inclined his head in acknowledgment.

I wanted to ask what the injury was—or had been—but decided that was too personal, so I merely said, "I'm very glad to hear it, then."

"Thank you, mademoiselle. The pork—it is to your liking?" He gestured with a fork.

"It's very good. Julia would be impressed."

He made a contented sound and reapplied himself to his meal, working his way through it efficiently and neatly.

"And the story about the knees?" I asked. "The man with the tattooed knees, with the faces on them at the Salève?"

"Ah, yes. The Ill-Fated Knees, as they are called. The way I have heard it is . . . there was, before the war, perhaps in the middle thirties, a man named Vladimir. He and his friend Boris were stationed in northern Africa, I believe. Algeria perhaps. Vladimir met a woman, Consuelo, and fell in love with her, but unbeknownst to him, his friend Boris was also dallying with her."

I hid a smile at the old-fashioned term of "dallying." Merveille was so amusingly—and frustratingly—proper sometimes.

"Vladimir eventually made plans to run off with his love but instead was arrested for some minor infraction and imprisoned for a short time. When he was released, he discovered that Consuelo and Boris had gone off together. He was, understandably, quite angry and caused more problems and was again thrown in jail. It was there he had his knees tattooed with the faces of his betrayers, and claimed—in what was almost a sort of curse, you see?—that 'as long as my knees are together, the two will also be together—but as long as I can move them and jump them around, their life will be just as disruptive and terrible.' And so Vladimir would go into these pubs, traveling aimlessly all around France, and make his knees and their faces dance for entertainment—just as the man was doing tonight at the Salève."

There was more to the story, but Merveille paused to finish the last bite of his meal, swiping a heel of the bread through the remaining juices.

I waited patiently, enjoying my own dinner and savoring the red wine—which was much better than what I'd been served at the tattoo parlor.

"One night," Merveille went on, "Vladimir was performing

with his knees as usual here in Paris—here in the Quartier, most likely on or near rue Xavier, for that is where these sorts of things happen, you see—when Boris and Consuelo straggled in. They were quite poor and destitute and also weary . . . just as, perhaps, Vladimir and his tattoos had cursed them to be.

"As one can imagine, there was a terrible moment when the three of them recognized each other—and Boris and Consuelo saw what he'd done to his knees—the caricatures of them, the laughingstock he was making of them.

"There was no altercation. Vladimir left the pub. But only a day or two later, he was found dead—murdered. But he had stiffened in place, you see, and his knees were drawn up to his torso with pain, and the men, they couldn't bring him down the very narrow stairs of the place he was found, because he was a very large man—and his legs, they were bent up.

"And so the decision was made to use a hammer and to break his kneecaps so they could straighten his legs." Merveille lifted his eyes to mine, with a little curving smile, as he took a sip of his whisky.

He was waiting for me to say something . . . for me to guess the punch line? The plot twist?

"And so the curse was broken once his kneecaps were shattered?" I said. "And Consuelo and Boris were able to find happiness?" I wasn't certain I liked that resolution—after all, they'd both betrayed Vladimir.

Still with the faint smile, Merveille shook his head. "No, mademoiselle. You see, some few days later Consuelo and Boris, they, too, were found dead . . . They had been crushed by huge blocks of rubble that had fallen on them from an abandoned lime kiln, which they had been using for shelter."

"Crushed. As if they'd been hammered . . . to death. Like his knees?" I shivered, then shook my head. "That is hard to believe, and yet . . ."

"And yet . . . this is Paris." He lifted his glass and finished off the rest of his drink.

I knew I had only a short time left to find out more of what I could about his take on the murders. I hoped he was feeling more relaxed now that the conversation had gone off in other directions—strange ones, but fascinating and thought-provoking nonetheless—and so I prepared to pounce once more—

But he beat me to it.

"Now, mademoiselle, I think it is time that we should speak of the elephant in the room. The one you have so obviously avoided during this entire meal."

CHAPTER 14

I froze and my stomach—which had been feeling comfortably full—dropped alarmingly. What did he mean? How could he know I had a thing for him?

Before I could think of something to say, he set down his empty glass and placed his elbows on the table, leaning forward slightly. His expression had turned somber, even stern.

"You were very nearly killed tonight, mademoiselle, and that is a direct result of your involvement—once again—in a police matter. There is little doubt that the person driving that truck intended to disrupt or even stop the investigation."

I eyed him back just as steadily, feeling wild relief that he was only reprimanding me for nearly getting run over instead of addressing the *real* elephant in the room.

"You were nearly killed, as well, Inspecteur. And I wasn't interfering in a 'police matter.' I had been given a message that someone wanted to speak with me, and so I went to speak with him—and I, prudently, did so in the presence of a police officer, might I add. *And*," I went on, relentless and calm, when he drew in a breath to speak, "Madame Vierca came to me and then asked me to visit her. Am I now to be restricted from interacting with people or visiting them if they are only *possibly* or distantly connected to a murder investigation?"

"After tonight I believe there is no longer any doubt that Madame Vierca is connected to this murder investigation," Merveille replied dryly. But I swore I saw a glint of appreciation or humor in his expression.

"I agree—but until tonight, no one knew for sure. And so warning me to stay out of a police investigation that I *haven't* been interfering with is just making you sound like a stuck record album."

"An off-putting demeanor and a stuck record album," he said, shaking his head. "You are so very complimentary, mademoiselle."

"Interfering, stubborn, and too curious for my own good," I retorted, fighting a grin as I reminded him of the ways he'd described me. Somehow his rebuke had turned into . . . something else. A gentle sparring match that neither of us seemed to mind.

"*D'accord*," he said. "Like the street cat you have adopted, *non*?"

The waiter appeared at that moment, asking whether we wanted a digestif or anything else to finish our meal.

Merveille looked at me and I declined, so he asked for the bill.

When I pulled out my little change purse—which wasn't bulging quite as much as it had been when I walked into the Salève—Merveille gave me an affronted look.

"You may put that away, mademoiselle. I will take care of it."

"You mean the 36 will take care of it," I said with a smile, tucking the purse back into my pocket.

"No, mademoiselle. *I* will take care of it." He seemed annoyed.

"Oh. Thank you."

We were silent on the short walk back to his car. The night had turned colder, and the air was still, carrying only the faintest tinge of cigarette smoke. A spray of stars glittered above, joined by a chunk of moon that had dipped lower since we'd walked along the quai hours ago.

"Thank you for going with me tonight," I said as he navigated the car onto rue de Bellechasse toward my street. "I hope it was helpful for the investigation. I'll leave the knife and the business card with you." I pulled them out of my pocket and placed them on top of the dashboard.

"*Merci.* And thank you for your help in procuring them. As I said, it was done more easily with your assistance. And so there is one thing I will tell you, mademoiselle, about the killer."

"You will? What is it?" I half expected him to say something like, "The killer is determined and dangerous, so stay out of his way."

But instead, he said, "The killer is left-handed. That is what the pathologist has determined, and Docteur Jackson is in agreement. Now, I will take this knife to them to confirm it was the murder weapon."

"Thank you for that information, Inspecteur." I hesitated, then went on, feeling as though I had to address the other elephant in the room, "It must be a challenge to be working on this case with your oncle and his pathologist friend sort of . . . watching every step you take."

He made a quiet sound, like a short laugh. "It is to be expected, and I appreciate my oncle's assistance. But . . . there are times when I would prefer he perhaps be less . . . present." He glanced at me, the tiniest of smiles twitching his lips.

"I can imagine. You are dealing with two civilians interfering with your work," I said. "Your uncle and me."

He laughed. *"C'est vrai."*

The car eased to a halt in front of my house, and it was the reminder of my messieurs that had a rush of worry swamping me.

"Please find the killer soon," I said, overwhelmed by that great emotion. "I'm so worried for Grand-père and Oncle Rafe. They aren't going to let me keep them under wraps and protected for long. They think they're invincible."

"Like someone else I know, eh?" He cast me a sidewise look in the shadowy light. "Mademoiselle, I must ask you please not to go to Madame Vierca's again, or rue Xavier until this matter is closed, *hein*? Not even if you go during the day or with someone, like Madame Child or the veterinarian boyfriend."

The mention of Jean-Luc took me by surprise. How had Merveille even known about him?

"I don't plan on going back there at all," was all I said. "But will you please tell me if you find out anything about Madame Vierca?"

"I will do that, mademoiselle. And if you like, I will make certain there is a police agent stationed at your house for the protection of your messieurs until this is resolved."

"Oh, *would* you?" I turned in my seat to face him. "That would make me feel so much better. *Thank you.*"

"I will do that," he repeated, looking at me in the close, dimly lit space. "It is not only for the protection of Monsieur Saint-Léger and Monsieur Fautrier."

His eyes held mine for a moment too long, and I felt a rush of . . . something—expectation, anticipation—shuttle through me. I couldn't breathe. Then he blinked and shifted a little, and our connection broke.

"Thank you," I managed to say as I reached to open the car door.

The cold winter night felt good on my hot cheeks. I gave Merveille a jaunty little wave as I walked into the house, wondering if he'd been about to kiss me . . . or had *I* been about to kiss *him*?

Zut!

It wasn't until I stepped into the foyer and my attention fell on the flowers from Jean-Luc—the flowers, and the card that came with them, which Julia had left sitting on the table . . . right where Merveille had been standing as he waited for me to get ready to leave this evening—that my question was answered.

So that was how the inspecteur had known about Jean-Luc.

"The funeral is at noon," I told Julia the next morning as we headed to the market, our empty canvas bags flapping against our legs. "And then I have a tutoring appointment at three on the Right Bank."

It was bright and sunny, with a clear blue sky, and the weather was feeling past balmy and even slightly warm. It was so gorgeous out, I was wearing only a light jacket over my skirt and blouse, and a little beret—more for style than for warmth—and no gloves!

"Monsieur Hauet's funeral is *today*? Already? That seems awfully quick," said my friend with a frown. "Usually it's at least a few days before they can make arrangements."

"I thought so too, but Grand-père sprung it on me this morning. Apparently, it was all arranged yesterday, when they called to reschedule with the priest. Grand-père said they're all too old to waste time, and the priest—who is also very old, apparently—was available today, so they decided to do it then. Not many people are going to be there," I went on. "Monsieur Hauet has no family and only a few friends left since the war. Just the Bluets—"

"You mean the remaining Bluets and the person who is trying to kill them," Julia said dryly.

"Yeah." I didn't like the idea at all, but I'd had no luck in convincing either of my messieurs to delay the memorial. Apparently, the morgue had finished with the body yesterday, and since it was being released, they saw no reason to wait. "At least Merveille has arranged for us to have a police agent at the house until things are wrapped up."

"If they ever are," Julia said, her tone still dry as a good Burgundy.

"Well, the killer is going to run out of the Nine Bluets eventually," I said grimly. "And then we'll know by process of elimination."

"Whoever's left—besides your gentlemen, of course—has to be the killer," Julia said.

"It sure seems that way."

I hadn't had the chance to tell her about everything that happened when Merveille and I went to find the ragpicker and Madame Vierca, because I'd first had to let her know I had to be back from our shopping early in order to get ready for the funeral. I wasn't going to let Grand-père and Oncle Rafe go without me. I was hoping the police agent—this morning Agent

Richot had been relieved by Agent Écuyer, who was very sturdy and solid and gave me great confidence in his abilities—would agree to come along, as well. Grand-père would fuss, but I would have my way.

As we walked to the market, I quickly filled in Julia about everything that had happened last night—even the almost-getting-run-down-by-a-truck part, though I knew it would make her waggle her eyebrows over Merveille's heroics.

"So I promised him I wouldn't go back to Madame Vierca's," I said, ending my narration. "Even with company."

"Good plan," Julia said with a little shudder. "That whole place felt off to me the other day. Not creepy, just . . . *off.* Strange and a little otherworldly. But at least you *know* for sure Madame Vierca is involved somehow. If you weren't sure, the bluet sitting on her table would be a good sign."

"Yeah," I said thoughtfully. "What was she doing with a bluet, anyway? And where did she get it? And is she okay? I'm mostly worried that something has happened to her."

"Do you really think she was leaving you a message with those cards?" Julia asked.

"I don't know. It definitely struck me that one of them was *Roy d'Épée*—King of Swords. It very creepily fits with Paul Hauet's death, with him getting his throat slit. And the fact that Madame Vierca foresaw the slicing of the blade through the air . . ." I gave a little shiver. "If the killer realized she's been seeing visions of the future, he or she might worry that she can also identify him or her."

Julia hugged herself as if she, too, shivered—and I knew it wasn't from the weather, because it was so pleasant.

"This is a weird investigation, Tabs," she said as the market came into view. "Normally, you have more interactions with the suspects so you can try and suss out what they know or any motive they might have had. But so far, you haven't really been able to talk to any of them."

"That's my plan at the funeral today," I told her. "They should all be there—the killer, too, I'm sure—and I'll be watching everyone carefully—especially since Merveille told me the killer is left-handed!—and also trying to talk to each of them. I'm not really sure what I'm going to say, but I'll figure it out."

"Maybe you can get each of them to sign something or write something down," Julia said. "Then you can see who's left-handed." She suddenly gave an energetic wave. "Bonjour, Madame Marie!" As we approached the wizened old woman and her produce cart, she added, "I think there might be a real hint of spring in the air today, eh?"

"*Bien,* and thank our good God for that, eh?" Madame smiled as I greeted her, as well. "Bonjour, Mademoiselle Knight. And you spoke to Papa yesterday, *hein,* mademoiselle?"

"Yes, thank you for sending him to me. The ragpicker was very helpful. And here," I said, pulling a little paper bag from my market tote, "is some fresh parsley, chervil, and thyme from my grand-père's garden as a thank-you."

Madame beamed with pleasure at my offering, then turned briskly to business—without even mentioning my love life! I was shocked. "Madame Child . . . wait until you see what I have for you today."

"More strawberries?" Julia said hopefully, her eyes dancing.

"Alas, no . . . but I have these asparagus and two pretty tomatoes."

Julia cried out as if she'd just been given a three-carat diamond ring, swooping down upon the slender bright green stalks of asparagus and the plump, dark red tomatoes.

Grinning, I left her to her raptures, excusing myself to Madame Marie. I would think about what to make for dinner later.

"Bonjour, Mademoiselle Yvette," I said, approaching the flower cart. "What do you have today that could brighten my grand-père's salon?"

"Ah, mademoiselle, I am so happy you have asked. See, I have some forsythia branches. I have already prepared them so they will bloom inside." She showed me some long, graceful, slender branches—thinner than my pinkie finger and two to three feet long—with many smaller twigs erupting along them, all with hundreds of tiny brown buds. "If you put them in warm water at home, they will bloom with many little yellow flowers in perhaps four or five days. It will be like a little miracle—these dead branches will suddenly spring forth with so many flowers—like magic!"

"That sounds lovely," I said, very pleased with the idea. "Yellow is such a happy color. I'll take five stems, please, mademoiselle."

As she wrapped them up, I noticed that the bottom inch or so of each branch was smashed, as if with a hammer. When I asked her about it, she explained that it was to help it absorb the water, which would force the forsythia to bloom a month or two before they would bloom outside. "Remember to put them in the *warm* water."

"Merci beaucoup," I said, taking the package. And then I went on to my real purpose for speaking with her. "Mademoiselle, could you tell me . . . How easy would it be for someone to get a fresh, living *bleuet* right now, in early March? And where could I find one?"

I was wondering where and how Madame Vierca might have obtained the blue flower we'd seen in her parlor.

"Eh, mademoiselle, that would not be so very easy," said the flower seller. "Perhaps at Les Halles, there might be the chance of finding some there. They have the bigger shops and more shipments, you see. But they are a summer flower, mademoiselle, and so they are not so very common right now, even in the greenhouses."

"*Bien.* Thank you." That only confirmed my theory that the killer *had* to have been at the dinner party. "Oh, and one more question," I said, turning back after having started away. Something Merveille had said yesterday had stuck in my mind. "What about finding lily of the valley? Did you know it was poisonous?"

Mademoiselle Yvette's eyebrows popped up so that they touched the red knitted cap she wore over her dark hair. "But of course I know all the flowers that are poisonous. The lily of the valley, she is beautiful and elegant, and she smells like heaven, but she *is* very, very toxic. All of the parts of her are poisonous—the leaves, the flowers, the berries—but especially the rhizomes."

"The rhizomes? Do you mean the roots?"

"*Oui*," replied Mademoiselle. "They are very, very dangerous. And to find the flowers right now, here in March, eh, it would be impossible in Paris for at least another six weeks. We have the big celebration on the First of May with the lily of the valley, and so there will be plenty by the end of April. But now . . . no."

"But the roots . . . they could be found at any time," I mused, more to myself than to Mademoiselle Yvette. Now I had to think about which of the other members of the Bleuets would have a garden—or be near one—where lily of the valley might grow. It was another trail to follow.

"*Oui.*" Mademoiselle Yvette gave me a little smile. "Are you thinking of poisoning someone, then, mademoiselle?" She laughed, letting me know she was joking. "Or are you investigating another murder, eh?"

"Yes," I replied with an enigmatic smile as I tucked the stems of forsythia under my arm. "Thank you very much. I know Grand-père and Oncle Rafe will love these yellow flowers."

"Ah, but you must take care with the cat," Mademoiselle said quickly just as I once more started away. "*Les chats*, they love to bat at the branches, for they see how prettily they arch and the flowers will dangle—and they will knock them over. It will not hurt Madame X if she should nibble on the flowers, but she will make a mess if she overturns the vase." Yvette smiled, her eyes dancing and a little dimple appearing next to her mouth.

"Thank you for that," I replied, and, giving a little wave, went off to join Julia, who'd made her way on to the fishmonger.

"Don't forget to put them in *warm*, even hot, water," Yvette called after me, and I waved again to let her know I'd heard.

"Oh my *God*, Tabitha, you won't believe what I'm going to make tonight," Julia gushed, brandishing a freshly wrapped package from the merchant as she walked over to meet me. "*Sole en papillote*, wrapped up with these *gorgeous* asparaguses—or shall I say asparagi? Is that the plural? I suppose I ought to know, shouldn't I?"

She belted out a laugh, gay and free, as only Julia Child could be when faced with the opportunity to cook something magnificent in the kitchen. Getting fresh summer produce unexpectedly in the winter was, to Julia, like finding a big fat pearl in a ratty, old oyster. "I'm going to wrap them all up together in parchment paper packets—the fish, the tomatoes, the asparagi, some garlic and a bit of lemon and *lots* and *lots* of butter—and I'll need to get some of your Grand-père's little babies—thyme and tarragon and dill, of *course*, to sprinkle on them—and pop them in the oven. They're going to be the most *delectable* little packages of *deliciousness* tonight! Paul is going to think he died and went to heaven—*again!*" she crowed.

"Sounds delicious, and very fancy—and *very* complicated," I said with a grin.

"But it's not! Not at all! Even you—I mean, *you* could do it, Tabs. I can show you how. Let's get you some fish from Monsieur Jacques and you can use thin-sliced potatoes and carrots with it. I'll give you some parchment paper. It'll be *divine*, I promise, and it doesn't take long to cook at all!"

I allowed myself to be convinced, and purchased some thick fillets of cod, which, according to Julia, were not so delicate as the sole she'd purchased (and, therefore, more appropriate for me so I wouldn't ruin them).

Although Madame Marie didn't have any more asparagus or tomatoes, she did have tiny new potatoes and big, thick carrots that Julia assured me would be "*stupendously perfect*!" for slicing thin and layering beneath the fish.

"Add some dill and chervil from your grand-père's greenhouse and lots of butter—maybe a *splash* of white wine—and you're going to have a *feast*!" Julia told me excitedly as we started back to rue de l'Université. "I'll show you how to make the little packets for the fish, too, Tabs. They're just like little envelopes. We can do them together in my kitchen and then you can just take them home to slip in the oven. Easy-peasy, and they don't take long to cook *at all*."

I loved easy-peasy, and I told her so. "I'll call you when I get home from the funeral and come over then."

We parted there on Université, Julia's market bag much heavier and bulkier than mine due to some other treasures she'd found, and I ran across the street and darted into the house.

Bet and Blythe were there, and I gave one of them the task of setting the forsythia branches in hot water and putting the fish in the refrigerator. Agent Écuyer—who was sitting in the kitchen with a mug of coffee—agreed without hesitation to come to the funeral with us, and so I hurried upstairs to break the news to my messieurs.

To my surprise, they didn't argue with me about the police escort, so, feeling more optimistic, I rushed up to get ready to go.

As I changed into a nice dress and shoes and fixed my hair, I was acutely aware of how many funerals and memorial services I'd attended in the last eight years—since the beginning of the American entrance into the war. Funerals for far too many friends and relatives and acquaintances. Some with coffins, some unable to even have that bit of comfort, of having the body returned no matter what condition.

It had been so difficult at first to attend the services. Everyone was grieving, and in my opinion, grief is one of the most difficult challenges for us as humans. It's unspeakably awful living and dealing with the loss of a loved one, but it's also difficult being a bystander when the loss is not of someone close. You don't know what to do, what to say. . . . It's uncomfortable and awkward.

But it was my grand-mère who told me that it was important to be present for those who grieved as often as possible. "It's a kindness," she told me, "and you don't have to say anything brilliant. Just be there. And know that the funeral is for the *living*. Not those who are gone. They will be grateful you gave up your time to come."

And so I'd attended many, many funerals with those wise words in my mind.

Today's service would be far less of a difficulty for me than most of the ones I'd attended, but my presence was no less important—for I was there because of my *messieurs* . . . but, yes, also because of murder.

When we arrived at the tiny church, whose name I don't even remember, I made certain to greet every one of the sparse attendees. We milled around, speaking in low voices, before the mass began. Messieurs Lussier, Taban, and Sénac were present, as well as Madame Munzel. Devré was there, as well, which was no surprise, but I didn't see Docteur Jackson.

The mass was about to start. Light filtered in through a small stained glass window, and flames danced on candle stands throughout. Monsieur Hauet's coffin sat in front of the church's tiny altar and people were beginning to take their seats.

"Oncle Rafe, Madame Demailly isn't here," I said, looking around the nave of the tiny space that was really no more than a closet-sized chapel attached to a larger church.

"She is not here? Eh, perhaps she is only late in coming. We sent word to her, as we did to the others yesterday," Oncle Rafe said, looking around with a frown. "Berthilde got the message—she sent back word she would be here."

"Surely she wouldn't miss it," I said, even as an unpleasant prickling skittered down my spine. "After all, she was there . . ." My voice trailed off as my throat went dry.

Madame Demailly *had* been there; she'd been the one to see Monsieur Hauet fall to the ground, clutching at his fatal wound, dying on the street. . . .

What if she had seen something else? Something important—something she didn't realize she'd seen?

Or, worse, perhaps the killer *thought* she'd seen something. . . .

"If she said she would be here, she would be here, wouldn't she?" I said, fighting back the rising worry. "Does she have a telephone?" Oncle Rafe shook his head, and I went on. "We should send someone to find out—to make certain she is all right."

"Reece." Oncle Rafe went to Grand-père, who'd already taken

a seat in the first row of the pews, and murmured into his ear as he beckoned to Devré to join them.

Just then, the somber bellow of the organ filled the small space. The funeral was beginning. Devré nodded and stepped away from my messieurs and started down the side aisle so as to avoid the priest processing in. I was content that he had the matter of Madame Demailly in hand.

I made my way to a seat in the pews several rows back, by myself. I wanted to be alone, to put space between myself and the four remaining Neuf Bleuets because one of them—one of these people, sitting here in this church, pretending to grieve for Paul Hauet, to honor his life—had to be a killer. I wanted to watch them.

I wanted to know more about each of them, too.

For example, I wanted to find out which of the Neuf Bleuets lived in a place with or had access to a yard that could grow lilies of the valley. Merveille's offhand comment about the poison probably being arsenic, but that there'd once been a case with lily of the valley as the poison . . . well, it had stuck in my mind.

I had no reason at all to believe whatever had poisoned Philippe Capron was lily of the valley, but the idea wouldn't let go.

Call it instinct. Feminine intuition. Or my niggling little sprite, who didn't like to let things go.

Mademoiselle Yvette had mentioned how potent the roots were. It would be simple to dig them up, even now in March, for the ground wasn't quite as frozen.

And so I wanted to know who had a patch of yard and could dig up lily of the valley. And I wanted to know where everyone had been last night, when Merveille and I were nearly being run down by a delivery truck.

Delivery truck.

My spine stiffened and my breath caught as my attention fell on Monsieur Sénac. His head rose taller than everyone else's around him, even with him leaning on a cane.

Hadn't I told Julia I didn't know much about him, except that I thought he drove a delivery truck? That would make it second nature for someone like him to find and use a truck to try and run Merveille and me down.

I eyed Madame Munzel and Monsieur Lussier and Monsieur Taban, as well, trying to remember things, little details, other bits of conversation during dinner two nights ago. During the entire service, my mind dwelled and poked and stewed on thoughts of murder rather than the idea of Paul Hauet resting in peace . . . but he couldn't really rest in peace until his killer was identified and brought to justice, could he? I thought he might forgive my inattention for that reason.

At last, the final blessing was pronounced, and the coffin, swathed in a white cloth shot with gold threads, was wheeled out of the nave as the priest followed behind.

I wasted no time following. I wanted news about Madame Demailly.

When I saw Inspecteur Devré's face as he stood at the back of the church, my heart lurched.

I hurried over to him. "Madame Demailly?"

He shook his head, his expression grim. "There was a fire at her house yesterday. They found her inside. She is dead."

CHAPTER 15

Another Neuf Bleuet dead.

"Was it an accident?" I asked Devré.

He pursed his lips. "Given the circumstances, my nephew does not think so. I am inclined to agree, mademoiselle." His attention slid to my grand-père and Oncle Rafe as they made their way down the aisle, far more slowly than I had, because of their age and also the conversations in which they were engaged. "The target on them grows tighter and closer, eh, mademoiselle?"

"Yes," I said, my stomach churning unpleasantly. I glanced over to assure myself that Agent Écuyer was still at his post, watching. He was.

I wanted to talk to Merveille. I needed to know what he thought, even though I knew he wouldn't tell me anything. But Devré was right—there were only six Bluets left, and two of them were men I loved dearly . . . and one of the other four had to be a killer.

I wondered if a *bleuet* had been found in or near Madame Demailly's house. Since her home had been set on fire, leaving a blossom by her body wouldn't have worked as a message, so did the killer leave it outside somewhere? Or not at all? Or had the fire been an accident, after all, and there was no flower to be found, anyway?

My eyes wandered over Messieurs Lussier, Taban, and Sénac,

then to Madame Munzel. One of them had killed three of their colleagues and was methodically working through some sort of list, driven by some obscure motive that no one seemed able—or willing—to pinpoint.

Was the list in order of importance or need, or was it based on opportunity? Could the first victim simply have been whomever the killer happened to be with that first night, on the street?

Each death had occurred by a different method, too, which made it more difficult to predict what would be next.

A sword, poison, fire.

Roy d'Épée.

King of Swords.

A little prickle went down my spine.

King of Swords—*Roy d'Épée*—had been placed between the Devil—*El Diable,* and *Le Morte*—Death . . . and the three of them left there on the table, away from the rest of the deck of cards.

Surely the arrangement was purposeful.

Le Diable.

Roy d'Épée.

La Morte.

The Devil had used a sword to start this entire reign of death. . . .

But I already knew that. Was Madame Vierca trying to tell me something more?

Madame Vierca . . . The thought reminded me of something else . . . something that whispered through my memory, as insubstantial as a remnant of smoke . . . something I couldn't snatch back before it dissolved.

"Mademoiselle?"

I was jolted from my thoughts to find Monsieur Lussier standing there, his shock of pure white hair drawing the eye as it fell over his forehead and brushed the shoulders of his dark suit. His gray gaze was filled with concern and, I thought, sadness. I recalled he did electrical work . . . and had played piano during the war.

"I am so sorry about Madame Demailly," I said, reaching to touch his hand. "Did you know her well? She was a piano teacher, wasn't she? You play piano, my grand-père told me." I smiled quietly at him.

He shook his head, his brows lifting in surprise. "Ah, no, mademoiselle, I don't play the piano." His own lips curved, and I could see the glint of a patch of silvery whiskers he'd missed shaving this morning. "But during the war, I was a secret radio operator for the Resistance—which was called being a piano player. It was not so far from here, the house where I lived and worked the radio. Near Châtelet.

"I would go onto the roof, you see—I could get there from my own flat's window without being seen, and I could send radio messages all the way to London . . . Every night at five o'clock, I would transmit for ten minutes. I was safe as long as the Germans didn't find me by detecting the radio waves."

"Did they?" I shivered a little. I suspected I knew the answer—for if they had found him, Monsieur Lussier would not be standing here.

"*Non,* mademoiselle. You see," he went on, "the flat where I stayed in Châtelet was so near Les Halles and all of the refrigerators there, the lifts, the electrical equipment—all of that made such interferences that they couldn't . . . ah, what is the word . . . *parse* . . . they couldn't parse out the radio signals, or recognize them, from all of the other activities.

"And so I was able to send many, many worthwhile messages to London and even to Marseilles, and other places—and not be caught." He gave me a jaunty little smile and at that moment, I hoped very strongly that he was not the killer. He seemed so nice, and at the same time, cloaked in sadness.

"And Berthilde Demailly . . ." he went on, "we did not know of each other until after the war, as difficult as it might be to believe. We worked in separate cells of the Neuf Bleuets, you see . . . but surely your grand-père has told you this."

"*Oui,* but he has not spoken very much about those times. I think it is very difficult for him."

"For all of us." He looked around, his expression tightening. "I don't understand why this is happening. We are long past the war, and during it, *oui*, together we did so many things . . . bad things, good things, brave things, stupid things . . . but now why?"

"Did you go to see Monsieur Gavril's old house? The safe house?" I'd momentarily forgotten I needed to follow that thread of the investigation—to find out who had had an appointment with Monsieur Capron for the morning he died.

"*Non.* I was meant to go today." He shrugged. "We had an appointment, Philippe and I. But I am not even sure why I should go. I would like to forget all of that time and live out the rest of my days quietly, only petting my cat." He glanced around, grimacing, and I knew he was wondering whether he would even live much longer.

"Maurice and Rafael, they want to go back. Now . . . I don't know if I will." He shivered. "I would like to put all of this behind me. I am old and weary." Thoughtfully, he glanced over at my messieurs, who were speaking to the priest. "One begins to wonder whether this has happened because of them. Because of them bringing us back together again after these years."

Now I shivered. I didn't like to think that was the case—that the blame lay with Grand-père and Oncle Rafe.

"Mademoiselle. Renald."

I turned, and Monsieur Taban was there, blinking behind the round glasses he wore as he greeted both me and Monsieur Lussier. His specs were still as crooked on his nose as they'd been at dinner.

It occurred to me suddenly that he had to be fairly agile and confident in order to be an apartment measurer: climbing stairs and ladders, crouching and stretching to measure, being on his feet quite often. . . . Someone like that could probably wield a knife and slice someone's throat.

"It was so very good of you to come today, Mademoiselle Knight," said Taban, patting my hand. "It's so good to see the young people honoring and acknowledging the old ones. But now I have only just heard about Madame Demailly. What is happening? Who can be doing this?" He looked at Lussier, his eyes wide behind those crooked round glasses. The corners of his eyes crinkled deeply with pain and age.

Lussier shook his white head soberly. "I do not know. But I think I will be locking my door very tightly and being very careful where I go—and with whom—until this is over."

"Locking her door did not help Berthilde," said Taban grimly. "I think I might go away for a time."

"Have you been to the old safe house recently?" I asked. "The one Monsieur Gavril let the Neuf Bleuets use in Charonne?"

"Me? No, no, not yet. I was thinking I should see it one last time . . ." Taban looked over. "Ruth." His expression changed into one of abject sadness, and yet I saw something else in his eyes. Hope? "Did you hear—poor Berthilde."

Madame Munzel, who was already very slender and fair, appeared almost skeletal in her grief. She had been widowed long before the war, and now she helped her sister and brother-in-law run a little brasserie a few blocks away. Plans had been made for everyone to gather for a post-funeral luncheon there.

"I've only just heard. I cannot believe it . . ." Her pale blue eyes blinked rapidly as her gaze darted from Taban to Lussier and back to me. The tip of her pointed nose was red. "Mademoiselle Knight. I am so very sorry it's during such terrible times that you've come to know us. Thank you for coming."

"I'm so sorry for all of this," I said, waving my hand around. "I'm sorry for the loss of your friends . . . and everything else." I hesitated to put into words what we all knew: that one of them was meant to be next.

She echoed the same thoughts as the others. "Who is doing this? Why is this happening? Can the war *never* be left behind?" Her eyes glittered with tears, and Monsieur Taban reached over to take her hand. I realized then, with a start, that I saw something more than mere comfort in his eyes. Love shined there.

"If only we had not all come together," Madame Munzel said. She hadn't pulled away from Monsieur Taban's hand; in fact, she leaned closer to him just a little . . . just enough to suggest she welcomed him, his presence. "If only Gavril had not gone and died and then we all came together, everyone would have forgotten about it all, and we would have just gone on with it."

"What do you mean?" There was something there that seemed important. "What does Monsieur Gavril dying have to do with this?"

"But . . . it has everything to do with it," she said a little sharply. I didn't take the least bit of offense. We were all filled with emotion, including fear. "It brings it all back—the memories. The terror, the things we did. Hiding people, sneaking around, lying. All of the lying. And the killing. I am so old and so tired of it all."

Tears streamed from her eyes, and Monsieur Taban drew her into his arms, murmuring into her ear.

"Perhaps we ought to go and exorcise the demons, eh, Ruth?" said Taban as he released her from the embrace but still held her hand. "See the house, one last time, and put it all to bed. To rest."

"Did something happen there?" I asked, a little prickle running down my spine. "At the house?"

"Many things happened there," said Lussier in that vague way I was really beginning to find frustrating.

"Did someone die? Did someone kill someone? Did someone betray someone? Did something in particular happen there at the house that might be the reason for all of this?" I asked, trying to keep my rising exasperation under wraps. "We need to find out *why*—"

"Ah, mademoiselle, there you are."

I looked up as Monsieur Sénac approached, gritting my teeth with renewed frustration at being interrupted just when I was hoping to pin down my companions and get some actual details. I was beginning to get the feeling that somehow the motive for this series of killings was related to the safe house.

After all, Monsieur Gavril had died and the house became empty *before* Grand-père and Oncle Rafe had their fête at Maison de Verre. Whoever had killed Paul Hauet had planned it—for they brought a knife with them.

Louis Sénac was the delivery truck driver, and he conducted his tall and slender figure easily with the help of his cane. He wore a neatly trimmed and groomed Van Dyck–style mustache and beard and carried an unlit cigarette, as if he was anticipating getting outside and lighting it as soon as possible. "And what is all of this?" He looked around the little group of us, obviously noting Madame Munzel's tears. "It is sad news about Berthilde, *non*? I cannot quite comprehend how—and why—this is happening."

"Do any of you know Madame Vierca?" I asked, trying to regain control of the conversation and acquire at least something that might help determine who was behind all of these deaths.

Even as I said this, I realized with a stark and cold shock that I was standing there with four people and *one of them* was a killer.

And I was just *standing* there, talking about the terrible deaths that had been occurring, having just finished honoring one of the victims . . . and one of these four was responsible.

It was a strange and unsettling feeling. I hoped my expression didn't give away the sudden shock I felt.

"Madame Vierca. The medium, *hein*? Ah, that is a name I have not heard in a while," said Taban, his eyes crinkling at the corners behind his glasses. "She is well known in the Quarter . . . and elsewhere. You used to see her, Ruth, did you not? For the messages from your husband?"

Ruth Munzel nodded, her head bowed. "*Oui*, but it has been years since I've spoken to her."

"Berthilde knew her," said Lussier. "She said something—it was at the dinner. Did anyone hear it?"

"What do you mean?" I tried, and probably failed, to keep my voice from sounding desperate and sharp.

"It was something . . . *Merde*." His eyes widened and his face, already pale, went sheet-white. "She said—she was laughing when she said it, you see. You must understand. I'd forgotten about it until just now because she was so very . . ." He shook his head, his eyes filled with shock. "Berthilde said that she was thinking about leaving Paris because the woman—the medium, the fortune teller—had told her she would end her days in the heat. Where it was very warm."

CHAPTER 16

I found Grand-père standing outside the little church, smoking a cigarette while speaking with a few other funeral goers who were not members of the Nine Bluets.

"I have to see to something—I want to speak to Inspecteur Merveille," I said in a rush when Grand-père turned to me. "Agent Écuyer will stay with you, all right?"

"*Oui, oui*—but what is it, Tabi?" He must have seen the shock and stress on my face, despite me trying to hide it.

"I just thought of something I have to tell him," I said, which was partly true. "I'm going to find him at Madame Demailly's place—I think he is probably still there. If not, then I'll go to the 36 and hunt him down. You go on and eat lunch with everyone as planned at Madame Munzel's place. I'll speak to Merveille, then grab something to eat and do my tutoring appointment at three, and then I'll see you at home, all right?" I glanced at my watch. It was getting close to one thirty, but I'd have plenty of time.

"*Bien.*" Grand-père hugged me, and I felt the gentle tremors in the muscles deep beneath his skin. Feeling comforted as well as terrified for him, I hugged him back hard and kissed him on both cheeks, then did the same when I found Oncle Rafe standing next to me, as well.

I had already spoken to the police agent about staying with my messieurs and making certain they arrived safely at home in their Bentley—which no one was allowed to drive except Oncle Rafe. I had impressed upon Agent Écuyer that one of the four friends who attended the funeral was most likely the killer and to keep a close eye out, especially at the brasserie. Devré was planning to go to the luncheon also, so I knew I left my beloved gentlemen in good hands. I couldn't imagine that the killer would claim his next victim with so many witnesses.

Since I was in a hurry, I splurged on a taxi to take me to Madame Demailly's address. I hoped Merveille was still there.

When I got out of the taxi, I smelled the smoke that still hung in the air, wafting from embers in the house. Whatever crowd might have been there earlier had been dispersed, and a few police agents were busy taking statements or examining the crime scene.

I was relieved when I spotted Merveille speaking with someone who looked like a neighbor. The inspecteur was wearing a new dark-colored fedora. I wondered how many of those he owned looked exactly the same.

Madame Demailly's residence was a narrow, flat-fronted, two-story town house made of limestone and brick, so the structure remained. But the windows were blown out, and the frames around them black with soot and smoke, and I could see that the inside was completely destroyed. The tile roof had dark patches on it where the heat from the flames had broken through. Smoke still curled from one of the windows.

It seemed that the houses on either side had mostly been spared, other than a few burn marks on their roofs and one charred wooden shutter on the residencc that was attached to Madame Demailly's. There was a narrow walkway on the other side of her townhouse that led behind them, possibly to a courtyard or alley.

Merveille looked up suddenly and saw me. I stood patiently, waiting until he could make his way to me a few moments later.

"*Merci*, mademoiselle," he said by way of greeting.

I was so surprised by this that at first I was speechless.

He didn't smile, but neither was he exuding exasperation. "It was your concern over Madame Demailly that had me called to the scene. My oncle telephoned the 36 and urged me to investigate. I might not have known the connection for a day or more if you hadn't raised the alarm.

"The fire was yesterday," he said before I could ask. "In the evening, when she would have been inside, perhaps cooking her dinner. Her husband is dead from before the war, and so she lived alone. They found her body in the kitchen."

"Was it an accident, then?" I asked, looking at the destruction.

"I do not think so, mademoiselle." He withdrew an envelope from his pocket and opened it to reveal a crumpled *bleuet.*

My heart jumped. "But where was it found if the house burned inside?" I asked, looking around.

"There." He pointed to the ground in front of one of the windows. "And there was another one in the back, in the garden. It seems our killer wanted us to know for certain that he or she has been here."

"The garden?" I thought instantly of lily of the valley. "Could I look at it?"

His gaze measured me for a moment. "You are thinking about what, mademoiselle?"

"Lily of the valley," I said, then started toward the narrow passage between the houses. Careful of my funeral-appropriate dressy frock and heels, I managed to pick my way along the tiny walkway strewn with ash and remnants from the fire. The alley was, thankfully, neither slushy nor muddy due to the spring-like weather and lack of precipitation, so my shoes and nylons would likely come through clean of splatters. However, my hat—an appropriately sober navy—would possibly pick up some of the floating bits of ash.

Merveille didn't join me. I assumed he had other things to do, and that was fine. I was perfectly capable of looking for a sign that someone had dug up some lily of the valley rhizomes. And there it was.

My heart jolted a second time when I saw the small, freshly dug hole in the tiny, barren courtyard. I couldn't know for certain whether lily of the valley had been growing there, but someone could surely verify either way.

This realization got me thinking as I came back around to the front of the house. *If* I was right—or rather, if Merveille was right, for he'd been the one to mention lily of the valley first—then someone had to have dug it up before yesterday morning, when Philippe Capron was poisoned.

It was reasonable to assume that the rhizomes had been steeped or boiled in a liquid or ground into a powder, which was then added to whatever Capron ingested—coffee, tea, anything. This was yet another sign that the killer had planned this reign of terror.

If someone had dug up lily of the valley here, that someone had visited Madame Demailly at least a day or two before the fire was set. I assumed the authorities would be questioning neighbors and possible witnesses about who might have been seen visiting the dead woman.

I explained all of this (except my assumption about him questioning the neighbors) to Merveille, who listened with an unreadable expression. I didn't stop to wonder how much of what I told him he'd already deduced.

"That is all quite possible, mademoiselle, unless Madame Demailly dug up the flower roots herself," was all he said.

I blinked. "Why would she do that?"

"Perhaps she was doing some early gardening, and the poison was not, in fact, from lily of the valley, eh, mademoiselle? One must consider all possibilities. The medico-legist has not yet reported on the type of poison used."

I gave him a look, barely refraining from rolling my eyes. A little breeze kicked up, bringing a fresh waft of lingering smoke on the air. It was surprising how long a fire like that could smolder . . . and how strong the smoky smell still was over twelve hours later. My coat and hat—and hair—would probably smell like—

"*Mon Dieu.*" My eyes popped wide, and forgetting myself, I

grabbed the inspecteur's arm, then released it almost immediately. But not before I'd felt the hard muscle beneath his coat.

"Qu'est-ce que c'est?"

"Yesterday—last night, I mean—at Madame Vierca's—there was a sweater that smelled very strongly of woodsmoke. It was in her bedroom. Did you notice? When did the fire start here, exactly? Do you know?"

His eyes sharpened as he looked at me, nodding. "I have been told they noticed the smoke and saw the flames when it was six o'clock or thereabout."

"That was well before we got to Madame Vierca's," I said, mostly for myself, as I was working through my suddenly wild and jumbled thoughts. My stomach fluttered and pitched as even more ideas and suspicions began to fall into place: *click, click, click* . . .

A very smoky sweater. Madame Vierca, gone, and obviously in haste . . . leaving her tarot cards behind.

A new theory began to form in my mind, but I didn't want to put it into words. Yet.

It was crazy. It couldn't be right. It didn't make *sense.*

"I came here to tell you that Madame Vierca told Madame Demailly that she foresaw her—Demailly—ending her days in a very warm place," I said slowly. "I thought it was just a prediction, like she had given about the bluets dying or wilting—an *accurate* prediction. She predicted the swipe of the blade, too—the throat cutting. But what if . . ."

"What if Madame Vierca was not predicting but was *planning*?" Merveille said calmly, taking the wind out of my sails. "What if she was merely telling what was to happen, what *she* was intending to do, eh, mademoiselle? That she has a smoky sweater because she set the fire that killed Madame Demailly?"

"Right," I said, hiding my disappointment that he was either on the same page or had been ahead of me. "But why would she have warned me and tried to warn Grand-père and Oncle Rafe?" I sighed, then plunged on. "Someone should check Madame Vierca's place again and see . . ."

"See what?"

I heaved a sigh. "I don't know. See whether there is any sign she came back after we left last night? See whether the smoky sweater is still there? All along, I kept saying the killer had to have been at dinner at Maison de Verre—because there only being eight bluets remaining on the table was the killer's message that the Neuf Bleuets were . . . well, were being eliminated—"

"But now you are reconsidering, eh, mademoiselle? Because the *bleuet* found in the medium's parlor means that someone else could have flowers. That there are others in Paris besides the ones in that vase. And this someone else could have left *their* flowers with the bodies of Monsieur Capron and Monsieur Hauet and Madame Demailly."

"Yes. And I suppose that *anyone* could have taken the bluet from the dinner table that night."

He looked at me as if to say, *But of course, mademoiselle.*

"You thought that all along," I said, giving him a grim look.

"My mind is open to all possibilities always, mademoiselle." His eyes narrowed. "Please, I implore you once again—do not return to Madame Vierca's place. I know you are curious now and think there might be more clues there, but if your theory is correct, the medium could also be there, and she is obviously dangerous."

"I won't go back there." I meant it, too. I started to speak again, then hesitated.

My conversations with the remaining Neuf Bleuets after the funeral had got me thinking that perhaps something about the old safe house had something to do with the killings . . . but if Madame Vierca was the murderer, I didn't understand how she could be connected to it all. She hadn't been a Bluet, and no one had given any indication that she'd been close friends with any of them.

And why, why, *why* would she have started this whole thing by warning us?

Was she simply trying to throw off suspicion from herself? It would be a clever tactic . . . like something an Agatha Christie character would do. I shook my head.

"Could the safe house have something to do with it all?" I

said after a moment, speaking my half-formed thoughts aloud. "Everyone I've spoken to has mentioned it—all of the other Neuf Bleuets I saw at the funeral today mentioned it. They each had different feelings about it, but they all seemed to want to put the past behind them."

Merveille made a quiet, thoughtful sort of grunt. But then he said, "And did you determine today which of the suspects is left-handed, so that you know which one might be the killer?" His voice was dry, and his brows had lifted to just beneath the edge of his hat.

"No." I didn't want to admit I'd forgotten about that, dang it.

"Very well, then, mademoiselle. You still have work to do, eh? As do I. Is there anything else you wish to tell me?"

I shook my head.

He bowed his own head in acknowledgment. "*Bien.* Please be assured I will be in contact if there is anything you need to know—or Messieurs Saint-Léger and Fautrier. And the police guard will remain in place as long as necessary."

I thanked him and was ready to leave; then realized I needed either a taxi or to find a *métro* station.

"Do you need a ride home, mademoiselle?"

I heaved a sigh. I disliked feeling unorganized and appearing helpless. "I came by taxi. I can take the train—"

"I will get you a ride home." He beckoned over a police agent, and the next thing I knew, I was climbing into an official car. Merveille politely closed the door for me—to make sure I actually got in, I thought wryly—then gave a sharp knock on the roof, signaling the agent to leave.

Then the inspecteur returned to his task of handling death.

I almost asked the police agent to take me to the safe house. It would be the perfect opportunity for me to look around uninterrupted, to see if I could determine what about the place might be the catalyst for killing off les Neuf Bleuets. How much safer could I be, being in the presence of a police agent while doing so?

But I reined in my internal sprite—who was all for it, of course, because of this crazy theory that wouldn't let me go.

Honestly? The main reason I didn't ask was because I was pretty sure Merveille had told the agent to take me directly home, and I didn't want to embarrass myself by asking for something the driver would not only decline to do but also would probably rat me out to the inspecteur about my request.

Instead, I did the mature and responsible thing: I had Agent Parqué drop me off at a café near the house of my tutoring client. He didn't seem to balk at not taking me to rue de l'Université, so maybe I'd been wrong about Merveille's order—or maybe he'd just told the agent not to take me to the Latin Quarter *or* to the location of the safe house. Still. I did have a job to do—my tutoring—and so I would do it.

I was able to have a quick bite at the café, then went on to my appointment, which was with one of my favorite students. Judy Packard was about my age and newly married to a very sweet but shy man who worked with Paul Child at the embassy, and she, too, as it turned out, had worked in one of the airplane plants during the war. We always had a lot of fun during our lessons because we had so much in common, and she liked to learn all the slang words and idiomatic phrases the young people used—some of which were a little off-color.

When I left, I was in such a good mood and the beautiful weather was holding so nicely that I decided to walk back home. It was just over the bridge and down a few blocks, and spring was in the air. I knew my messieurs were safe at home with Agent Écuyer, so I didn't feel the need to rush. Julia would be expecting me at her house to make the *poisson en papillote,* but not before five, so I took my time and enjoyed the little slice of spring that had been given us in this early week of March.

When I got home, I was more than a little surprised to find that the Bentley was not parked in its place under the portico. But then I remembered it was Paris and there was a meal . . . and those could go on forever, as I well knew, so it wasn't all that surprising. Still . . . I had left Grand-père and Oncle Rafe almost three hours ago. . . .

I let myself into the house and immediately sensed that something was wrong. It was too quiet. The hair on the back of my neck prickled so sharply that I dug the Swiss Army knife out of my pocket (yes, it was in the pocket of the dress I wore to the funeral—I truly never leave home without it).

I took two steps, silent ones through the foyer, listening carefully for anything that might suggest why I felt apprehensive. Bet and Blythe would have left by three thirty or so, and with the Bentley not in its place, that meant the house should be empty.

Empty and eerily quiet and still.

I realized with a sudden cold and terrible start that Oscar Wilde was not rushing down the stairs, barking his head off, to greet me.

Something was definitely wrong.

I took two more steps, my heart thudding in my ears, and then I heard a faint yip. It was coming from the ground-floor study, a room we never used that was tucked back beyond the kitchen.

I listened, and there was another yip. It had to be Oscar Wilde, but what was he doing down here? Usually he sprawled on the chair by the furnace in the salon when there were no opportunities for treats.

"Oscar Wilde?" I called, starting down the hallway. This was very strange. My palms were damp, and my hair stood on end. Then I heard a dull thump, and the yip became a volley of wild yapping and whining.

At least I knew Monsieur Wilde was unhurt—but he must be locked up somewhere. And Madame X—well, she was probably hiding away, as cats are wont to do.

The door to the study was closed, which was not usual and could explain why Oscar Wilde was trapped inside. Maybe he'd sneaked in while Bet and Blythe were here and they closed the door—but they would never do that. The door is always kept open.

Prickling skittered over my shoulders. I held my breath and turned the knob slowly. There was another thump and more crazed, desperate yipping.

I gently pushed the door in, standing to the side in case . . . in case something had happened.

Nothing happened.

Then I heard a low moan and a dull thud. I looked around the corner into the room, which was unlit and shadowy.

Oscar Wilde appeared from nowhere, launching himself from the depths of the room, barking wildly as if to welcome me and thank me for showing up. But it was the fallen chair that caught my attention—and the form with it.

I turned on the light and saw that Agent Écuyer was there, bound and gagged, tied to the chair that had fallen over, his eyes wide and rolling with extreme emotion as he tried to communicate.

I wasted no time utilizing my knife to cut him free. Gag first, so he could tell me, haltingly and with great self-loathing, what had happened. It was obvious he'd fallen over and hit his head quite soundly and was just regaining consciousness. He was a solid man—not bulky but solid—and had fallen hard.

Even so, he managed to speak. "We arrived here, and it was no problem, mademoiselle. We came inside . . . and we were taking off our coats . . . and all at once she was there."

"She?" It was a question, but I'd already known. I'd already expected it. I was still sawing away at his bonds, which I recognized as the thick tieback cords from the curtains in the room. They were a little loose, suggesting he'd made some progress in attempting to free himself, and that was probably how he'd managed to tip over and knock himself out or at least stun himself.

"*Oui.* She was waiting here, inside. We had no warning. I am sorry, mademoiselle. I am so very sorry. She had a gun, and she pointed it at Monsieur Saint-Léger, and she said if we did not do what she told us, Monsieur Fautrier and I, she would put a bullet in his head. I am so sorry, mademoiselle—" He winced, obviously in pain as well as remorse for being taken by surprise.

"We need to call Merveille," I said, my heart lodged in my throat, a terrible roaring filling my ears. I shoved back the panic.

Later. I could be terrified later.

"Tell me what she made you do," I said, even as I rushed from the room before I'd finished freeing Écuyer. I needed the telephone.

In that instant, I had gone strangely calm. Focused. Probably because I couldn't bear, didn't *dare*, to think about what could happen, what could be the worst case, where Grand-père and Oncle Rafe were, what she was doing to them, the fact that she had a *gun*. . . .

I had just been connected to the front desk at the 36 when Agent Écuyer stumbled into the foyer, mostly having finished freeing himself. There were still loose ropes around his ankles, and in the light, I could see a nasty swollen cut on his forehead from when he'd tipped over in the chair.

"This is Tabitha Knight," I said into the phone, giving my address and telephone number as I beckoned frantically to Écuyer to speak. "I need to speak to Inspecteur Merveille."

"She made Monsieur Fautrier tie me to the chair. I think he did his best to keep the ropes as loose as possible. I think I might have gotten free, but then I fell over, and . . . I don't remember anything until you got here." Écuyer rubbed his wrists. "They left. Together, the three of them. I heard her say Monsieur Fautrier was to drive and Monsieur Saint-Léger would sit with her in the back in order to make certain no one tried anything."

"Where did she take them?" I said to Écuyer as the agent at the police station said over the line, "I'm sorry, mademoiselle, the inspecteur is not here. I will leave a message for him. What would you like it to say?"

"Wait one moment, please," I said to the man on the line, then beckoned wildly again for the policeman to continue speaking.

"I don't know where she was taking them."

I thought *I* might know, but what if I was wrong? There were two possible places she could go.

"Did they say *anything*, monsieur?" I asked the man in front of me, holding my hand over the telephone mouthpiece. "Anything that might give a clue?"

"She just said they had old business to discuss," he replied, even as the police agent on the other end of the line squawked, "Mademoiselle? Are you still there?"

"Yes, just one little moment, please," I said into the phone, then once more turned to Écuyer. "How long have they been gone?"

"Perhaps thirty minutes. We got home before five, and it is not half past now." He had just finished unwinding himself from the cords that sagged around his ankles.

I turned my attention back to the phone and left a brief but detailed message for Merveille with what had happened and the two places I thought she might have been taking them. I impressed upon the man on the other end that it was imperative this message get to the inspecteur immediately. That it was life and death, and then I went on to say that former Inspecteur Devré would need to be notified as well and asked the agent on the phone to send word to him right away.

And then I hung up and ran for the door. My hand was on the knob when I stopped, drew in a deep breath, and turned around. I bolted up the steps to the salon as Agent Écuyer called after me, confused by my frenetic activity and a little slow due to his head wound.

Miraculously, Oscar Wilde was subdued and quiet during all of this, watching silently as this happened around him. I suspected he knew what a grave situation his master was in and that there were to be no biscuits or other treats until that was rectified. He might not even get dinner on time.

I found what I needed in the salon, then dashed up to my bedroom to get the flashlight that should have already been in my pocketbook. I couldn't take the time to change out of my funeral clothing. When I ran back down the stairs, Agent Écuyer was on the telephone, speaking rapidly and tersely. I didn't know who he was talking to or why—his boss maybe?—and I wasn't going to wait for him to finish his call. He knew the two places I had in mind; he'd heard me say them in the message.

I ran out of the house, ignoring his shouts after me, and dove into my little Renault. I was peeling wildly out onto rue de l'Université when I saw him burst out of the front door, waving me down.

I shouted out the window, telling him where I was headed and for him to go to the other place, as I drove by. I could have waited and let him get in the car with me, but I wanted both locations covered.

One of us would be going to the right place.

I hoped.

CHAPTER 17

It was nearly five thirty, which meant the traffic was terrible.

I chafed over the delays, swore at the other drivers, prayed that I'd get there in time, promised myself I would no longer be ruled by my internal sprite—all the while leaning as far forward over my steering wheel as I could, as if that would get me there any faster.

It was a miracle I actually remembered how to get to the safe house where the Nine Bluets had plotted to resist the Germans. Somehow, each time, I knew where to turn to get there, even though it was in an area of the city not familiar to me.

It was almost as if some spirit or intuition was guiding me. Later, I realized that spirit had been helping me through this entire investigation.

Even so, the whole way, I prayed not only to get there in *time*, but I prayed even more desperately that I was going to the right place.

Madame Vierca's flat was closer, but I knew . . . I just *knew* . . . that she had taken them to the safe house. It was the only thing that made sense. Still, I hoped Agent Écuyer had heard me and had gone to rue des Grands Degrés as I'd begged him to do as I drove away.

When I saw the Bentley parked on the street near rue Saint-Blaise, a rush of relief flooded me. They were here.

I leaped out of my car, barely remembering to take my keys,

and grabbed my pocketbook. It was heavier than usual because I'd put Oncle Rafe's pistol—the one he'd kept beneath the cushion in the salon—in there.

I considered for a moment, then removed the gun, checked the safety and that it was loaded, then shoved it into my dress pocket and tossed my purse back into the car. My father, the cop, had not only taught me how to shoot but also how to be safe with a firearm. Even so, I don't think he ever imagined I'd be running down a tiny lane in Paris with a pistol in my dress pocket.

When I got close enough to the house that I could be seen, I slowed and edged close to one of the buildings. The street was so narrow there was nowhere to hide: anyone watching would see a person approach. I supposed that had probably been very helpful when the place was being used to hide people from the Nazis, but it didn't help me now.

"Bonsoir, mademoiselle!" came a cheery voice from behind me, and I nearly jumped out of my skin.

I whirled to see a little old man standing there, wearing a bemused expression. The homburg perched on his head was battered and had a crooked brim, and he was holding a dark cigarette, from which smoke streamed.

"Bonsoir," I said, stopping for the moment from my trek to the house to face the man. If she looked out, she might not recognize me and would only see two people talking on the street. "I'm looking for my grand-père. Have you seen anyone come down here recently? He gets a little confused sometimes," I added, feeling guilty for throwing my sharp-minded Grand-père to the wolves. "And he might be lost."

"Ah, *oui*, I see, mademoiselle. There was a man who came along some time ago. The street is very busy tonight, eh," he said with a gruff laugh. "So many people walking through. I suppose it's the weather, eh? Everyone thinks the spring is here."

"He was alone?" I asked.

"*Oui*, and he was not old enough to be your grand-père," he said with a grin as he dragged on his cigarette.

"Right. Thank you. Well, I'm going to walk a little farther along and see if I can find him, anyway."

"He didn't want to talk to me, either, mademoiselle. He was in a great hurry, you see. Like you are, eh? Why are the young people always in the rush?"

I couldn't stand there and chat with him any longer, so I bid him a polite bonsoir and continued on my way, hoping and praying that the killer hadn't noticed me from the windows.

Night was near, and the shadows were growing long on this narrow street, which helped as I drew closer, staying as close to the shadier side of the lane as possible. The house that was my destination was dark, although as I made my way nearer, I saw a faint glow of light that seemed to be coming from deep inside—possibly the kitchen, where Philippe Capron's body had been found.

That thought filled me with both hope and terror: hope that they were in a back room and therefore weren't looking out the front and wouldn't see me, and terror from the reminder that a cold-blooded, versatile killer had my messieurs under her control.

I decided to focus on the hope—because what else was I going to do?—so I dashed toward the house, trying to keep my heels from clopping too loudly on the stones and from turning my ankle on the uneven ground. I should have changed my shoes.

When I got close enough, I waited, leaning up against the stone wall, slowing my breathing so I wouldn't announce my presence. I was near a window, and although I'm not a tall woman, I was able to see inside.

I was looking into the front room that had the piano and the shrouded furnishings. No one seemed to be in that room, but there was definitely light spilling from down the hall, where I knew the kitchen and some other room were located.

I considered for a moment. Did I try to sneak in the front door, or should I creep around to the back of the house and look inside the kitchen window and assess the situation? The problem with that idea was I didn't know where anyone was sitting or arranged in the kitchen, and the last thing I wanted was to look in a window and have the killer facing me.

But creeping inside the house was even more challenging because it was an old building and the floor surely creaked, and I didn't even know whether the door was unlocked.

If I were a killer bent on revenge, I think I would have locked the door behind me.

But my messieurs were inside, and I didn't have time to dither—I needed to do something.

The front door was closer, no one was around, and I knew my way from there, so it was the obvious option. My heart lodged in my throat as I stepped up onto the tiny porch and eased toward the door. I listened hard and could hear nothing but the distant murmur of voices from inside—*voices*, plural and masculine—so that gave me a lurch of hope, and so, crouching, I stealthily reached for the doorknob.

Please be unlocked.

I spewed out a breath when the knob turned easily. *Thank you.* My heart, still in my throat, pounded so hard and fast I thought it would choke me as I pushed ever so gently on the door.

It moved, and I eased it a little more, my ears attuned to the slightest sound of a creak or a scrape or a shout of discovery. Nothing happened, so I pushed a little more, slowly, as beads of sweat ran down my spine and my feet began to ache from my crouched position while wearing heels. I definitely should have changed my shoes.

More, more, carefully, more . . . until the door was open wide enough for me to fit through. I stayed low, listened and heard the voices still in rumbling, even tones from the back of the house and, holding my breath, slipped inside.

I crouched there for a minute, catching my breath, waiting for the boom to fall . . . but nothing happened. I carefully closed the door and rose to my feet, staying out of sight from the kitchen.

Since I was inside, I could hear the actual conversation. I didn't care about the words. I cared that I recognized both Grand-père's and Oncle Rafe's voices. A rush of relief flooded me, making my knees weak and my belly flutter.

This new information, confirmation that my messieurs were alive and well, propelled me to action—not quick, impetuous action, but action nonetheless. I touched the pistol in my one pocket and my Swiss Army knife in the other—hoping it was only the latter that I would need to use—and drew in a deep breath, then began to inch my way toward the short hall that led to the kitchen.

I had a gun and the element of surprise, and those gave me big advantages over an older woman, even if she was armed and desperate.

At last I could see partway into the room, and very carefully, I maneuvered myself to manage a look into the kitchen while still remaining out of sight from its occupants.

The first thing I saw, which had me smothering a gasp and rearing back, was the killer. She was, thankfully, standing with her back mostly angled to me. She still held the gun, even though it was gripped in a hand dangling at her side.

I recognized her even from behind and felt a rush of satisfaction that my wild, crazy, unbelievable theory had been right, after all.

Berthilde Demailly was not dead.

CHAPTER 18

Madame Demailly was not only not dead, she was holding my beloved messieurs hostage.

And she had already killed three people—including Madame Vierca, who, I was certain, had not only been the body found in Madame Demailly's kitchen, but had also left me a very strong clue as to who the killer was. It had just taken me a little too long to figure it out. And once I had, I'd been able to see how Madame Demailly had done it all . . . and tried to make it look like Madame Vierca had done it.

But I still didn't know *why*.

"Ah, Berthilde, it was so very long ago. The war, it is over. Perhaps it is time to let all the things go and live our lives without these memories." It was Oncle Rafe speaking in a smooth and steady voice. I couldn't see him, but I could tell he was sitting or lying in front of her, just outside of my frame of vision. "There is no reason for more death and violence, eh? We saw enough of that back then."

"It's too late now, isn't it?" Madame Demailly replied. Her words were calm and steady. "One more death doesn't matter. One more death, one more betrayal, one more person to be avenged. And then I can be free."

I moved a little closer, angling myself carefully to stay out of her peripheral vision. I wanted to actually see my grand-père and Oncle Rafe so that I could assure myself they were well.

A little closer, a little more to the right . . .

And then I saw the man sitting in a chair, the first chair I could observe from my angle, and my heart dropped to my knees. I don't know how I managed to keep from gasping in shock, but somehow I did.

Merveille.

What was Merveille doing here?

A hundred thoughts and questions ran through my mind, but one stuck out and answered all of them. The old man I'd run into on the lane—he'd said a younger man had come through a while ago and hadn't wanted to talk to him, either.

That had to have been Merveille.

So had he already been here when Demailly and her hostages showed up? Or had she seen him coming from down the lane and taken him by surprise?

Not that it mattered, but having known Merveille for a few months and never seeing him get taken by surprise made me confused and a little worried that maybe the situation was going to be more difficult than I'd imagined.

That also meant not only was Merveille *not* going to arrive and help save the day due to my message, but I had to rescue him, as well.

I must have moved into view enough that the inspecteur could see me, for all at once I noticed his shoulders jerk, tensing. He snapped his gaze away so as not to alert Demailly, but I could fairly see the tension ripple through his shoulders even from where I stood. And when, a moment later, he flashed me a look—not necessarily an *I'm so happy to see you, Tabitha* look, but more like *What in the hell are you doing here?*—it was quick enough that his captor didn't notice.

Still holding her gun—in her left hand, of course—Demailly was pacing and talking. Her attention seemed to be focused on Oncle Rafe and his arguments, which Grand-père joined in, in what was an obvious attempt to distract her and delay any violent plans. Keeping the villain talking so they spilled all their plans was a great plot device in novels and movies, but I wasn't certain how long it would work in real life.

Either way, this distraction left Merveille unobserved and able to cast me a straight, deadly, intense look that clearly said, *Go get help*.

I had a lot of respect for him, but the man was nuts if he thought I was going to leave and take the chance Demailly would put an end to everything by shooting my gentlemen. Instead of backing away, as Merveille clearly thought I should do, I shifted in the hallway and withdrew the pistol from my pocket so he could see it.

His eyes widened so that even from here I could see the whites around his irises, then quickly shuttered as he looked down in order to hide his reaction from the murderous woman. Only then did I realize that he was tied to the chair, one hand bound to each arm of it. His feet were also tied to the front legs. Apparently, Madame Demailly was taking no chances.

Based on that and what had happened at home, I made the logical assumption that at least one of my messieurs was also restrained. That meant at the most, only one of them—the one who'd done the rope tying, assuming he wasn't also tied up—would be mobile and able to assist in an escape.

But Berthilde Demailly had not anticipated Tabitha Knight, former airplane-part riveter and imp-motivated amateur detective, and her determination. And her oncle's pistol.

Merveille had lifted his face again and was giving me the most compelling, urgent, desperate look that clearly said, *Are you crazy? Go get help*!

I shook my head and took another step down the hall, pistol in hand. Merveille gave me one last wild look designed to change my mind—it didn't—then started coughing. I realized after half a second that he was doing it to help camouflage any sounds I might make on a possibly creaky floor. So I moved faster.

Unfortunately, him doing so drew Madame Demailly's attention to him. Fortunately, that meant her back was directly to me and I was able to take three more quick steps down the hall. This put me right at the opening of the kitchen.

I pressed up against the wall on the left so that if Demailly turned to look at Oncle Rafe—whose feet I could now see at the chair next to Merveille's—she wouldn't catch me from the corner of her eye.

She still held her gun, but loosely, almost carelessly. She certainly wasn't aiming it at anyone, and she even gestured with it a little when she demanded of Merveille, "What's wrong with you?"

He coughed again, then shook his head and seemed to recover. He lifted his face and did not look toward me. "Madame Demailly, you don't want to hurt anyone else, do you? You could just put that gun down, and—"

"You don't know what you're talking about," she snapped and tightened her grip on the firearm. She lifted it, and the hair on my body rose in a great sweep of terror as she pointed it right at Merveille. My heart stopped beating, and I froze.

"Berthilde, wait . . . please. What was it you were saying about the—"

"All of you! *Silence*! I know what you're trying to do," cried Madame Demailly, cutting off Grand-père, her arms flailing. The gun moved away from Merveille. "I know you want to distract me, to delay the inevitable. But I tell you, I will have my revenge. I will—"

"Freeze, Madame Demailly. Don't move."

I hadn't even been conscious of making the decision to move. The next thing I knew, I'd taken one quick step, and then another, and suddenly I was right behind her.

It was almost as if someone had prodded me from behind. . . .

Madame Demailly froze. (Thank goodness.)

"I have a gun, and I know how to use it," I said, shocked that my voice came out so calm and steady—and that the pistol, which I held properly with two hands as I'd been taught—was also just as steady. "Very carefully, I want you to lower your left hand and place the gun on the ground."

I stepped closer, and she must have been able to feel my proximity. The barrel of my pistol was nearly touching her back. She did as I directed, and the moment her gun was on the floor, I stepped over and picked it up . . . and breathed a sigh of relief.

"Tabitha!" cried my grand-père. "What are you doing here?"

"I came to get you, of course," I said, still keeping my eyes—and pistol—trained on Madame Demailly. From the corner of my eye, I could see that Grand-père had not been tied to his chair and had risen, albeit slowly and jerkily, to his feet. I pulled out my Swiss Army knife and handed it to him so he could cut the ropes on the other two.

"Where did you get that gun, Tabitha?" cried Oncle Rafe as Grand-père went over to free him from his restraints. "Eh, now, take care with the blade, Reece. Your hand is shaky."

"And you are surprised about this? After all of this? Sit still, then, will you, and I may not cut you," Grand-père retorted as he went about his business. "I did not even make the ropes very tight, Rafe."

Apparently, thanks for saving their lives were *not* in order according to my gentlemen.

"Tabitha, where did you get that gun?" Oncle Rafe demanded again.

"From under your seat cushion in the salon. Madame Demailly, I think you ought to sit down." I was getting tired of holding up the pistol (they're heavier than you think), and a delayed reaction of terror, followed by a wild rush of relief that everyone was safe, was making me shake.

The only person who had not spoken was Merveille. I glanced at him as Madame Demailly took the chair Grand-père had vacated, but the inspecteur was not looking in my direction. He was watching Grand-père saw away at Oncle Rafe's ropes. I winced because, as I've mentioned, my grandparent is a little rickety. It would be a miracle if he didn't draw blood the way he was going at it. I could have done it, but I was managing Madame Demailly, and even though I had her gun, I wasn't confident enough to look away.

"I don't see any reason to tie you up, madame," I said. "Please don't give me one."

She merely looked at me with sad, empty eyes and settled into the seat as if all her will was crumbling away. Whatever madness or anger had been driving her seemed to have evaporated. Now she looked only old and fragile.

As Oncle Rafe, now free, got up from his seat and came toward me, I gratefully returned the pistol to him, then hugged him hard and long. "Will you watch Madame? I'll take care of freeing the inspecteur. Grand-père, sit down and rest a little now that you're safe."

"I don't need to rest," Grand-père growled.

I shook my head, smiling, and held out my hand for the Swiss Army knife. He gave it to me, casting me a dour look. "You're making me testy, *ma chérie*."

I smiled and pulled him into a big, hard embrace. "You're always a little testy, Grand-père." I squeezed him tight, and my eyes stung with tears. I was trembling, and so was he. Thank God he was safe.

Merveille cleared his throat. "Mademoiselle?"

Right. He wanted me to cut him free.

I needed a distraction as I carefully cut the ropes from his wrists, so I looked over my shoulder for a moment and said, "Madame Demailly, I don't understand why you did all this. Why? Why were you killing les Neuf Bleuets?"

"Mademoiselle, if you please," Merveille said quietly, but urgently, and I realized I'd taken my attention from the very sharp blade that I was using to saw at the rope around his wrist.

"*Excuse-moi*," I murmured, returning my attention to the delicate matter. Fortunately, whoever had tied him—Grand-père, presumably—had done a relatively clumsy job of it. I could see that Merveille had made good progress in loosening one of the knots; he'd probably only been able to do it when Demailly wasn't looking at him.

"Yes, Berthilde . . . we still do not understand why you would do these horrible things—to kill Paul and Philippe and . . ."

"Madame Vierca," I said, stepping back as the last of Merveille's ties fell away. "It was her body that was mistaken—purposely—for yours in the house fire, Madame Demailly." I didn't look at Merveille; I assumed he'd already figured that out.

Demailly shrugged. "*Oui.* I had to get her out of the way. She was seeing too much, *hein*? In her visions, she saw too much. She didn't remember often what she said, and that was how I could lure her to my house. She didn't know she was in danger. And I needed to die, as well, of course, so that I would not be the suspect. Once every one of the Neuf Bleuets was dead, whoever is left must be the culprit, eh?"

"*And Then There Were None*," I murmured, thinking of the brilliant Agatha Christie novel. "And so you had to fake your death so you could go on killing the rest of your comrades."

"*Mais oui.*"

"What did you use to poison Philippe Capron? Was it arsenic or something else?"

Her eyes narrowed craftily. "The poison roots of a flower. Lily of the valley. It is very, very toxic, and the ground is not so very frozen, and so I could dig it up. I did not want to chance being seen buying the arsenic or any other poison, eh? No one would suspect the flower."

I glanced at Merveille, and he shifted his brows in acknowledgment of our conversation. But instead of taking up the interrogation, I supposed you'd call it, he allowed me to continue on with my chain of thoughts.

"But Paul Hauet . . . How did you manage to cut his throat right there on the street?" I asked. "That had to be a risk . . . and you must have brought the knife with you. You had planned it all."

She nodded. "Ah, *oui*, of course I planned it. I had a small knife in my pocket—large enough to do the job. I had used it before. During the war." Her eyes looked into the distance, seeing something from her past. . . . Then she came back to us. "I came up to him and asked if he would walk with me—no one was around, I made certain of that. And then I stopped along the street, pretending to be upset. He hugged me, and as I stepped back, out of the embrace, I had the knife in my hand and . . . *tranche*." She made a slicing motion. "Along the side of his throat. There was all the blood, of course . . . but I wiped it away. And what was left, eh—it was from me trying to revive my friend, *non*?"

I shivered. There was a wild look in her eyes now that suggested this wasn't the first time she'd used her knife in that way. I took a deep breath. I might as well continue.

"And so you tried to frame Madame Vierca for all of the killings. You left a smoky sweater in her flat so that we—I mean, the police—would think she set the fire that supposedly killed you, and came back home afterward to pack her things and flee.

"And you made it look as if she'd gone in a hurry, but there were things that weren't right. You left her tarot cards behind, and Madame Vierca would never have done that. And that was when I began to wonder, just a little. And then—it was you who tried to run the inspecteur and me down on rue Xavier, wasn't it? In the delivery truck?"

Madame Demailly merely looked at me, her eyes bland. The wildness had faded from them, to be replaced by weariness.

"And so, *why*? Why did you do all of this?" I asked. "Killed your comrades, kidnapped my grandfather and oncle?"

"The twelfth of August, nineteen forty-three." Madame pronounced those words, that date, like a death knell—as if it meant something.

It meant nothing to me or, as far as I could tell from his expression, to Merveille. But Grand-père and Oncle Rafe had reacted with interest and confusion.

"*Oui*," Oncle Rafe said, taking a seat in the chair Merveille had vacated. He had pocketed his pistol, probably assuming the police inspecteur had things in hand. "L'Opération Onyx." He glanced at me as I remained standing. "We had ten people coming here—some of them Jews, some of them only men who needed to leave so they would not be conscripted to Germany, and one who was an agent who'd been compromised—and they were to be here overnight. And then in the morning, the next day, they were to be sent off with four different guides to get out of the city and to safety out of France. But, Berthilde, you were not even here for that. You had made a trip to Nice and were not part of the operation."

"*Ten* people, *oui*," Demailly spat. "But only nine of them came, eh? There were only nine who could go, eh, Rafael? You made certain of it—*all* of you, you made certain of it. You took only the nine. You *saved* only the nine."

"Pourquoi?" Oncle Rafe looked at her with confusion and perhaps a dawning comprehension. "But the tenth one, the agent—I don't know his name, for he was known only as Le Canard Noir—he did not come. He did not arrive at the meeting place.

"He was one of the best agents in Paris—young, brave, daring. I understand he helped to bring so many to us who needed to flee, and shared so much communication. But then something happened, and he was seen somewhere he shouldn't have been. And so he was in danger of being exposed. We would help him get out of the city; we would put him with the group coming here. He was to be the tenth, *oui*. But when he didn't come to the meeting, we thought he realized some danger and stayed away to be safe—for himself and for us."

"Of course he did not come! He was in hiding!" cried Demailly. "And then two days later, he was captured by the police. He was taken away, and I have never seen him again. And it was you—*all* of you—all of you *Bleuets*—who caused this to happen."

"But, Berthilde," said Grand-père in a quiet voice, "you know that cannot be true." He looked at me, grief in his eyes. "I do remember that day. I was not closely involved, although I did run the paperwork through the bank's courier network—the false papers and identifications for the ten. We knew le Canard Noir was in danger."

"We waited, Berthilde," said Oncle Rafe. "I was there, with Paul, you see, and we waited at the brasserie, and he did not come . . .We waited longer than we should have. But he did not arrive. We had to go—"

"*Oui*," she spat, "*you* had to go—back to your safe houses, your homes, where you had no fear of being dragged from them and placed on a train to slave for the Nazis or sent to a camp or prison! You could not have stayed another ten minutes for him, you could not have looked for him, tried to find him—"

"We had to go, or the entire operation would be compromised," Oncle Rafe said quietly. "We had also the other nine to think of, Berthilde."

"And *yourselves,*" she cried. "You thought only of yourselves and your safety."

"That is not true," Oncle Rafe replied in a cold, steady voice. I could see his hand tremble. "We did everything we could to keep as many people safe as possible."

"Berthilde. I am so sorry," Grand-père said. Tears glistened in his eyes. "We did not know. No one knew. It was so very dangerous, and no one gave their real names during this time . . . Who was he to you, this Canard Noir?"

"He was my *grandson,*" she choked, tears streaming wildly. "My *grandson.* Félix Charmont was his name. He was all I had left from my daughter . . . and you let him *die.* You didn't wait for him, and he was taken—and they tortured him."

There was no sound but her harsh sobbing breaths. My heart felt heavy, and her grief seemed to reach out and claw at me.

"Your grandson," Oncle Rafe said quietly, pain in his voice and eyes. "I am so very sorry. So sorry. We did not know . . . Berthilde, we did not know—we *could* not know—that your grandson was le Canard Noir."

She lifted her face, which was streaked with tears, and looked at him with a level gaze "You did not ask. No one asked. No one cared. I gave up so very much for this *Résistance.*" The last word came out bitterly. "I traveled so many times to the south. I sewed coins—so many heavy ones—into my girdle so I could bring money here to Paris without being found out.

"I could have left and gone away many times, and I would have been safe, but no, I stayed. I risked my life. I stayed, and with my husband gone, and my daughter and her husband dead, as well, I had no food, no money . . . but I stayed, and I helped so many people go to safety, and you could not help the *one person* . . . I needed to help . . . the most . . ." Her last words were nearly unintelligible, mixed in with her wrenching sobs.

"I am so very sorry, Berthilde," Oncle Rafe said, reaching over to touch her quaking shoulder. "We should have known. We should have done something more."

"You should have. You *should* have." Her eyes blazed when she looked up. "Gavril told me. He told me just before he died how it happened. How there was a meeting—how there were messages about the one who did not come. Canard Noir. The agent, the compromised one—my grandson. And how the decision was made that you could not wait for him for another day. That the guides were coming, and the operation had to go on . . . and so it did.

"*All* of you! All of you decided that the operation was more important than my Félix! And so when he told me this, when Gavril told me this—he was dying, you know—I knew that you all had to pay for it. You had to *pay* for letting my grandson die in prison . . . tortured."

Her words echoed from the peeling, water-stained walls. No one spoke for a long moment.

Then Merveille took a step toward the sobbing woman. "Madame Demailly, I am very sorry for the loss of your brave, patriotic grandson. It is a tragedy that happened during an awful, untenable, unspeakable time in our lives. I believe everyone here is remorseful and grieving with you . . . but I am afraid you must come with me now, madame. You must come with me."

Madame Demailly didn't fight the inevitable. She rose, beaten and subdued by her grief, wrung out from her anger and desire for vengeance. Her shoulders caved, and she moved as if in great pain as she grasped the back of the chair.

I was the person closest to the front door, at the end of the hall by the kitchen, so I was the first to see shadowy figures approaching the front of the house. Night had fallen, but I could still make out the shapes of several men coming toward the house in a furtive manner, similar to the way I'd approached.

I went out to greet them and found Agent Écuyer and several other policemen, along with, unsurprisingly, Inspecteur Devré.

"The killer has been apprehended," I told them. "Madame Demailly is prepared to leave quietly."

Grand-père and Oncle Rafe and I sat in the kitchen on the chairs as Merveille spoke to the police agents—who would take Madame into custody—then began to fill in his great-uncle on the events of the evening.

As she was being led away, Madame Demailly paused in the doorway. "You were wrong about one thing, mademoiselle."

I looked at her. "What was that?"

"I did not leave the tarot cards behind in Vierca's flat. She had them when she came to see me at my house—that was last night, of course. She was preparing to do a reading for me when I came up behind and hit her on the head. I hit her hard enough to knock her out, and then I set the fire. When I left, you see, the flames were eating up the tablecloth and the cards where she sat. So, you see, there is no possible way the tarot cards were left in her flat."

CHAPTER 19

I stared after Madame Demailly as she was led away. If what she said was true . . .

I shook my head. I couldn't really make sense of it. I had seen the cards, and so had Merveille. What was she talking about?

"We did not realize our decision would lead to le Canard Noir's capture and imprisonment," Oncle Rafe said wearily, breaking into my jagged thoughts. "We thought only that he had been delayed and didn't make the meeting on time, because he didn't wish to endanger us if he was being watched. It is what the agents are taught to do—to keep the risk to others a minimum."

"And what else were you to think, believe, *do*?" Grand-père asked quietly. "All of the decisions made during that time—during the war—they were often required to be quick and desperate, Rafe. And no matter what choices were made, someone would be captured. Someone would die. Someone would be compromised. No decision, no choice, was perfect or without risk. But they had to be made."

"You—les Neuf Bleuets—did the best you could do," I said, my heart swelling with pain for my messieurs. They suddenly seemed so much older than they'd ever been. "That's all any of us can ever do—only our best."

"If we had known . . ." Oncle Rafe said.

"No," replied Devré, who was suddenly standing there, listening. "*Non, mon ami*, you could have made no other decision. You know it. You could not risk the other nine, and you could not know whether le Canard Noir had been captured, killed, or had merely gone into hiding.

"And, I will say this, too, eh, although it might be harsh. Le Canard Noir—he knew the risks he took. As we all did. He knew it. He was willing. And his last bit of heroism, of patriotism, was to protect you, and les Neuf Bleuets, by avoiding the meeting. And so you saved nine other people, *hein*?"

I looked up at Devré, surprised to feel the sting of tears in my eyes. He was right. I sent him a look of appreciation and saw that Merveille was watching his uncle closely, as well. He certainly wasn't blinking back tears, but his expression was somber and thoughtful.

"Ah, thank you for that," said Oncle Rafe after a moment. He dug a handkerchief from his pocket and vigorously rubbed his nose. "Thank you. I still feel the grief and the regret, but you are right. We did only the best we could do, and we saved many lives." He hauled himself to his feet.

Merveille indicated he wanted to examine the entire safe house before he left. "I suspect here is where Madame Demailly stayed last night, after her house burned. She could not risk staying long at Madame Vierca's, where someone might see her. There may be evidence as to her plans."

Although I think Merveille expected us to leave him to his task, Devré and I—as well as my messieurs—insisted on going through the house with him. Merveille couldn't deny his great-uncle, and so he was stuck with all of us. I used the flashlight I'd taken out of my purse when leaving the car, and I could tell he was grateful to have another light besides his own.

We found the place where Demailly had slept last night, along with a little money and some other things—photos, a trinket, a book—packed with some clothing she had obviously wanted to save from her ruined house. There was an empty bottle of wine that suggested she'd had a moment of self-reflection or perhaps celebration . . . but there was nothing further that I considered incriminating.

"Ah! I almost forgot. There is one more thing we must do, eh, Rafael?" said Grand-père when we had finished looking through the entire house. He seemed straighter than he had been earlier, and with a little more energy in his movements. He'd mostly stayed in the front parlor while the rest of us snooped around, sitting on one of the chairs and looking through a curio cabinet to see if there were any pieces he wanted to buy. It was clear the worry and apprehension that had weighed him down since Paul Hauet's death was gone . . . or at least had eased.

"Ah, I'd almost forgotten, as well. There has been so much excitement, eh?" Oncle Rafe nodded, and I was surprised to see the faintest little gleam of delight in his eyes. "We intended to do it yesterday, but unfortunately, poor Philippe deserved our attention."

"Do you think it's still here after all of this?" Grand-père said as he went back into the kitchen, where there was a small, narrow door in the back. He opened it, and I saw that it belonged to a slender, deep sort of pantry.

"That I do not know. And of course we have no flashlight, eh?" said Oncle Rafe, mild disgust in his voice as he peered over Grand-père's shoulder. "There is only the few working lights in this damned place—"

"I have one," I said, giving him the one I'd been using during the exploration of the house.

And apparently, I'd been correct in my suspicion: yesterday my two gentlemen had sent me upstairs here at the safe house so they could rummage around in the kitchen undisturbed. I *knew* there'd been another reason we'd come to this house besides just having them look around.

They dug around in the pantry, shining the light, swearing, and making all sorts of thumping and bumping sounds, until at last I heard, "Voilà!" and more scrabbling sounds and even the groan of one of my messieurs as he seemed to be fighting to extract something from the depths.

I exchanged glances with Merveille, who had been strangely quiet and who had not said one word to me since his mild warning to pay attention when I was cutting the ropes from his wrists. He shrugged and remained silent, watching the activity in the pantry.

At last, Grand-père stepped back, looking a little dusty. But Oncle Rafe came out and was even worse—covered with cobwebs and appearing very disheveled. It was probably good he was bald, or all of that would be clinging to his hair as well as his clothing.

Oncle Rafe was holding a large glass canning jar, sealed with a rusted metal ring top, which was also very dusty. It contained something that looked disgusting: a sort of blobby, milky gray substance that neither sloshed nor moved inside its vessel.

"What is that?" I asked.

Oncle Rafe glanced at Grand-père. "It was left here by a Jewish friend of ours when he and his family had to leave the city in a hurry. They stayed here for two nights before they could leave, hidden in the bedroom upstairs. It is, I was told, a salve—a sort of balm or cream that is a secret family recipe. He asked us to keep it safe for him in case they returned."

"I had forgotten Rafe told me that David had left it here at this house," Grand-père said. "And then when Gavril died, it reminded me."

"Did you hear from the friend who left? David? Did the family return?" I asked, eyeing the jar. It didn't look like any salve I'd want to put on my skin. Why on earth would a person fleeing the country care about leaving behind a jar of homemade medicinal balm? And why would my grand-père and oncle be so determined to retrieve it?

"*Non.* We have not heard anything from them since they left in July of nineteen forty-two. I think there is not good news, and so we will keep this jar and perhaps . . ." Grand-père eyed the gray matter grimly. "Perhaps we will use the lotion . . . someday. In the honor of David Milhaud. I did not realize it was so ugly looking, Rafael." He frowned.

Oncle Rafe gave a little laugh. "Perhaps it smells nice, anyway. I am certain it will be worth the little trouble we have gone through, this salve. We did as they asked, *non?*"

Merveille cleared his throat, drawing everyone's attention. "*Bien.* I think now perhaps we can bid this place adieu?"

Everyone was in agreement, but as we began to leave the safe house, I said, "I know it's late, but I would very much like to go to Madame Vierca's flat. There's no danger any longer, and I'd just like to look around."

"You want to see the cards that were left there," said Merveille, sounding none too pleased.

"Berthilde claimed that the cards burned in her house fire, but you saw them after?" said Grand-père. "Then I think we should all go to see these cards if they helped you to identify the killer."

I heard a thin layer of skepticism and a bit of affable indulgence in his voice, but I didn't care. If his support got me to Madame Vierca's home, I was all right with it. I knew what I had seen, and Merveille had, as well.

There were no tarot cards in Madame Vierca's flat.

Neither the three that had been laid out on the table nor the rest of the deck, near the chair in the corner.

I stood there, staring, silent, unable to believe what I was seeing—or, rather, *not* seeing.

Unlike the previous two times I'd been in Madame's salon, I did not feel that strange sense of disquiet . . . of *something*. The place simply felt empty and dull. Abandoned. Even the scent of her thick, musky perfume had faded. Only a faint smokiness remained.

I wondered if that was because she was dead . . . but she had been dead when we were here the last time, hadn't she?

I shivered and hugged myself, even though I was wearing a coat and the temperature was still mild.

"They are gone, mademoiselle," said Merveille unnecessarily. "The cards we saw."

I cast him a look, grateful that he'd confirmed he'd seen them, as well. "Who would have taken them? Who came in here after we did last night and took only the cards? We know Demailly was at the safe house."

He shrugged—that Gallic movement that indicated a lack of interest or knowledge—and I gritted my teeth in frustration. He might not care, but *I* did.

"*Bien, ma chérie,* there are no cards—and so perhaps now, at last, we can find someplace to get a drink, eh? And some dinner?" said Grand-père.

"*Mon Dieu,* it's after eleven o'clock," said Devré, looking at the timepiece he kept tucked in his pocket like my grandfather did. "It takes much longer to catch a killer than I remembered, eh?" he said with a little laugh. "But that is why I'm so hungry. It's a long and difficult business, that of the detective, eh, Étienne? But now we must eat—and drink to the success."

All at once, I realized I was exhausted—both mentally and physically. I was still wearing my funeral dress and heels. I suspected my jaunty navy hat was sagging from its long day of catching a killer, and my lipstick was long forgotten, but I was suddenly starving.

I really can't say how it happened, but the next thing I knew, I was sitting in a little pub just at the corner of rue Xavier-Privas and Saint-Séverin with my messieurs, Inspecteur Devré, and Merveille. We were crowded at a tiny table right next to the bar counter.

Even so late, the place was thick with smoke and noise, the tables were so crowded the single waitress couldn't get through between them, and so drinks and food had to be passed from one end of a table to the other and sometimes from one *table* to another.

I'd been a little leery about eating in a place that looked as if it had been around since medieval times (and hadn't been cleaned since then), but Devré assured us all that the proprietress offered an excellent fish stew, and a chicken soup if one preferred that, and that he didn't know anyone who'd died from eating there.

It occurred to me, very belatedly, when Oncle Rafe poured me a healthy-sized glass of red wine that Julia was probably wondering where the heck I had gone off to, for we had been supposed to make *poisson en papillote.* I would have a lot of explaining to do to her tomorrow. I hoped she wasn't too worried.

I finished my stew—the chicken one, which had fat dumplings and slices of carrot and tasted like ambrosia—and felt much more human afterward. My two glasses of wine had probably helped. I was also feeling more relaxed now that I knew my messieurs were no longer in danger of being murdered by someone they'd once trusted with their lives.

But the missing tarot cards still niggled at me.

"I just don't understand where they went," I said. "The cards."

"It is of no consequence, mademoiselle," said Merveille, who sat across and down the table from me. It was a small table, however, so the five of us were packed so tightly he might just as well have been sitting across from me.

"But there has to be an explanation," I said. "They were a message—a clue that helped me figure out that Madame Demailly was the killer. And now they're gone."

Devré shook his head. "*Non,* mademoiselle, there does not have to be an explanation. After all, this is Paris—as we have told you." He gave me a kind smile to take any sting from his words. "She does not always care to give the explanations."

I settled back into my seat and sipped my wine, even brooded a little, as they chatted and drank and smoked. The older gentlemen seemed to still be going strong, while I felt like all I wanted to do was get prone and sleep for a day. But why didn't the rest of them care about these disappearing cards?

"It is possible," came a voice from behind me, right near my ear, "that the cards you seek have served their purpose, *hein?* And now they are no longer necessary, and so they have gone away. And perhaps it is also so with the photograph that is no longer on the desk, *non?*"

I turned slowly, all feeling draining from my body.

The speaker was a man of indeterminate age—somewhere over forty, somewhere under seventy. He had a beard that just brushed the second button of his shirt, and he wore a heavy dark coat and a cap. He was sitting on a stool wedged up against the wall behind our table—a stool that I was certain had been vacant a moment ago.

I was just as certain that no one had pushed their way between me and the wall and the bar counter to sit on that stool.

"*Pardon*?" I said, not quite certain I'd heard what I thought I'd heard.

"*Les cartes, hein*? They were provided to you when you needed to see them, but now you do not, and so they have served their purpose." He sipped from a glass of wine and eyed me over the rim of it. Smoke from his cigarette curled between us like a spectral wisp. "And now they have returned to be with their mistress, wherever she may have gone."

"I see," I replied, still reeling from the shock of this man's sudden appearance and his impossibly intuitive statement. How could he have known? He *might* have heard us talking about the cards—although in the din of this place, I highly doubted it, and he *definitely* hadn't been there only a moment ago anyway—but there was simply no way he could know about the photograph missing from Merveille's desk. Maybe I'd heard him wrong. "What did you say about a photograph?"

The man's beard and mustache curved. "But it is gone, *non*? If it is gone, then, mademoiselle, the man no longer has a need for it, eh?" His attention flickered to something—or someone—behind me, then back to me. "You see?"

"I—I don't know. Thank you. I suppose . . ." I shook my head to clear it.

Even if what he was saying was true—that Marguerite's photo was missing from Merveille's desk because their engagement was over (and why did I automatically think it was *that* photograph the man was referring to?)—it didn't change the fact that I'd had absolutely no indication that Merveille had any interest in getting to know me any better than as the sometimes helpful, sometimes interfering (in his opinion) amateur sleuth.

I turned back to the table at the sound of a burst of laughter from my companions, who'd obviously found something one of them said to be uproarious—or maybe it was just the amount of wine that had been imbibed, and the sense of relief that had overcome us all—and took another sip of my own drink.

"But which photograph are you—" I turned to speak to the man again, but there was no one there.

He was gone.

With a sudden rush of comprehension, accompanied by a strange prickling sensation, I looked at my watch.

It was fifteen minutes after midnight.

I looked up and found Devré watching me. He wore a warm little smile beneath his neat white and gray Van Dyck. He winked, then went back to his cigarette and conversation, and I realized he'd done it on purpose.

He'd arranged for us to come here so that I'd meet the Old Man Who Appears After Midnight.

Merveille insisted on walking me to my car, which was parked only a short way down Saint-Séverin from the nameless pub where we'd eaten.

We stood next to the Renault, and I could see Devré waiting for his nephew across the road and down the block. The younger inspecteur would drive the older one home. My messieurs had already bundled themselves into the Bentley and driven off.

"Mademoiselle Knight, I find myself in the unexpected position of having to thank you for a second time today," said Merveille. He sounded so formal, but there was a flicker of humor in his tone that told me he wasn't actually annoyed about it nor was he being graceless about expressing his gratitude.

He was missing his hat again—likely due to his encounter with Demailly—and so I could see his eyes without them being shaded by the brim of a fedora.

"Things might have ended differently if you had not arrived when you did and . . . eh, not refused to go and get help. Which would have been the prudent thing to do, mademoiselle, as I am certain you know."

"I wasn't going to leave the three of you there with a killer and her gun," I said.

"You put yourself at risk, as well."

I shrugged. "Yes, but—"

"You had a *gun*," he said in a little explosion of frustration. "That only made the entire situation more dangerous. Surely you see that, mademoiselle."

"My father taught me to respect and use a firearm," I said evenly. "I wasn't flailing around with it, as you well know. I had control of it the whole time."

"Oui." The agreement sounded as if it had to be forced out.

"And you helped by distracting her and covering up my movements."

"It was the least bit I could do since you would not leave." He sighed and, in an uncharacteristic moment of exasperation, shoved a hand through his hair. "Mademoiselle, I confess, I do not know what to do in your regard. There are moments when I would like to shake you, to berate you for your foolishness—and there are moments when I think I only should make love to you. *C'est intenable*!"

I gaped at him.

He made a sound of disgust and frustration, then pointed to my car. He looked wildly romantic, like a Byronic hero, with his dark hair mussed and winging about in every direction, his eyes dark and annoyed. "Get in, mademoiselle, if you please. Go home. Be safe. Bonsoir."

CHAPTER 20

I had an awful lot of explaining to do to Julia the next day. Fortunately, she had been coming across the street to find out why I wasn't answering the telephone and ran into Agent Écuyer as he was leaving. Though he was obviously in a rush, he gave her enough information and assurance that she wasn't terribly worried about my unexpected absence.

Still, it took a good two hours over coffee in her tiny kitchen for me to give her all of the details. Meanwhile, something on the stove was cooking, and I was dying to find out what it was—and if I could taste some of it.

But I controlled myself and told her everything (almost) that happened last night. And instead of ending by relating what Merveille had said—I absolutely did *not*—I finished the story by explaining about the jar of salve.

"Grand-père and Oncle Rafe have been so weird about it. They want to have everyone there when they open it," I said, shaking my head. "An old jar of some family remedy."

"Of course I'll be there," Julia said with a grin before I'd even asked. I was glad she automatically included herself in "everyone."

Then she said, "No, no, no—instead, tell them I'll cook dinner. Bring them over here to La Cuisine de Child, and I'll stuff you all full with this *gorgeous* coq au vin I've been *dying* to make again. It smells *divine*, and I like to add a bit of *cognac* to it, along with the wine, to make it just that much more *delectable*.

"I *just* got the mushrooms from Monsieur Michel this morning. You'll be salivating the minute you step into the house and smell it, I promise. And *la soupe à l'oignon*! With crusty bread and Gruyère melted on top . . . Tabs, I've been caramelizing the onions all morning . . ."

"Is that what I smell?" I said, looking toward the stove, a little desperate for a taste.

"It is. Those precious little darlings are just about ready for the broth to be added—it's broth left over from when I made that boeuf bourguignon, do you remember? That stock is darker than the cave where Monsieur Michel grows his mushrooms, and it's so rich even Midas would be jealous. You can just *see* the little circles of fat dancing on the top . . . It's going to be *spectacular*. Make sure *everyone* comes. I mean *everyone*."

Everyone came.

My messieurs and I, of course. Inspecteurs Devré and Merveille. And also Messieurs Lussier, Sénac, and Taban, as well as Madame Munzel: the remaining Bleuets.

We couldn't all fit into Julia's kitchen, so we squeezed into the next room, sitting on chairs and sofas, with tables scattered about. Paul Child was there, the jovial host. He poured generous servings of wine from his excellent collection as well as from the bottles Oncle Rafe had brought with us, and assured everyone that "Julie" was going to "completely delight our tongues" with the meal she'd cooked.

We were merry and loud, and I avoided looking at Merveille (too much, anyway). He'd taken off his hat, and his hair was back to its normal smooth, combed style. He looked relaxed and slightly less official than usual, with a sweater over a shirt and tie instead of his usual coat. Even so, he was still in somber-colored clothing: dark gray and blue.

"But I still don't understand how the tarot cards that disappeared helped you to figure out it was our Berthilde," said Monsieur Taban.

I noticed with a little tickle of pleasure that Madame Munzel was sitting on a divan next to him . . . very close . . . and that she no longer looked quite so pale and wan or sad. I hoped that meant something.

"It took me longer than it should have," I confessed. "And I didn't really even consider Madame Demailly as being the killer until after the fire at her house, when I saw the hole dug in her garden. But the tarot cards . . . they were laid out like so: *Le Diable . . . Roy d'Épée . . . la Morte.*"

"Devil, King of Swords, Death. It seems obvious to me they were speaking of the Neuf Bleuets' killer, as the first death was made with a sword of sorts . . . but if it had been the Queen of Swords, might it not have been more obvious that it was poor Berthilde?" said Monsieur Lussier. He, like the others, like my messieurs, could not help but feel some sympathy for his former colleague, despite her murderous actions. They had, after all, faced a war together.

"It actually didn't matter whether it was the Queen or King or even the Ten or Two of Swords. It was the *E* of *Épée* that mattered. It wasn't *Bâtons* or *Coupes* or *Deniers*—it was *Épées*. You see, the cards spelled out D-E-M. D—*Diable,* E—*Épée,* M—*Morte.* D-E-M. Demailly," I explained. "I thought it was a crazy theory at first, but then the more I thought about it, the more it made sense . . . She was, after all, the person to find Monsieur Hauet's body."

"*Oui,* mademoiselle," said Merveille. "She was indeed."

"You suspected her as well?" I said, eyeing him narrowly. I knew he had come to the same conclusions I had—I just didn't know how or when. "When did you become suspicious of her, Inspecteur?"

"Me? But I am always suspicious of everyone. Always," he said, making all of us laugh. His eyes lit with humor as he looked at me, and then he sobered. "But, you see, I suspected Madame Demailly immediately . . . because of the blood all over her."

"But she'd been helping Monsieur Hauet—of course she'd have blood all over her," I replied reasonably. I had originally dismissed her as the culprit for that reason.

"*Bien entendu.* And Madame thought that, as well, that she would camouflage the blood that sprayed on her when she cut his throat, eh? She would lean over him and get the blood on her coat and dress. She would wipe the dots and splashes off her face, see? But it was the splatters of blood on her *hat* that suggested the real story. Of course, if someone cuts the throat of a person, the blood, it sprays everywhere. But there is, I thought to myself, no other way to get the little splashes of blood like that on the hat, *hein*?"

My mouth had fallen open a little, and I closed it quickly. "Why, yes. That makes sense. So you suspected her all along?"

"I did not know for certain it was her until the fire. But by then I was sure, even without the small hole in the garden. It was the two *bleuets* that convinced me, you see. It was . . . too much, *hein*? The killer was so very concerned that the connection be made to the other killings.

"And when I returned to the office afterward, I got the report that the poison that killed Capron—it was not arsenic or anything else so very common, and so I reminded the pathologist of the case of the lily of the valley poisoning, and he agreed to test for that as well. But already by then I knew, and I suspected Madame would soon be at the house where she'd poisoned Philippe Capron. She needed a place to stay, eh?

"I did not, however, suspect that I would arrive to find her already there with the hostages. And she had the gun, and I did not, and . . . you know the rest, mademoiselle."

I nodded.

Before I could say anything else, Julia appeared in the doorway. "Although I have a *delicious, delectable* dinner prepared for all of you, Monsieur Fautrier has asked that I cook one other thing on the stove before we start to feast. And so, if you might all come into La Cuisine de Child to see it?"

I glanced at Grand-père, who gave me an enigmatic smile and gestured for me to follow everyone into the kitchen.

The space was, as I've mentioned, *tiny*. There was barely room for all of us to crowd in there, and the smells of the food . . . I was drooling.

But at the moment, Julia was not about to serve or even prepare anything that looked like it smelled that good. To my surprise, she was joined at the stove by Oncle Rafe, who had the canning jar he and Grand-père had retrieved from the safe house pantry.

"We're going to dump this . . . *salve,*" Oncle Rafe said with a mischievous smile, "into this pan and heat it up. And then we will see."

It looked disgusting. Like a marbled fat or greasy wax that had solidified. Julia scooped it out with a large wooden spoon, and it plopped into the pan.

Grand-père had suggested that maybe the unguent would smell nice, even if it didn't look nice . . . but it didn't. As we stood around, none of us got very near the stove . . . but even so, I could smell the contents of the jar. It was not pleasant.

"It's lard or some kind of animal fat," said Julia, sounding far more interested than I would have been—but she's a cook, after all. "I could use it in my cooking." She was stirring the contents of the pan.

"You are heating it up, eh?" said Oncle Rafe. He was standing there, his eyes gleaming. "Watch."

"It's melting," Julia said, still stirring. "And . . . there's something in it . . . *oh my God.*" She reared back from the pan and stared at Oncle Rafe. "Is that . . . is that . . . is that what I think it is?"

Everyone pushed closer, despite the rank smell of melting animal fat . . . and we saw it. Or, rather, *them.*

As the fat melted, it became transparent. And sitting in the bottom of the pan, in the midst of melted lard, were sparkling *diamonds.*

"Yes," said Oncle Rafe quietly. "Those are real diamonds. David Milhaud was a jeweler. He knew he could not take those when he fled—they would only be seized from him when he tried to leave. Those at the borders, they searched and took what they liked, you see, as payment to cross over.

"He said to me that this was a jar of some family recipe skin salve, and that I should keep it safe for him. And if he never came back, I should use the salve as I see fit." He shrugged. "It was the look in his eye, the way he said it, that made me wonder about it all. I wondered if there might be more than only a lotion or balm in the jar.

"But then he left, he and his family, and the war got worse and things turned bad . . . and then it ended and things were better, and . . . I'd forgotten about it all. I never heard from David or his family again. It has been five years since the war, and I know that if he was alive or if any of his family were, they would be here to retrieve this . . . family legacy. God rest their souls."

We had a long moment of silence for the Milhaud family.

"And so, you ask, what is to be done with these diamonds?" said Grand-père after the pause. "Each of the Bleuets will have one, and then the rest of them we will give to l'Oeuvre de protection des enfants Juifs . . . the organization that is helping the children, the orphans of the Jews here in Paris."

Everyone applauded quietly, and I happened to look over at Merveille. Our eyes caught and held for a moment, and I felt a definite sizzle of something rush through me. My internal sprite egged me on to give him a quirky little smile; then I turned away as Julia spoke.

"Since we will not be serving the diamonds for dinner," she said, "I will invite you all to get yourselves a bowl. I'll ladle up this *magnificent* coq au vin—look at those sassy brown mushrooms!—and we can enjoy a feast while toasting the bravery and dedication of our Neuf Bleuets!"

Then Julia cried, "Bon appétit!"

AUTHOR'S NOTE & ACKNOWLEDGMENTS

Thank you once again for traveling back to post-war Paris and the world of chef-in-training Julia Child for the fourth installment of the An American in Paris Mystery Series. I loved diving into the "noir" tales and traditions of this wonderful city, and I hope you enjoyed them as a backdrop to the story.

Before I get to all of the people I want to thank, I'd like to share a few comments about some of those stories and anecdotes.

I knew I wanted this book to have an element of the otherworld, the supernatural, the paranormal (hence the title), but it wasn't until I came across the engaging, disquieting, and sometimes disturbing memoir by Jacques Yonnet, titled *Paris Noir* (original French: *Rue des Maléfices*), that I found the "feel" I wanted for this book.

Yonnet's stories, all recounted from his own years living in the Latin Quarter during the Occupation and shortly after (he worked as a radio operator for the Résistance), were creepy, fascinating, and compelling—and I used many of his experiences for this book, including The Old Man Who Appears After Midnight, the Ill-Fated Knees, and the story of the Sleeper, Monsieur Lancelin. I have no reason to suspect these tales are fictional, for I, too, believe that a city as old and as imbued with tradition and experience as Paris has no need—as Devré says—for explanations. Things simply happen.

As the backdrop for this book was, more than the previous ones in the series, focused on how the Resistance actually worked during the war, I spent a lot of time with some other non-fiction accounts as a basis for many of the anecdotes and descriptions herein. Some of my favorites were *A Woman of No Importance, The Paris Girl,* and *When Paris Went Dark.* The young woman mentioned in the book named Andrée, who worked at the police station in Paris and secretly made copies of underground newspapers and stole blank ID cards, was a real person and did exactly this. The story of the fake blank ID cards that came from England that were printed on too-fine of paper to be believed and used was also true, as was the sewing of coins into a woman's girdle (Andrée had that brainstorm) in order to secretly transport money into Paris. Jacques Yonnet was the radio operator who worked out of the rooftop over his flat near Châtelet and was never caught by the Germans because of all the other interference nearby, as described by Monsieur Lussier.

And, finally, the story of the diamonds kept in the canning jar of lard is also a true tale. A Jewish jeweler did just as I described in the book—he stirred up his diamonds in a quantity of melted lard, put it in a jar and asked that this "family unguent" to be kept for him until after the war. In my book, the jeweler never made it back, but in real life, the jeweler did make it safely back to Paris. When he went to the house of the man who'd saved the jar for him, the man had completely forgotten about it, and, as in this book, the forgotten jar had to be retrieved from where it had been put away. When the jeweler melted down the lard, as Julia did in this book, the man who saved it was astonished. He was gifted the largest diamond of the bunch as a thank you by the jeweler.

Another quick note about the food that was served at Maison de Verre's little soft-opening fête: the Magret de Canard that is described as the entree was borrowed from Chef Andre Daguin, who first created and prepared this dish in Paris in the late 1950s—so Chef Debord's creation for Maison de Verre's reopening would have beaten him to it. ;-)

For those curious, the deck I chose for Madame Vierca's Tarot cards is the Tarot of Marseilles. And the unusual name of Keep-on-Smiling was inspired by a person who appeared quite often in Yonnet's book, known as Keep-on-Dancing.

If you're intrigued about the homicide investigated by Inspector Devré in which lily of the valley was the poison used to commit murder, you can read the entire story in my stand-alone novel *Murder on the Champs-Élysées.*

Now, onto my thanks and gratitude for these books, which I find so very enjoyable, even delightful, to write.

Always, I appreciate my ever-so-patient agent, Maura Kye-Casella, who is unflagging in her support and confidence in me, as well as manages all of my writerly—shall we say "issues"—throughout our interactions. I can't thank you enough for the various ways you calm and support me!

The team at Kensington Publishing has given me the absolute best publishing experience, and I'm grateful every day for every last one of them. My editor Wendy McCurdy tops the list—she is my constant champion and advisor, and even lets me completely change the plot of a book on a last-minute whim (I hope you agree that this version is much better than what I'd originally proposed!). Larissa Ackerman continues to be the best publicist In the World, and she's the most amazing cheerleader for my books in both of my series with libraries, booksellers, conventions, and every other opportunity for publicity. She's creative, energetic, organized, and always in a good mood and she and Sofia Szyfer make an excellent team. Sarah Selim keeps the entire process moving so very smoothly. Seth Lerner continues to create *magnificent* covers. The entire subrights (Susie and Jackie), production (Robin and team), and marketing gurus at Kensington are top notch. Thank you to everyone who has supported this and my other series.

I also want to thank my sister, Kate, for being an early reader of this and all of my other books. She doesn't let me get away with anything (but that's what sisters are for, right?). My dear friends Darlene, Gary, Erin, MaryAlice, Dennis, Diane, Diane, Donna, Bob, and Rosie always cheer me on and support all of my writing endeavors in a number of ways. I especially need to thank Darlene and Gary for helping me figure out a plot detail for this book that was giving me fits.

I'm not a French speaker, and so I rely on others to help me *not* make mistakes with my French, particularly Miriam Miller, who has been gracious enough to give the books a very close once-over to check my French, and Marty Lewis, who is always available for a quick French question by text as needed.

My husband Steve and my children all are so used to listening to me moan and blabber on about my plots and character arcs and motives and clues. . . . I love you all and thank you so much for always letting me rant on and on, even if I don't make much sense sometimes.

The independent bookstores that support this series are legion, and too many to list here, but I offer particular thanks to 2 Dandelions Bookshop, Bay Books, Murder by the Book, The Poisoned Pen, Gathering Volumes, Schuler Books, Inscribe Books, Fountain Books, Fenton's Open Book, and so many more. I'm grateful to each one that has hosted me for an event, offered my book as a book club offering, displayed, hand-sold, and/or otherwise promoted this series. Libraries continue to support this series nationally, and I'm supremely grateful to those librarians and patrons who've read and talked about my books. I support them in every way possible, especially during these difficult times.

And, last and most importantly, I thank you, dear reader, for being here with me, for hanging out with Tabitha and Julia, and, very possibly, for rooting for Merveille to finally make a move. I'm waiting for it just as eagerly as you are!

Thank you again for reading. Please find me online at colleencambridge.com and check my website for appearances and events. I love to hear from readers and to meet them at events.

—Colleen Cambridge, May 2026